PERFECT OPPORTUNITY

PERFECT OPPORTUNITY

Steven F. Havill

SEVERN
HOUSE

First world edition published in Great Britain and the USA in 2024
by Severn House, an imprint of Canongate Books Ltd,
14 High Street, Edinburgh EH1 1TE.

severnhouse.com

British Library Cataloguing-in-Publication Data
A CIP catalogue record for this title is available from the British Library.

ISBN-13: 978-1-4483-1167-5 (cased)
ISBN-13: 978-1-4483-1168-2 (e-book)

All Severn House titles are printed on acid-free paper.

MIX
Paper from
responsible sources
FSC
www.fsc.org   FSC® C013056

Typeset by Palimpsest Book Production Ltd.,
Falkirk, Stirlingshire, Scotland.
Printed and bound in Great Britain by
TJ Books, Padstow, Cornwall.

Praise for Steven F. Havill

"One of the most vivid worlds in mystery fiction"
Booklist

"Enticing . . . fans of the astute Estelle will enjoy the ride"
Publishers Weekly on *No Accident*

"A fine, complex mystery in an always-satisfying,
long-running series"
Booklist on *Less Than a Moment*

"A character-driven procedural . . . Strong sense of
place and family ties"
Kirkus Reviews on *Less Than a Moment*

"Compelling . . . Series devotees will eagerly welcome the
latest installment"
Library Journal on *Lies Come Easy*

"Irresistible . . . Havill's inviting world welcomes newcomers
and keeps fans happily coming back for more"
Publishers Weekly on *Lies Come Easy*

"Meticulous plotting, multidimensional characters, sharp
dialogue, and a vivid sense of place. This is one of
the very best entries in a consistently excellent series"
Booklist Starred Review of *Easy Errors*

About the author

Steven F. Havill lives with his wife of more than half a century, Kathleen, in Datil, New Mexico. A former high school teacher of biology and English, Havill is the author of more than thirty novels, including the Dr. Thomas Parks historical mystery series, the long-running Posadas County police procedurals featuring retired Sheriff Bill Gastner and Undersheriff Estelle Reyes-Guzman, and several standalones.

For Kathleen M. Havill

ACKNOWLEDGEMENTS

Special thanks to the folks who manufacture devices like Bill Gastner's four-wheel drive wheelchair, helping the elderly stay independent and in touch with their world.

ONE

B ill Gastner welcomed the day *after* being the focus of a big birthday anniversary bash. The cheerful, laughing, congratulatory guests had gone home, leaving their wishes for many happy returns of this day. *Well, maybe,* Gastner thought. After eighty-seven birthday anniversaries, who knows how many more would return, happily or otherwise. Still, he ruminated, for eighty-seven, only three years shy of four score and ten, he was almost mobile, still in possession of most of his faculties – those that mattered, anyway. He still enjoyed his own company, and the quiet of his own home, a sprawling adobe twice as old as he was.

The party had been pleasant, if crowded. The green chile lasagna had been memorable, the cherry crisp concocted with Luke Martinez's home-grown Regál cherries was award-winning, and even the coffee was perfect. Gastner had admitted that he didn't feel eighty-seven, as long as he sat still.

To help celebrate the day, Gastner's daughter Camille and her oral surgeon husband, Mark Stratton, were visiting Posadas, New Mexico, from Ann Arbor, Michigan. Camille – the oldest of his four children – behaved herself. During the year, she had telephoned often enough to approach pesthood. Her hints were none too subtle. There was this nice retirement village just down the road from their home in Ann Arbor, replete with lots of huge shade trees, spreading flower beds amongst the abundant flowering dogwoods, and acres of manicured lawns. And they had a vacancy *now*.

But summer always ends, the trees lose their leaves, the lawn shrivels, Michigan winters descend. True, the mosquitos and black flies and snowbirds did whatever they did to escape the powerful winters, a small consolation. Gastner shivered not so much at the prospect of interminable Michigan winters, but rather at the intrusions of graduated in-house medical care with stethoscopes threatening around every corner, hovering dietitians, and yes – lots of old people. Gastner had politely, and repeatedly, declined.

For his gift, Gastner's younger son, Air Force Colonel Bill Gastner Junior, had offered to take the old man for a commemorative flight in an A-10, a twin-engined tank buster that the service had threatened to retire a couple of times. The thought of the flight in the Warthog didn't bother Gastner. His son's air base was home to several two-seat trainer versions of the A-10. Ground crews would figure out how to get Gastner into the damn thing, and hopefully out of it again.

In fact there were spots in Posadas County that he would have liked to see from the air, enjoying the view from the A-10's big, bubble canopy. But the ride would require a long, tedious road trip to the airbase in Texas, and all the paperwork necessary for a civilian to take a military fly-along. He had politely refused that offer, too.

On this festive birthday anniversary, both his son and daughter seemed to realize that Bill Gastner was content right where he was – in his own secure badger-hole, tucked away in one corner of one of the least populated of New Mexico's counties, surrounded by people he treasured.

Not that he had done much to help with the festivities other than being there. The dishes were cleaned up and put away without him raising a finger to help. When all the chattering and clattering stopped, with the kitchen clean and tidy, he was treated to the most amazing rendition of the tune 'Happy Birthday' that he'd ever heard – a mix of Haydn, Mozart, Bach, Gershwin, and a few other musical bigwigs, their motifs intertwined around, over and under the traditional birthday melody.

With the double studio doors yawning open, Gastner's godson, the maestro Francisco Guzman, led the charge on his new piano. A gigantic nine-foot-long sea of ebony, the concert grand Steinway lived in the new music studio that had been built as an addition to Gastner's historic adobe. Francisco had played on Steinway concert grands in most corners of the world, but it was the first such beast to take up residence in tiny, culturally isolated Posadas.

Several years before, seeing no reason to cling to property to the bitter end, Gastner had given his old home (keeping residential rights to one wing of the place) to Francisco and Angie Guzman. They were neither son nor daughter by blood to him, but Francisco was one of two treasured godsons. Francisco's mother, Estelle Reyes-Guzman, at first had been skeptical that her son and daughter-in-law would actually embrace the village of Posadas as home base. But they had done so effortlessly.

They'd done a first-class job with expansion and renovation of

Gastner's historic adobe, incorporating their new living quarters and the music studio. When the two musicians needed a break from their hectic recording and concert schedule, they found Posadas a powerful draw. Francisco's Mexican genes, Gastner supposed. But Angie, a product of Kansas City, seemed to feel right at home as well in the high desert.

Gastner had given them the house free and clear, but had kept a nifty couple of rooms as his own suite. The additions and modifications to the adobe began, all designed by Francisco's younger brother Carlos, Gastner's second treasured godson. It was all an exciting process for an old man who enjoyed acting as sidewalk superintendent. Carlos had preserved the basic character of the adobe, though, managing to incorporate the major addition without losing any of the home's character as 'Bill Gastner's House'.

The birthday tune was no sing-along, Gastner thought thankfully, since no one other than Maestro Francisco on piano and Angie on cello had a clue about where the music was headed. Once in a while, fragments of 'Happy Birthday to you' would surface to keep the audience oriented. Each time that happened, Gastner's five-year-old great-godson, William Carlos – Francisco and Angie's son – would wiggle in his perch on Gastner's lap and giggle. He'd twist his black-haired head around to make sure the old man had heard those few bars of musical artistry.

About the time all the guests should have gone home anyway, Gastner went to bed – Francisco, Angie, and little William Carlos in their end of the sprawling house, Gastner in his.

For once, insomnia didn't win. Gastner slept straight through until just after four the next morning, awakening in the silent old adobe house that hours before had so rocked to music, merriment, and noshing on the best food on the planet.

Still in his most fashionable flannel jammies, Gastner made his way out to the spotless kitchen, making use of the stainless-steel handrails that had been added to the walls in strategic spots. Once in the kitchen, he stopped short. The coffee maker gurgled softly, the carafe full. He peered down into the sunken living room and saw Angie, Francisco's wife, curled in one of the huge leather chairs, a quilt drawn up under her chin. The thick manuscript of a musical score was nestled in her lap.

'You warm enough, sweetheart?' Despite the temp outside in the low seventies, the house was cool these June mornings.

'Perfect, and good morning to you.' She put down the score and patted the round mound of her belly. 'Just too much rich food yesterday. I'm not sure the baby likes green chile all that much.'

'That would be tragic.'

'The coffee is ready if you want some. I'm having tea, hold the tea.' She nodded at the cup of hot water on the table near her elbow.

'I do. Thank you.' In the distance, beyond the heavy insulation and the closed studio doors, he could hear quiet piano, more like a faint suggestion of music rather than a noisy imposition on the early morning hour. 'Sounds like he's getting an early start.'

Angie smiled. She was a beautiful young woman and Gastner found her smile luminous. 'He has to make up for the time out yesterday, you know.'

'I suppose. I've never fallen prey to such dedication.'

'Oh, sure, *Padrino*. So, what are the grand plans for your day?'

'I try not to have grand plans,' Gastner snorted, then concentrated on hitting the mug with the coffee stream. 'I promised an old friend I'd meet him for lunch at the Don Juan. And I think I'll take a drive this morning. That's kind of a ritual for me.'

She didn't presume to admonish Gastner for doing something so uneighty-seven-ish. Instead she said simply, 'Roaming your county.'

'Sure. You never know who or what is going to be out and about.'

'You do miss it, don't you.' Angie had the most amazing violet eyes, Gastner thought, and her gaze was so steady as to be disconcerting.

'Sure. In some ways, I suppose I do. It's an old habit. But I have to see what shenanigans the ravens and roadrunners are up to.'

Angie paused. She never had any trouble speaking her mind, and Gastner could see that she was winding up this time as the delicate frown lines deepened above her eyebrows. 'Camille worries each time you go out, *Padrino*.'

Gastner snorted. 'Worry, worry, worry. That's Camille. She hasn't come to terms yet with the reality of the situation, Angie. What the hell. I'm eighty-seven years old, come yesterday. What difference does it make at this point in time whether or not I trip over a rock somewhere out in the boonies and break my neck?'

'Surely you jest, *Padrino*.'

'I'm halfway serious. At the moment, my challenge is to get myself dressed and out of the house before Camille gets out of her bed down at the Posadas Inn and starts trying to enforce her geriatric restrictions on me. You watch. The phone will ring before you know it. And there Camille will be.'

'She means well, *Padrino*. You'll be back after lunch? Should I snitch on you?'

'Sure. In an emergency, I always have the goddamn cell phone. I think it's in the truck somewhere. Whether or not it's charged is another question. And then if nine-one-one doesn't work, the radio does.'

It had been a lot of years – decades – since he'd been first a deputy, then undersheriff, then sheriff of Posadas County. When he retired, he had never asked the county powers-that-be for permission to keep a department radio in his personal vehicle. He just did it. The current sheriff didn't seem to object, sensing that Gastner knew perfectly well both the law and his own limitations. And what the hell, Gastner had always rationalized. How could it hurt to have another set of eyes and ears out there? Obviously the current first-term sheriff, Jackie Taber, wasn't going to argue the point.

The faint music whispered to a halt, and one of the studio doors opened. Francisco Guzman appeared, looking more like a fit middle-weight boxer than a much-lauded concert pianist. He wore only gym shorts and slippers, and greeted his wife and Gastner with his radiant smile. 'Work day,' he whispered. He knelt beside Angie's chair and rested a hand on her belly. 'How's our girls?'

'We're fine,' Angie said, and then made a face. 'And you need a shower, Cisco.' She pronounced it *Seesko,* with her Kansas version of a heavy Mexican accent.

'I've been hard at work,' Francisco explained. 'Since when, you ask?' He twisted around and looked at the antique clock on the fireplace mantel. 'Since two.' He grimaced. 'So no wonder.' He stood up and stretched his six-foot frame. 'You're headed out this morning?'

Gastner nodded. 'Thought I would.'

'Carlos has your wheels, though.' His brother, Carlos Guzman, was making slow but steady progress in his rehab after a nasty bike-truck incident in California the year before. For even a year before that, he'd been infatuated with Gastner's 'back country' wheelchair, a four-wheel drive monstrosity designed with broken soldiers in mind.

'He's welcome to it,' Gastner said. 'If I have to leave the comfy lieutenant's chair in the Suburban, the duck-footed cane will do just fine.'

'He's not sleeping very well these days, so he's probably up,' Francisco said. 'You ought to rope him into going with you. Take his mind off things.'

'Maybe I'll do that.' Gastner refilled his coffee cup and turned back toward his bedroom. 'Cover for me while I get dressed, just in case my daughter-the-warden tries to head me off at the pass.'

A few moments later, Gastner's Suburban whispered down the streets of the neighborhood, through the silent heart of Posadas. A Sheriff's Department patrol unit paused to let his Suburban pass before the deputy pulled out of the Handiway convenience store to head southbound, and the officer offered a pulse of the roof rack gumballs in greeting. Or maybe the officer was a she, Gastner thought. He couldn't tell in the vague dawn light and the window tint. Forty years ago, he mused, there had been no such thing as a female road patrol officer in Posadas County. Now even the sheriff herself had busted that adobe ceiling.

The sky was just beginning to show some definition to the east, without a cloud to be seen. It would be another blistering June day. He turned south on Twelfth Street by the Don Juan de Oñate restaurant on the corner of Bustos and Twelfth, and immediately saw the two familiar figures up ahead, moseying down the sidewalk of the quiet residential neighborhood.

Carlos Guzman's cane-assisted limp was pronounced, but his recovery showed incredible progress. A year before, while riding a tandem bicycle, he'd been pounded to pieces, nearly to death, during an assault by pickup truck. His fiancée, Tasha Qarshe, was riding with him and was injured as well, although Carlos had taken the intentional brunt of the crash. And yet here he was, almost whole. His mother, Undersheriff Estelle Reyes-Guzman, strolled with her left hand cupped through her son's right elbow.

'Nobody in the whole goddamn family gets a full night's sleep,' Gastner said aloud.

Like his brother, Carlos topped six feet, broad through the shoulders, big and brawny enough to make his mother appear almost waif-like. His T-shirt and shorts were just enough to cover most of his scars. Most. Despite the mild morning, he wore a navy blue wool watch cap pulled down to his ears. Estelle was in what passed for a uniform for her – a desert tan, tailored pants suit with a black PCSO ball cap, her favored Beretta 92FS high on her right hip, the gold undersheriff's badge on the leather keeper on her belt.

Quiet as the Suburban was, Estelle still heard it the moment the vehicle turned the corner. She and Carlos stopped, and Gastner was once more impressed with the disparity in height between mother and son. Undersheriff Guzman was five foot six, and maybe a hundred and twenty pounds after all the food yesterday. Her son Carlos shared the same dramatic swarthy good looks with his older brother – for whom he'd been confused more than once. Add thirty years to his visage, and he'd look exactly like his father, Dr Francis Guzman.

Carlos raise his cane in salute, and Gastner lowered the passenger side window.

'*Padrino!*' the young man greeted, as if he hadn't seen Gastner for most of the day before. He took a step forward, stepping gingerly off the curb and into the street so he could rest his right forearm on the windowsill of the Suburban. 'The remains of the lasagna await, if you're up to it.'

'Not at five in the morning, thanks just the same. I've got some serious cruising to do before I eat anything else.' Estelle had remained on the sidewalk, and she took advantage of the extra height of the curb to rest her elbow on her son's shoulder. 'Francisco is already working up a sweat, and Angie was up and about, so here I am.' He glanced at the dashboard clock and saw 5:10. 'Day's half over.' Before either of them could reply, he asked, 'How's Tasha? She seemed a little under the weather yesterday.'

'She just wants a chance to sleep in,' Carlos said. 'It's been a restless couple of days, and now she has a design deadline. She'll probably work most of the day, once she gets up.' He grinned. 'She's the only one in this outfit who knows how to sleep in.'

'Smart girl. Look, I didn't get a chance to corner you two yesterday and monopolize your time.' Gastner frowned at his youngest godson. 'The day was all about me, me, me. If you have nothing better to do just this minute, let me invite you to take a turn around the county with me? You can fill me in about what's what with you two. I'll buy you breakfast.'

Somewhat to Gastner's surprise, Carlos accepted the invite. 'Give me a couple of minutes to tell Tasha, or leave her a note or something. Do I need to bring anything? Food? Water? An Uzi?'

'I don't think so. My limo is stocked. With all of the above.'

'We'll be back by lunch?'

'Likely a little bit after that. I don't move very fast.'

He nodded and limped back toward the house. Estelle took up her son's position at the truck's door.

'You can come too, sweetheart,' Gastner said.

'I would, but I have a meeting with the sheriff and the county manager at eight that I really shouldn't miss.'

'Damn, even way back in the day, I could bring myself to miss all of those that I could,' he laughed. 'Leona is a sketch, that's for sure. How's she doing these days?' Leona Spears had been county manager for a respectable tenure – longer than any of the previous tenants of that thankless office. She amused the hell out of Gastner with her bubbling humor and general love of all mankind, habitually clothed in her trademark flowered Hawaiian muumuus.

'Always creative, always hands-on.'

'She talking retirement yet?'

'Always.'

'That's the scary part, how fast all that comes along,' Gastner said. 'We think we have forever, and it turns out we don't.' He shrugged and changed the subject. 'And I've seen the sheriff around town a few times in recent weeks. She's settling in nicely, is the impression I get.'

'Indeed she is.' Estelle smiled. 'The women are going to rule the world, *Padrino.*'

'They can't do any worse than the men,' Gastner scoffed. 'I saw one of your minions when I passed the office, headed south on Fifty-Six. Whoever it was recognized me and gave me a flip of the lights.'

'That would be Deputy Thompson,' Estelle replied. 'Graveyard is her preference.'

'She's still working through some issues, is my guess.'

'Exactly, sir.' Typically, Estelle didn't elaborate.

'She certainly roared through academy, though,' Gastner said. 'Surprised the hell out of me. I don't mean her success. I meant that she'd even go that route.'

Estelle glanced back toward the house as her son managed the front door and three careful steps down to the sidewalk. 'She had something of a head start over the other recruits.'

'For sure.' Lydia Thompson had grown up in upstate New York, Gastner knew, and experienced a brief career with the New York State Police. She'd been terribly injured by a young thug with a shotgun, and it had been her partner who had saved her life . . .

and married her after her extended convalescence. They'd moved to New Mexico, started a successful career in land speculation and development, and this time it had been her husband who had been a victim, leaving Lydia Thompson a young widow.

Lydia had taken some time to think about what path her life wanted to follow, but after passing a rigorous physical, she'd hired on with the Posadas County Sheriff's Department – surprising everyone. Like so many others, she had found solace in the vast, quiet expanse of the prairie, and Gastner understood that perfectly. The prairie at night – his favorite time – was to him a showcase of endless fascination.

'I have a Zoom conference at ten, Tasha reminds me,' Carlos said as he returned to the Suburban. He held up a gadget that looked like an overgrown cell phone. 'This'll work if we get involved.'

Getting in and settled took patience, but eventually Carlos flashed a smile. 'All set.'

'That seat comfortable enough?'

'Enough.' He clicked the seat belt in place, then slipped a small pillow under the chest strap that lay directly across his busted ribs. 'I have my pet pillow, but please . . . no sudden stops, *Padrino*.'

'Behave yourselves,' Estelle admonished. She didn't look worried, didn't try to tell either her son or his godfather that they should be vegging out, within easy reach of the nurse brigade.

'We will try.'

TWO

Other than a few wide, dusty streets with the curbs capturing the usual landfill of wind-blown trash, Posadas, New Mexico, wasn't much to admire. It had boomed during the copper mining days, when Consolidated Mining Operations had done its best to carve a chunk out of Cat Mesa, north of the village. Bars and saloons had flourished, the public school had swelled beyond capacity, and the village of Posadas supported its own police department, with the Sheriff's Department working the rest of the county.

Then a faltering economy cut the village's throat. Consolidated pulled operations, the school shrank, even most bars closed. What was left was a quiet, dusty little village of 3,000 people, more or less.

Out of old habit, Gastner still took his time, idling the Suburban along, looking into every nook and hidden alley. None of the buildings was old enough to be a landmark, none new enough to hint at prosperous growth. And neither he nor his godson were particularly blabby for the sake of holding the silence at bay. They cruised first east on Bustos, then turned south on Grande.

As they drove under the interstate overpass, Gastner said, 'I was going to meet Miles Waddell at the Don Juan for lunch, but I think I'll catch him at home for breakfast instead. You've eaten up there, haven't you?'

'Sure. Good stuff. Better than good. Five-star dynamite, in fact.'

'Indeed it is. And if you have to do that Zoom thing, he has the facilities.'

'For sure he does.' Carlos reached forward and stroked the screen in the middle of the Suburban's dashboard. 'So do you, right here.'

That screen, and all the other WiFi stuff in the truck, went unused as far as Gastner was concerned, their functions a mystery to him. He had badgered the salesman to show him how to turn the screen off so it didn't stare him in the face.

'I look forward to seeing Miles again,' Carlos added. At first, the community nay-sayers had had a field day with Miles Waddell's

NightZone project – a world-class astronomical center high above the surrounding prairie on Torrance Mesa, thirty miles southwest of Posadas. What they said couldn't be done *was* done, and then some. And then *a lot* more than just some. And on top of that, Gastner was proud that Carlos had had a hand in the design and acoustical engineering in both the mesa-top auditorium and the planetarium.

His godson sat with his right elbow on the door sill, resting his chin on his right fist. 'I miss the prairie,' he said as the village of Posadas fell away behind them. For the next twenty miles, not a single ranch house or business hinted at civilization.

'Out in California,' he continued, 'we get so used to all the humans packed in together, all the traffic, all the planes, all the concrete. We forget about all of this.'

'It was interesting to hear your mother talk about her adventures out there,' Gastner said. Undersheriff Estelle Reyes-Guzman had spent a nerve-racking week or two in California the year before, after Carlos and Tasha's bike crash – after the attack on them had put Carlos under medical care that took the better part of a year out of his life. To Gastner's way of thinking, the only good part of the whole misadventure was that the man who had attacked them ended up with a bullet in the head, his corpse unceremoniously pitched into a trash dumpster.

'Ma is nothing if not tenacious,' Carlos said.

'And good for us that she is. I wish I could have been there to join the chase.'

As they approached the jounce of the expansion strips on the Rio Salinas bridge, he slowed in deference to his godson's battered bones. The bed of the Salinas, thirty feet below the road surface, was the usual smooth gravel. During his forty-plus years in Posadas County, Gastner had seen water in the Salinas only a handful of times. Cattle used the streambed as a smooth thoroughfare between water tanks. Rattlesnakes snoozed in the culverts under the roadway, escaping the sun. Once in a while, some rancher's hot-rodding kid blasted up and down the dry arroyo bed in a four-wheeler, booming through the six-foot diameter culverts.

Carlos pointed up ahead, and without a thought, Gastner's first reaction at seeing the vehicles stopped on the highway shoulder was to reach over and turn the police radio on. The airwaves were quiet, so he'd missed the initial radio contact. As they drew closer, he saw a usual sight for this country – a sheriff's patrol unit, all emergency lights ablaze, pulled in diagonally behind a pickup truck. The truck hitched a battered livestock trailer, the trailer a twin-axle rig that could hold a dozen steers or half a dozen saddled horses. In the shadows of early dawn, Gastner couldn't tell if the trailer was loaded or not.

He slowed and pulled the Suburban into the left lane while they were still a couple hundred yards or more from the two stopped vehicles. The truck was a rancher's favorite, a massive Ram crew cab dually, who knows what original color under all the dust. The left back fender was torn, a chunk of bodywork missing.

Out of long habit, Gastner glanced at the dash clock and saw 5:27 a.m., still early enough to be dark with a wash of stars and the Milky Way across the sky, not yet light enough to see who was whom. Estelle had said that Deputy Lydia Thompson, the lover of the night hours, was on duty. If she was out of her unit, the deputy was hidden from view on the off-road side. The pickup's driver's door was ajar, just enough to switch on the inside light. As they passed, Gastner saw that the driver was also out of the truck. He apparently had walked around the vehicle and now stood with his right elbow resting on the passenger windowsill. His grungy Stetson turned as they passed. He might have lifted a couple of fingers in salute, maybe not.

'People find all kinds of interesting places for privacy, don't they,' Carlos observed. 'Maybe a little love interest going on there.'

'You think so?'

'His left hand was on the deputy's shoulder.'

'Couldn't prove it by me.' Gastner felt a pang of apprehension as his imagination laced memories together. Traffic stops didn't include buddy-buddy hands on shoulders – unless it was the deputy's hand that was clamped, forcing the suspect face down in the roadside gravel.

He glanced in the Suburban's big passenger-side wing mirror, but the pickup's headlights and the pulsing red and blue of the deputy's unit washed out any details. 'I don't know about that,' he said. The driver was out of the truck, shielded from positive view from the road. The deputy was on the same side of the truck, backlit by her own unit's headlights.

Gastner knew that the situation was none of his business, of course. As far as he knew, Deputy Lydia Thompson hadn't radioed for backup. She should have called in the plate before the stop, but Gastner hadn't turned on his own radio before the event, so wasn't privy to any on-the-air conversations.

'All this trips my busy-body switch,' he said, and nodded toward the Suburban's voluminous center console. 'Grab the phone for me.' At the same time, he let the truck coast, gradually slowing without the flare of brake lights.

When Carlos had the phone out, Gastner added, 'Speed-dial the SO.'

With the radio, he could have reached dispatch, but then everyone could hear the conversation, including the deputy and the rancher she'd stopped.

Carlos handed his godfather the phone, a gadget that Gastner's aging, arthritic fingers found challenging. He managed to thumb the 'talk' mode without driving off the highway, and the response was in progress before he had the damn thing to his ear.

'Posadas County Sheriff's Department. Deputy Burke.'

Lawrence Burke was a new face. Gastner had met him a couple of times and hadn't formed any opinions about him, one way or another. The kid was too young, maybe. Then again, almost everyone else was too young, too.

'Deputy Burke, this is Bill Gastner. I'm just beyond mile marker twenty-two on New Mexico Fifty-Six. One of your deputies has a traffic stop with a pickup hauling a stock trailer.' He paused. Burke didn't respond, perhaps thinking, *Who the hell is Gastner?*

Gastner gave him another five seconds and then said, 'Everything copacetic with that stop?'

Burke sounded puzzled, as well he should, Gastner thought. And he didn't answer the question. Instead he said, voice curt, 'Who is this again?'

'Bill Gastner. Three hundred.' His old car number didn't do the trick, either.

'What, are you with Grant County, or State Police or something?'

Carlos chuckled, the conversation amped by the phone enough that he clearly could hear the dispatcher's response.

'Just a concerned citizen. I didn't hear Deputy Thompson call in the stop.'

'She did.'

'All right, then. You have a good day, Deputy Burke,' Gastner said, and handed the phone back to Carlos. By now they were several hundred yards beyond the stopped vehicles. 'This is where we get to decide.' He swung the Suburban to the right, tires thumping on the shoulder, and pushed it through a U-turn. 'You said his hand was on the deputy's shoulder. Did I hear that right?'

'I believe so.' Carlos glanced across at his godfather. 'I knew I should have brought the Uzi.'

'We're just going to look, Carlos. Survey the scene. If the deputy wants backup, she'll ask for it.' With no other deputy on duty, the nearest backup would be a state trooper on the interstate. *Who am I kidding?* Gastner thought. Certainly not his godson.

'And then what do we do, *Padrino*?' He didn't sound nervous, perhaps believing that his trusted *padrino* wouldn't be so foolish as to put either of them in danger. Gastner truly hoped that Carlos believed that. But there was a balance going on here.

'Damn good question. Keep that phone handy. At least we have *that*.' He didn't mention that his well-worn Smith & Wesson .357 stubby rested in the center console.

'Three zero one, PCS. Ten twenty.' Burke's voice on the radio sounded bored. At least he had been prompted to check on Deputy Thompson's status, Gastner thought.

'Who owns the truck? Do we know?' Carlos asked.

'We may be about to find out. I think I know, if my memory comes back from vacation.'

By then they were within fifty yards and approaching head-on. Gastner felt a flash of irritation. The pickup driver's name was out there somewhere buried in his memory. 'I think I probably know every resident of Posadas County. But recall is another game entirely. It's been a while.'

At that moment, Deputy Lydia Thompson stepped out through the space between her unit and the stock trailer, evidently preparing to walk back along the side of her department Yukon. She didn't though, instead staying in the defensible space between the trailer and her Yukon, rather than trapped on the traffic side of her unit. She stopped, turning to watch the Suburban's approach. She would have heard the radio call, both from her vehicle and from the radio on her belt. But at the moment, she was more interested in other things.

Gastner slowed until they were directly opposite the patrol car. Just behind them, the pickup driver rounded the front of the ranch truck and reach for the front door. At that point, Gastner's porous memory kicked in.

With no traffic in sight, he fingered the window button.

'Good morning, Deputy Thompson. Is everything all right? Need a handy-man jack or something like that?'

Her smile was a little tight, but she nodded. 'We're just fine, Mister Gastner. You two are out and about early this morning.' After a glance in both directions, she took a step toward Gastner's vehicle.

'It's the curse of the aging,' he said. 'My godson and I have a breakfast date with Miles topside, and when I saw both you and whosits there out of your vehicles, I thought "Oh, well. Maybe the deputy needs another jack or something."'

Her expression loosened up just a tad. 'I appreciate that, sir. Big, empty country we have here. But we're fine.'

'It is that. Big, I mean.' Gastner lifted a hand in salute as he let the Suburban roll ahead. 'Have a grand day, Deputy.'

'You be careful out there, sir.'

As they eased away, Carlos observed, 'Good-looking deputy, that. She prefers the graveyard shift?'

'It would seem so.' After a few yards down the road and another U-turn, they resumed their excursion toward the NightZone mesa.

The truck/trailer and the deputy's unit hadn't moved yet as they passed them for the third time, but in a moment the radio crackled with Deputy Thompson's brief announcement. 'PCS, three zero one is ten eight on Fifty-Six, mile marker twenty-two.' Gastner grunted with satisfaction when the deputy didn't announce the name of the truck driver . . . not to him, not to the dispatcher.

'Graveyard shift always was my preference,' Gastner added. 'That cowboy, by the way, is a young fellow by the name of Johnny Rabke.'

'My mom knows him,' Carlos said without hesitation, and Gastner wasn't surprised at his godson's memory. His agile mind had astonished the old man since the kid was a year old.

'Indeed she does. That's how I happen to know who he is. Your mother responded to a bar scuffle at the Spur that ended with Rabke facing a grand jury for murder. He bounced a billiard ball off another guy's skull *after* the guy cut him with a knife. Fortunately for him it was *after* he was cut, and not before. On that basis, Rabke beat the rap. Grand jury let him walk.'

'Ma was right in the middle of all of that when we got into trouble out in California.'

'Yup, that's exactly right. Anyway, Rabke is a loose cannon, that's for sure. I was long retired when he started playing the field, feeling his oats. But I've heard all the stories. My busy-body nature would like to know what the deal here is – what Rabke and the deputy were discussing in the quiet of pre-dawn.'

'Maybe one of his taillights is out,' Carlos said. 'His truck's got that caved-in back fender.'

Gastner laughed. 'Maybe.'

THREE

The tramway up the mesa face was the most efficient, fastest access from the parking lot to the top of NightZone mesa, but Gastner had no love of dangling from cables high above the rocks, going light-headed as the winds played games with the tram cars. His favorite approach was the roadway – an ultra-smooth macadam engineering marvel that followed the north side of the mesa, then climbed around on the west before popping out on top. No highway signs marred the great views. What roadway directions that might have been necessary were painted right on the road surface in the European style.

The fancy access road was closed off with a handsome, sturdy gate, since casual visitors were required to take the spectacular tramway to the top, rather than cluttering the mesa with vehicular traffic. Developer Miles Waddell took the concept of 'dark zone' seriously.

And sure enough, as they turned into the lower parking lot and then approached the gate that blocked the mesa access road, a young woman with clipboard in hand stepped out of the small geodesic dome that served as a guardhouse. White shirt perfectly pressed with the NZ emblem on the left breast, black slacks with razor crease, polished boots, black baseball cap also sporting the NZ logo – she looked spiffy and official. She greeted them with an expectant smile. In deference to NightZone's ambiance, Gastner had already turned off his headlights, although a bright dawn was coming fast. Stargazers ruled the night, bird-watchers, hikers and rock climbers ruled the day. Some folks, like Bill Gastner himself, came for the five-star food in the restaurant – like most of NightZone's features, open 24/7. The place was always busy.

'Welcome, Mr Gastner.' Her smile grew wider.

What the hell was her name? He squinted and read 'Morton' on her name tag – all the prompting that he needed. She was a year or two younger than Carlos, which meant she was four or five years out of high school . . . maybe a recent college grad working over the busy summer season. Gastner made a mental note to try to

remember to ask her mother next time he saw Vivian Morton at his
dentist's office.

'Cindy, how's it going?' He glanced in the rearview mirror. Across
the parking lot, four enormous tour buses were parked side by side.
'You folks are going to be busy today.'

She rolled her eyes, then stepped to the side a little so she had
a better look at Carlos.

'You probably know my godson, Carlos Guzman,' Gastner
offered. 'We're planning to drive up.'

'Hi,' she said demurely, and then frowned as she leaned forward.
'You're OK, then?'

'I'm OK,' Carlos said. 'And please let Clay know I'm in town
for a little bit. I'd like to see him. Tasha and I are staying over at
my mom and dad's place.'

'I'll do that.' She noted something on the clipboard, then looked
at Gastner. 'I think Mr Waddell is expecting you, sir. You were down
originally for lunch, but then told Mr Waddell to make it breakfast.'
Cindy nodded uphill, to the deep shade beyond the gate where the
dawn had yet to touch. 'But I must warn you . . . we have a herd
of javelina who are hanging out on the mesa now. Watch for them
near the spring at mile marker two point one, over on the west side.
One of the workers reported them earlier this morning. At last count
there were nine of them.' She held her hands about eight inches
apart. 'The little ones are sooooo cute, like little wind-up toys.'

'We'll be careful,' Gastner said. 'Are you headed back to school
this fall?'

She touched a remote on her belt and the gate hummed open.
'Oh, sure. It never ends, sir.'

'You're at . . .'

'Texas Tech.' She wrinkled her nose as if that explained it all.
'Have a great day.' She favored Carlos with another thousand-watt
smile. 'I'll let Clay know as soon as I see him after work.'

Through the gate, Gastner kept the Suburban's speed sedate.
'Cute kid,' he said.

'Yup, she is. She was going to marry Wiley Scott. Remember him?'

'Have a heart, *hijo*.'

'He worked at the feed store for a while? Didn't graduate,
somehow got lucky and landed Cindy, but they never got around to
marrying. They had one son, then he put his delivery truck into a
bridge abutment.'

Always curious about things that just didn't matter anymore, Gastner asked, 'Which bridge, which year?'

Carlos tapped the windowsill. 'I graduated in eighteen, so she finished up in twenty or twenty-one. The baby was about six months old when Wiley got killed that summer after she graduated. He ramped into one of the interstate bridges on the way to Deming.'

None of that prompted a memory and Gastner thumped his forehead with the heel of his hand. 'No file comes to mind.' He shrugged. 'But she seems in good spirits now.'

'That, or she's a good actress.'

After a couple of minutes, Gastner slowed the Suburban to a crawl, then to a full stop. The mesa-side spring that Cindy Morton had mentioned fed a small oasis on the uphill side of the road, beautifully stoned and culverted. Sure enough, there they were, the whole grunting javelina family, doing their best to dig up every tender little cactus in sight. Two of the adults sprinted off into the rocks, but the rest remained, no doubt having learned not to fear the infrequent traffic.

'Some ranchers really like to have 'em around,' Gastner said. 'They wreak havoc on the prickly pear cacti.' He watched two of the little ones, each about the size of an over-inflated football, romp and root in the mud at water's edge. 'Other folks shoot 'em on sight, claiming they're a nuisance.'

'Open season on nuisances,' Carlos observed.

'Except they're considered a game animal with a formal season,' Gastner added.

As if they'd lost patience with the humans, the javelinas crashed off uphill through the brush, and Gastner urged the Suburban onward.

'You know, it's no secret that Miles Waddell wants your mother to work up here when she retires from the Sheriff's Department. I always thought she'd be a good fit.'

'Well, you did that yourself, *Padrino*. For a little while, anyway, kinda informally. Maybe it's a good tradition to continue.' Carlos didn't sound surprised, so Gastner gathered that the news about Estelle's opportunity at NightZone wasn't news to him.

'Sure enough.' They drove around the west end of the mesa, breaking out on top near the mammoth radio telescope installation, a compound that included the sixty-meter dish and assorted support buildings. Fresh sunshine washed the white upper rim surface of the dish, now pointed east, and it was bright enough to force a flinch.

'She could ride the train out,' Carlos said. 'Tasha and I did that the day before yesterday. Pretty snazzy. We didn't come up here, though. Just rode out and turned around to ride back. Really smooth ride with those hi-tech welded rails.'

'Your mom likes to have her "office" with her, close at hand, so I'm betting that most of the time, she wouldn't do that.' The train was convenient, an ultra-modern propane/electric narrow-gage pulling four fancy touring cars that would have made Andrew Carnegie envious. The train ran constantly morning and night, covering the twenty-six miles from Waddell's companion development at the Posadas Municipal Airport through rugged ranch and wilderness country to NightZone, each one-way trip taking a leisurely seventy minutes. Passengers not riding all the way to NightZone could elect either of two brief courtesy stops that accessed hiking trails or the bird-watching refuge and its fancy gazebo. Gastner had ridden the train several times himself, and despite the elegant ambiance of the ride, always ended up feeling claustrophobic, stuck on board with no easy way out.

Toward the east, across a couple miles of mesa top, the cluster of NightZone's buildings looked like a small village. A collection of observatories, including the newest solar observatory, surrounded the main facility that housed the auditorium, offices, dining room, and the arc of the hotel, all of them just close enough to the east mesa's rim to provide a view without the imaginary threat of them toppling off into the scattered rocks below.

Like his approach to roadway design, Miles Waddell eschewed signage, and nothing along the arced curb in front of the main admin building either encouraged or prohibited parking. With tourists discouraged from taking the access road up the mesa, traffic was kept to a minimum.

The only traffic this morning was Gastner's Suburban, and he snugged the big SUV close to the curb. He managed to slide out, grab his cane, and maneuver around to the front of the truck before Carlos had organized his own awkward dismount.

At the same time, the darkly tinted doors of the admin building glided open, and Miles Waddell appeared, clad in a narrow-brimmed Stetson, white shirt with his trademark purple scarf, blue jeans and fancy boots. Gastner was always delighted that inheriting a

billion-plus dollars from his financier mother hadn't changed Miles
Waddell much. Gastner had known him for thirty years, and had
had a ringside seat as Miles Waddell developed his dream on the
mesa top.

'My god, look at you,' Waddell exclaimed, and walked the last
fifteen feet to Carlos with his right hand extended. 'Long and slow
process, huh.'

'Yes, sir. But progress nevertheless,' Carlos said.

'Hey, I heard you and Tasha were on the train the other day. Why
didn't you come on up?' Gastner wasn't surprised that Waddell had
heard who was onboard his train. The man kept track of
everything.

'Next time,' Carlos said. 'We were both just taking a short work
break. We didn't even get off at the terminal. Just stayed on board
and let it glide us back home.'

'Work, work, work.' Waddell shook his head, then looked hard
at Gastner, offering the carefully modulated double-hand grip that
was both comfortably firm but respected the old man's arthritic
finger joints. 'Look, I apologize for not making it to your birthday
gig yesterday, but you probably saw those four buses down in the
parking lot? Big shots visiting from Nicaragua, along with big shots
from Japan.'

He tangled the fingers of both hands together. 'It's more stuff
with the radio-telescope world links. You oughta hear them all
talking to each other. Or trying to, anyway. Cracks me up. But I
couldn't break away.'

He heaved a deep sigh. 'Anyway. Chow time, yes? You need to
approve the new menu.'

'*I* do?'

He ushered them to the front doors. 'Of course you do.'

Gastner glanced at his watch. 'You're probably not even open
yet.' He was joking, but Miles Waddell took it as a cue for a
mini-lecture.

'Course we are. You know better than that, Sheriff. You come up
here at three a.m., we're open. Two p.m., we're open. Any time you
choose, twenty-four seven, three sixty-five. That's one of the secrets
of success.' He stopped inside and surveyed the lobby, his expression satisfied. He nodded at evidence of major construction along
one wall, the detritus kept tidy and contained, and held up both
hands. 'I had an epiphany.'

'It's been a week or two since you had one of those,' Gastner said, and Waddell laughed.

'This whole mesa project is one gigantic epiphany, an endless parade of ideas and dreams put into practice. That's my goal, and I hope it never ends.' He pointed with the index fingers of both hands at the construction. 'A while ago, I happened to hear this couple from Rhode Island discussing some camera problem they were having . . . some obscure something that I didn't understand. But then I thought, "Why not? Why should folks travel all the way here from Rhode Island, or Bangkok, or Oslo, and be frustrated by a cranky camera?" That makes no sense to me, no sense at all, and it's a problem I can solve for them.'

He stretched out his arms to embrace the entire north side of the generous foyer. 'That's how progress happens. Just imagine – a camera, binoc, whatnot shop, right here. Top of the line merchandise. Canon, Nikon, Swarovski, Zeiss, whatever else there is. And maybe a few lower-end camera models for the not-so-rich visitors. And not just sales. We're going to have a big-screen, top-of-the-line computer so customers can try out a camera, pop out the chip, and see the results right then and there. And an observation deck out the back side for anyone to try a spotting scope.'

Gastner started to say something, but Waddell carried on like a little kid pouncing on his Christmas presents.

'See that wall?' His reach included an area that also served as one wall of the spacious dining room. He rested a hand on Carlos's shoulder, delineating the scene with the other. 'This is going to take Tasha's talent, my man. I want a photo display of donated images taken right here at NightZone, sweeping across this wall. Top to bottom, one end to the other. And this is the challenge.' He held up an admonishing finger. 'Not just a hodge-podge. I want a theme here, real attention to detail. Real attention to *design*.' He looked at Carlos, leaning in close. 'Can she find a few minutes to talk with me about it?'

'That wall is, what . . . about thirty feet long? Nine feet high?'

'Exactly. And if it extends around that corner, even longer. I already have a file of photos that have been given to me over the years, even a couple that I took. Some images to get us started. And then we add to it as we go along, all images life-size. Make it an honor to have your picture or pictures chosen for the wall. Properly cropped, properly affixed to the wall so it looks as if we care about what we do. So you'll mention it to her?'

'Of course. You're thinking of permanent images, right? Not just some rotating display on a big-screen TV.'

'Maybe that. I hadn't thought of big-screen presentations. What the hell. Maybe both. But let's meet and see what we can come up with.'

He turned toward the dining room, where a young man waited politely. The fellow wore the white shirt with the black monogram, razor-creased slacks and polished black shoes that had come to be the NightZone uniform.

During Gastner's brief tenure, back in the Stone Ages, as a New Mexico livestock inspector, he'd apprehended this very youngster, Harve LeBlanc, for shooting a neighbor's steer that had chased the kid through a fence. Harve had been a skinny, awkward ten-year-old at the time, who couldn't talk to the cops without blubbering and spilling the beans. And here he was now, thirty-one or -two years old, all spit-polished, too handsome for his own good, and ready to serve.

'Good morning, gentlemen,' Harve said. 'Three for breakfast?'

'How about that four-top over by the exit,' Waddell replied. 'Who knows. I might have to duck out for a few minutes.' He reached out and took Carlos by the left elbow. 'And the wall thing? This is not a freebie, you understand. I don't want you to think that. If Tasha will do it, great. But once we agree on a design, once she starts, I want it to go up promptly. Not a little now and then. You know me.' He grinned. 'I'm willing to pay to make that happen.'

'I'm sure she'll understand that,' Carlos said.

'You both know how impatient I am,' Waddell laughed. 'And of course, that's the challenge. How to have a work in progress that always looks *finished*. Not like . . .' He hesitated and ducked his head. 'Not like some works in progress that don't actually *progress*.'

Then he charged out ahead of them, angling across the dining room to where its only other occupants were a party of three couples who looked as if they were ready for a day hunting in the bush. One of them even had a pith helmet nestled in his lap.

Waddell paused to exchange pleasantries, and as Carlos and Gastner caught up with him, he offered, 'These good folks are from Cleveland. They're ready for dawn on the bird trails.'

'Be safe out there,' Gastner said, unable to break away from the habits of a long career counseling tourists. He didn't mention the words *rattlesnake*, *scorpions*, *centipedes* or *cacti*. Good food and luxurious lodging had made sure that they missed the first hint of dawn breaking through the piñon and juniper.

Gastner and Carlos settled in for an amazing breakfast, both of them taking Waddell's suggestion to try the steak and eggs – the steak so tender it could be cut with a dull fork, the eggs fried in real butter exactly the way Gastner liked them, and the gluten-free walnut-raisin toast practically a meal in itself, aromatic in its own generous basket.

'I never would have guessed,' Waddell announced. He leaned forward, fists balled together on the table. 'This bird thing is growing exponentially, Bill. I mean, you wouldn't believe it. Literally, I have tourists come from all over the world to catch sight of roadrunners and harlequin quail. And sparrows? Don't get me started on them. Just incredible that there should be so many species. And *raptors?* And ravens, who seem to think we humans are putting on a show just for them.'

Waddell launched himself out of his chair to greet a Japanese couple as they came in. He obviously relished being host.

'You've heard the latest rumor?' he said at one point when he'd settled for more than thirty seconds.

'Which one of many?'

'There you go.' Waddell bobbed his head in exasperation. 'That's exactly right. See, we're building a sun pavilion over on the south-west rim, with a trail down about fifty feet so it's completely out of view of the mesa top. Just like the pavilion on the east rim.' He stretched back and waved his arms in both directions. 'Just a place to go kick back and soak up a dose of melanoma. A great view of the San Cristóbals, a couple of fixed-base viewing scopes, running water, even shade canopies. Some folks think it's a facility to spy on the drug intervention blimps that the Border Patrol flies along the border, but the latest rumor is that it's a spot reserved for nudists.'

He burst into laughter and smacked the table. 'I just love it.' His voice sank to a conspiratorial whisper. 'Waddell is turning the whole damn mesa into a nudist colony!' He munched a generous chunk of beef soaked in egg yolk. 'I mean, who spends time thinking up those crazy things?' He tilted his head in question. 'Though maybe it's not a bad idea, eh?'

'Depends on whose bodies are nude,' Carlos observed.

'There is that. And that's not the only thing I'm getting flack about, either.'

Gastner raised an eyebrow in question.

'When I purchased Lydia Thompson's acreage on our north border, I started to hear grumblings. I was going to do this, I was going to do that. At first, that wasn't so bad. But then when I fenced and posted the whole damn thing, *that's* when the grumblings turned up the volume. I even heard by round-about that I was indirectly responsible for Lydia's husband's death.'

'People say stupid things,' Gastner said. 'Is the dust-up just from boneheads in town, or are some of your neighbors none too happy?'

'Both, to put it mildly.' He glanced at Carlos. 'How about seconds?'

'I'm content,' the young man replied. 'The steak was just right. Spectacular, in fact.'

'Good to hear,' Waddell said. 'Nothing like New Mexico range-fed beef, is there? But back to the fence.' He dropped his voice. 'Wallace Boyd for one was truly pissed. He's complaining to anyone who will listen. As you know, Bill, his property adjoins ours in a spot or two, and of course he's hunted that turf for years. His dad before him. He's welcome to do what he wants on *his* land. But around here, we can't have hunters shooting bird-watchers or astronomers. I'm hoping Wallace will come to figure that out for himself. And maybe he has, because word has it that *he's* working on a massive fencing project of his own.'

Wallace Boyd's father, rancher Johnny Boyd, had smoked himself to death several years before, but his eldest son Wallace had taken over the ranch – a level-headed, well-educated fellow whom Gastner had known since Wallace was a toddler – and who had worked hard after his father's death to make the dusty, almost barren ranch land pay for itself. The Boyd property spread like a voracious elm tree, its branches winding around various Forest Service parcels, in places reaching all the way to state highway NM78, and crossing Forest Road 26 in half a dozen spots.

'He never did like my train, but when he heard how quiet it was, he grudgingly agreed it was an OK idea, especially since the tracks don't run on any of his property. Moving the tourists by train kind of keeps them all on a leash, so to speak. Keeps the road traffic down, keeps the dust down. And Wallace understands all that. But I think he sees the whole operation growing to be an infringement. He's old school, I guess, just like his dad. Likes open ranges, doesn't want anything blocking his sunrises or sunsets – not that we block anything. I mean, no tall structures. And our visitors aren't noisy, that's for sure.'

'You were there once,' Gastner gently reminded Waddell, the former cattleman. His boots hadn't carried the fragrant aroma of cattle manure for years.

'Yeah, I probably was.' He pushed his plate away. 'There's room for all of us, is what I'm saying. What, there's a few bazillion acres that I *don't* own in western Posadas County that's open to hunters and ranchers.' He leaned forward and lowered his voice. 'You remember Orrin Stance?'

'If I think hard enough, maybe.'

'Yeah, well. He wants me to include a riding stable on NightZone. With him running it, of course. Dude rides, pack trips, wagon rides . . . the whole ball of wax. *I* don't want anything like that on my property. There's the liability, of course. And the banker's hours that he wants. But I've been around livestock all my life. The *flies,* Bill. The horseshit.' He shook his head. 'No, thank you. Stance can go deal with the BLM or the Forest Service, if he wants.

'There's all the BLM lands, and if they ever develop the caves on the west side of the road, there'll probably be a Park Service footprint. You'd think that with all that, and the Forest Service besides? You'd think that would be enough. So I'm not alone in leaving a footprint.'

The muted squelch of a police radio sounded completely out of place in this lush oasis, and Waddell looked up, surprised.

'Well, my gosh. Look at this. It's a raid.' He rose and stepped past Gastner. County Manager Leona Spears, Sheriff Jackie Taber and Undersheriff Estelle Reyes-Guzman crossed the dining room, proudly escorted by Harve LeBlanc. Leona, a heavy-set woman in a bright sunflower muumuu, lugged both a black briefcase and a bundle of stuffed manila folders. Jackie Taber, robust and spiffy in the full, formal uniform that she'd adopted upon becoming sheriff, looked amused and favored Gastner with a wink. Undersheriff Estelle Reyes-Guzman, Carlos's mother, hung back, engaging Harve in a discussion that clearly was making the young man blush. Maybe it was just Estelle's subtle perfume, or her hand gently on his shoulder.

'You didn't tell me you were going to grace us with your presence,' Waddell exclaimed. 'You're headed for . . .' and Leona nodded toward one of the private meeting rooms off the back of the restaurant's open seating.

'Hubble,' she said. 'My friend Harve here says that it's free at the moment.'

'For you, any time.'

'You're such a sweety,' Leona cooed. 'We decided that we wanted something special to eat beyond greasy spoon chow, and it's been a while since I've visited this part of the county. So here we are. We need some room to spread out,' she added. 'And my heavens, look who Bill's got with him this morning. Carlos, you're looking better and better, day by day.'

'Thank you, ma'am. Lots of good food and clean air.'

'So UN-California,' she burbled.

'Let me lighten the load.' Carlos stepped away from his chair and reached for Leona's briefcase.

'No, no. If you take that, you'll disturb the delicate balance, and over I'll go. Just clear the way.' As the party headed off toward Hubble, one of the four well-appointed meeting rooms behind the dining room, Estelle detoured so that she passed directly behind Gastner. He could feel her breath on his ear and both hands on his shoulders.

'Your county is doing OK, *Padrino*?'

'It is, and I am,' Gastner said. 'I ate too much, but what else is new? And I did that yesterday, too, so there you go.' Estelle moved enough that he could twist around and see her face. 'What are you girls doing for fun this morning?'

'Budget,' Estelle said.

'Oh, now *that*'s fun. What playful new ideas does Leona have for you this time? She still aching to buy a fleet of Prius patrol units?'

'Solar powered,' the undersheriff said, but she managed to keep a straight face. 'You'll come over for dinner tonight? Tasha is making a really interesting Somali dish.'

'I sure would. But remember, sweetheart, I don't do insects.'

She punched his shoulder lightly. 'You'll be amazed, *Padrino*. And just a heads-up . . . Jackie and Kevin are coming over as well.'

'Kevin . . .'

'Kevin Parks?'

She said the name as if Gastner should know him. Instead, he held up both hands in surrender. 'I'm drawing a blank.'

'Kevin works with Prairie Sky Realty,' Estelle said.

'He *is* Prairie Sky,' Carlos added, and Estelle nodded. Carlos laughed at his godfather's blank expression. 'It's good that you don't remember ever arresting him, *Padrino*,' he said.

'Did I?'

Carlos looked up at his mother. 'I'll fill him in, Ma. Don't be late for your meeting.'

Miles Waddell intercepted her just as he had the county manager and sheriff, escorting her to the meeting room, then hustled back to rejoin his breakfast companions. 'Three great people,' he observed, and glanced back at the now-closed meeting-room door.

'Yes, they are,' Gastner said. 'And what should I know about Kevin Parks, other than that he's joining us for dinner and I don't want to be left wondering?'

'He's handling the title snarls for my great-uncle's property, just across the county road from here,' Carlos said.

'Whoa, and snarls there are,' Waddell added. 'I tried to buy it a number of years ago. I was going to use the place as storage . . . sort of a boneyard type of thing for all the stuff that we collect up here that needs to be out of sight and out of mind. Didn't go through, and I got busy with other things.'

'Reuben Fuentes,' Gastner mused. 'Damn, *that* name brings back a ton of memories. Other than an occasional visit from your mother, that place has stayed vacant for a lot of years.'

'Like twenty-six,' Carlos said. 'He died the year before I was born.'

Gastner laughed. 'I thought it was last week.'

Waddell nodded. 'You know, I remember old Reuben. He had quite a rep as a bandit of sorts. I mean, years and years ago.'

'He shot one or two people back then, but both deserved it,' Gastner said. 'He was caught up in some ruckuses down in old Mexico. Nothing in the States. About the time,' and he nodded at Carlos, 'this young man's older brother Francisco was in diapers, Reuben was just a quiet old geezer, in retreat from the world.' Gastner toyed with a small remnant of his hash browns. 'I liked him, though, old *bandito* that he was. And your mother,' and he glanced up at Carlos, 'your mother treasured him. She checked on him all the time.'

'She would have liked to see him move to town,' Waddell said. 'He was out there all by himself.'

Gastner grinned. '*Maybe* she would have.' He shrugged. 'The youngsters always want the old geezers to move into town. But see,

Estelle knew that Reuben wasn't cut out for town living. It would have killed him. We know how that goes, right? If you're not lucky enough to die quick and easy, the next thing you know, you're shuffled into assisted living.'

Waddell cupped his chin in his hand and his expression was an interesting mix of sympathy and amusement. 'Been mulling these things over, have you?' he chided good-naturedly.

'Too much free time now, Miles. And too many goddamn birthdays. Time to ignore 'em.'

FOUR

The next day, with the air-conditioned comfort of NightZone's hospitality almost forgotten, Undersheriff Estelle Reyes-Guzman stood in the center of County Road Fourteen's gravel surface, the rising sun of that Friday morning already hot on her back. Fifty yards to the north, Johnny Rabke's Ram pickup was nosed into the bar ditch, its stock trailer blocking half of the roadway. A few yards ahead of that, a white Ford F-350 was parked on the west shoulder, also facing north. Its flatbed carried a welding unit with a welter of support tooling. The driver, Jake Palmer, had found himself a seat on the tailgate, boots swinging free.

'Jake Palmer is the one who called this in?'

'He did. He hasn't left the scene since. I told him that we all needed to talk with him before he left. He's been sitting right there the whole time. I think by now he's working on his third pack of cigarettes.' Sheriff Jackie Taber pivoted at the waist, looking at the spreading emptiness around them. 'Lonely spot for dying that Mr Rabke found himself.'

'You're sure it's him?' Estelle Reyes-Guzman hadn't approached the rancher's pickup truck yet, in no hurry to intrude on the scene. She gazed back down County Road Fourteen. As the day progressed, there would be constant traffic on the gravel road, increased now by the attraction of the NightZone complex on top of the mesa. As if reading her mind, the sheriff said, 'I have Sutherland up at the intersection with Seventy-Eight, blocking traffic.' She nodded at her own unit, now pulled crosswise to the road. 'Linda is on the way. But I also put in a call to the state. I wouldn't object to some help, from what I can see here.'

'How many?'

'Two victims. Our friend Johnny Rabke is in the truck, the second victim is outside in the ditch. Both thoroughly deceased.' A charcoal-gray Dodge Durango approached, its dust trail blowing away to the east. 'And here's your hubby. You want to grab some photos first, before Linda gets here?'

'Just in case,' Estelle agreed, although she knew that the

department's photographer, Linda Real Pasquale, would respond promptly. Estelle glanced at her watch. 'What time was the call?'

'Dispatch caught me at six-oh-two, right after taking Palmer's call. I was rolling south anyway, so I took it. Deputy Thompson is on the road for a hearing in Albuquerque, or she would have responded. I was on the scene at six twenty-one.' The sheriff took a deep breath and pointed with the flat of her right hand. 'I walked straight up the left shoulder of the road. Palmer was walking toward me, and I told him to stay with his truck. He's pretty shaken.'

'I can imagine,' Estelle said.

Taber nodded. 'When I was sure Palmer understood me and would not be an issue, I left him at his vehicle and walked back to the victim's truck. The driver's side window was open, and the victim is behind the wheel, slumped a little toward the passenger side. Cool to the touch, no pulse, eyes dry. Rigor is significant.'

Taber held up her phone and selected an image. 'The second victim is outside, just a few feet behind the truck, in the ditch. The passenger door is open. Lots of blood, inside the truck and out. An obvious head wound.' She accepted the phone back. 'I made just the one circuit, to establish what we had.'

'ID?' Estelle felt a sinking feeling in the gut. Rabke's truck and trailer were local, and well-known. One year before, Estelle had responded to a bar fight at the Broken Spur Saloon, and found Rabke with blood gushing from a deep scalp wound, his opponent unconscious and dying on the floor.

Taber shook her head. 'I didn't touch anything. The driver is Johnny Rabke, no doubt about that. I don't know the other fellow.'

Estelle exhaled loudly. 'Aye. Shot?'

'The one in the ditch, most likely. Rabke has what looks like a Ka-Bar rammed into his chest.'

Dr Francis Guzman walked up the center of the road toward them, a black rucksack over one shoulder. 'Well, OK,' he said as he drew close. He stopped and reached out to rest his left hand on the back of his wife's neck while extending his right hand to Taber. 'Sheriff, what's the bad news?'

'One in the truck, one in the bar ditch, doctor.' Her radio crackled, as the EMTs called in their ETA. Almost immediately, photographer Linda Pasquale reported that she had just crossed the Rio Salinas, twenty minutes out.

'Let's take a preliminary look,' he said. 'But no question in your mind?'

'They're both as dead as they're ever going to get, doctor. The driver is Johnny Rabke. I don't know the second fellow . . . the one outside in the ditch.'

'Rabke, you said?'

'Yes, sir.'

'He hardly had time for that knife slash across his forehead to heal, did he.' He let the rucksack slide off his shoulder and held it in one hand. 'We'll wait on Linda before we disturb the scene.' He peered past them at the truck. 'One inside, one outside.' He grimaced. 'Let's see what we can do.' He headed for the yellow crime-scene tape that extended from one right-of-way fence to its companion across the road.

Dr Guzman avoided touching the victim's truck, but spent a long moment staring through the open driver's window. 'How about that,' he said finally. 'An interesting scenario for you folks. The truck's stalled in gear, the ignition is on, radio is turned low. I see one, two, three, four cartridge cases on the seat and the floor, and a cocked automatic just over the transmission hump on the passenger side. Huh.' He glanced back at the two officers. 'Rabke was in the habit of carrying a gun?'

'Don't know.' Sheriff Taber nodded at Estelle. 'Estelle took him on as a project a time or two in the past.'

'When he worked, yes. Even when he wasn't. He was always armed, as far as I know,' Estelle said. 'Some time ago, he and I had a discussion about his carrying a firearm into the Broken Spur. The saloon was his home away from home, but he understood the law and left the gun locked in the truck. But on the job, he had this thing about snakes, *Oso*.'

'Huh,' Dr Guzman said again. 'Well, a rancher's kid, why wouldn't he.' He reached in through the window and rested the fingers of his right hand on Rabke's neck, frowned, and drew away. Uncoiling his stethoscope from the rucksack, he donned it and listened, slipping the instrument's diaphragm between two of the upper buttons of the victim's shirt. As he listened, he touched the blood-soaked shirt below the knife and rubbed the blood between two fingers. 'What's the blade length of these things usually?'

'Marine Corps Ka-Bar standard is seven inches,' Taber said. 'If this is a knock-off, it could be anything.'

'Could be anything,' Guzman repeated. 'And had to hit him pretty hard, driven right to the hilt that way. Right through the breastbone like that. Tip might even be in the spine.' He relaxed the stethoscope and reached out to run his hand through Rabke's blond hair, then drew back. 'Just the one fatal wound, probably. Not counting what looks like a grazing wound in the thigh.'

'It'd be enough.'

'For sure. And number two?' The second victim lay across the ditch, body awkward. 'Do we know who?' Guzman asked.

'Yes,' Estelle offered, and her husband raised an eyebrow at her cryptic answer.

'Huh,' he muttered without offering the obvious question. He made his way around the big rig, and approached where the victim lay crumpled in the ditch. 'Now this is interesting.' He turned and regarded the open truck door, the inside surface and the lock plate, all heavily marked with gore. He straightened up and stood with his hands on his hips. 'Linda's ETA?'

'Momentarily,' Taber said.

'That's good,' and then he added with a straight face, 'I hope she brings a lot of film.' He turned to regard his wife. 'As best as I can guess until I have the clothing removed, Rabke's thigh wound is nearly contact. And then . . .' He shook his head and pointed across toward the truck, index finger tracing little circles in the air as he mused.

'The victim lying on the ground . . . did you say that you know this man as well?' He pushed through a tangle of chamisa and crouched near the body.

Estelle knelt beside her husband. 'It's Arturo Ramirez.'

'Well, damn. From Janos? The same family?'

'Yes. I've met Arturo a couple of times, *Oso*. Both he and his brother would come up across the border from time to time. Odd jobs and the like. His family lives in Janos.'

'Lived,' Dr Guzman corrected. He reached out with one gloved index finger and touched the entry wound just behind the victim's left mastoid, blood clotting Arturo Ramirez's long and tangled black hair. 'A heavy hitter.' He bent sharply at the waist, bringing his head down so he could look Ramirez in the face. 'Exit is explosive, just over the right eye.' He pushed himself back. 'Are there any more Ramirez brothers? Besides this one and the brother who tangled with Rabke at the saloon last year?'

'No. Two younger sisters. One's about eleven, the other is maybe six or seven.'

'Well,' the physician said, voice weary. 'I guess I can imagine what started all this.'

He glanced over at Sheriff Taber. 'Last year, as I'm sure you remember, this young man's brother collected a billiard ball to the temple, if I remember correctly. During a scuffle at the Spur with our other friend there, Mr Rabke. Young Ramirez died a day or so afterward.'

'Exactly.'

He regarded the man's blood-soaked left shirtsleeve, the spots of blood on the upper right chest just below the collarbone. 'They sure went at it, didn't they. This looks almost like bird shot.'

'Snake shot,' Estelle corrected. 'Rabke kept snake shot in his forty-five.'

'You talked to him about that?'

'He was always eager to discuss his firearm habits, *Oso*. At the time, I had no concerns. Nothing he did was illegal, or even threatening.'

'Until this, anyway. At least one round wasn't intended for snakes,' Dr Guzman said. 'That's no snake shot, or bird shot, through the Ramirez boy's skull. Like I said, you have your work cut out for you with this one.' He pushed himself upright. 'Some things I'll want to see as Linda works.'

FIVE

'Him again.' Linda Real Pasquale's exclamation was as much resigned as anything else. She balanced on the running board of Rabke's truck, standing on her tiptoes so that she could look inside the cab without touching anything. After a moment she shook her head in resignation. 'Such a waste.'

'I couldn't agree with you more,' Estelle said. 'The waste part, I mean.'

Linda stepped down from the truck's black rubber-coated running board. 'Did Jake somehow have a hand in this mess?' She glanced north toward where Jake Palmer, the lone spectator, still perched on the tailgate of his ranch truck, still smoking one cigarette after another. The tone of Linda Pasquale's husky voice reminded Estelle that her department's photographer lived with a nearly photographic memory of the myriad incidents she had photographed over the years – a scrapbook of whom she called the county's 'unfortunates'.

'He called it in. First on the scene,' Estelle said. 'At least he's the first who will admit to being first on the scene. That's why he has the ringside seat.'

'Ah. I guess it's conceivable that someone might drive by and not look too closely. Just pass by without stopping.' Linda stepped back until she was standing in the middle of the road, her mind turned to other issues beyond Jake Palmer's presence. 'Sheriff,' she said, turning to Jackie Taber, 'I need to shoot from above a bit before you open the driver's door. Kind of establish things.' She looked down at the hard gravel road's surface. 'I don't think we'll lose anything if you pull your vehicle up parallel, Sheriff. Right about where I'm standing. If I climb up in the back of your unit, I should have a clear shot. Before anything is disturbed. Then we can go from there.'

'Whatever you need,' Sheriff Taber said.

'And then ditto from the other side, maybe just with that door hanging open. The ground is a little higher beyond the ditch. That should work for me. We don't want you driving your unit all over the soft prairie.'

'And while you do that, I need to talk with Jake,' Estelle said. 'Then we can get him out of here. He doesn't need to see the whole circus.'

'Unless his hands are covered in blood,' Linda offered.

'Of course.'

The sun was already hot on the side of Estelle's face as she walked up the county road, leaving behind the stalled ranch truck, its dead occupant, and the dead Mexican national in the ditch. Jake Palmer slid off the high tailgate as he watched her approach. He lit a fresh cigarette from the butt of the last one, afterward scuffing the butt out carefully in the dirt.

His grubby white straw hat was pushed back far enough that the tan line on his forehead was stark. Just over six feet tall, he was a good-looking kid, Estelle thought, except for his blond beard and mustache, both sparse and scraggly, so much in fashion these days.

'I knew he was a goner the minute I saw him,' he said as Estelle drew close. He held up both hands as if in surrender, anticipating her question. 'I didn't touch nothin'.' His sweat-stained denim shirt was every bit as grubby as his faded blue jeans, both articles of clothing carrying an assortment of nicks and tears, typical of his work with barbed wire. He looked more as if he were finishing a day's work than well-rested and about to start one. He smelled that way as well, the odor of juniper smoke strong.

'Jake, I'm sorry you had to walk into the middle of this mess.' Estelle didn't offer to shake hands. She knew the young man well enough to call him by his nickname, rather than the 'Jason' that she knew was in his juvenile file. She glanced at his hands, his shirtsleeves, and blue jeans. Johnny Rabke's blood might have sprayed on a lot of things, but not on Jake Palmer's clothing. 'When you first arrived, the victim's vehicle was parked just the way it is now?'

'Yes, ma'am.'

'And when you first climbed out of your truck and approached his vehicle, you opened his driver's side door?'

'No, ma'am.' His reply was immediate and accompanied by an emphatic shake of his head. Equally interested, she watched the shake in his hands as he tried to find a way to hold the cigarette that looked both cool and collected.

'Didn't reach in to turn off the ignition key?'

He shook his head emphatically. 'Look, Sheriff, I didn't touch *nothing.* I mean, the truck was stalled out, the way it was in that bar ditch. One look, and I called it in.' He slid his cell phone out of his back pocket and held it up. He'd carried his phone in his left hip pocket for long enough that the jeans' fabric would be faded to shape. 'That's how it worked. I mean, I know better than to mess with things.'

His face, carrying several days' worth of blond stubble in addition to the silly little beard and the attempt at a mustache, was also touched with too much sun below his hat line. The fingers that held the phone shook. 'So . . . I mean, I could tell, Sheriff. Hell, he's got that big-ass old knife stickin' straight out of the middle of his chest. He ain't going to walk away from that. And the other guy, with that big old hole through his head . . .'

Estelle took a deep breath. 'So you walked around to that side of the truck as well?'

'Well, I mean I could *see*, you know? He's layin' right there. So yeah, I walked around over there, 'cause until I did that, I couldn't tell what the deal was. But I didn't touch nothing.'

'What time was that, Jake?'

He frowned and looked at his wristwatch. 'Had to have been right at six when I came by. Within a couple minutes either way.'

'I'm glad you called it in, Jake. And we're glad that you had the sense to wait here until someone could respond.' She looked past him at the load in his truck. 'You were headed out to work when you found him?' More than a dozen reels of barbed wire were crowded in the truck bed, along with several bundles of wire stays, a dozen or more bags of wire clips, and a mound of six-foot steel posts. Two jerry cans of water and half a dozen bags of ready-mix concrete added to the load.

'Yes, ma'am.'

'Nobody else stopped to see what was going on?'

'No, ma'am. Pretty quiet place out here this time of day.'

'And coming right up at six.'

'Right about. I start early, see, 'cause I need to get all this shit delivered so the crew can jump right on it when they see fit to start.'

'Including Johnny Rabke? He's working with you?'

Palmer hesitated. Estelle gave him time. 'Yeah, he is. I mean, he woulda been, you know what I mean. He'd come out to work a little later, same time as the rest of the guys.'

'And what time is that?'

'On the job at eight sharp, ma'am. We're building a section fence up north of Waddell's. Up around the north and east side of what was the Thompson property?' He turned and pointed his cigarette. 'Better part of two miles or so up that way, off the county road. The two-track goes off to the east a bunch of ways. You'll see our tracks where we've been going in.'

'That's hard ground. Right along the rimrock.'

He puffed out a burst of smoke in agreement. 'You got that right. About solid rock in most places.'

'That's all owned by the Boyds?' He nodded. 'So you and Johnny Rabke and who else? Who all is working with you busting through all those rocks?'

He held up his left hand, cocking the little finger down, then appeared to have second thoughts. 'I don't want to get no one in trouble, Sheriff.'

'I understand that. But we have two young men here as dead as it gets. If Johnny Rabke was working with your fencing crew? That makes sense. That explains what he was doing here in the first place.'

'Yes, ma'am. But look. See, I was surprised to find him out here when I come by. I mean, he's been here a while, ain't he? Like most of the night?' When Estelle didn't respond, he shook his head in puzzlement. 'I expected him to show up at eight. A couple of them are camping out to save the drive. Three of them are. I was thinking to do the same, maybe.'

'How about the other victim?'

He flinched at the word 'victim'. 'No, ma'am. He sure wasn't with us. I mean, not on our fence crew. Not with me and Johnny and the others. Maybe he was headed our way to work. I don't know.'

'Did you ever see him before?'

Jake took a long time answering, gently flicking the ash off the cigarette with the curled tip of his little finger. The shakes had settled down a little. Finally, he looked up at Estelle. 'Sure. A time or two. Mexican, ain't he?'

Estelle didn't respond to that. 'So you knew him.' Again, the bare hint of a nod. 'From where?'

'I mean, I *seen* him around from time to time. I know that for a while he was doing some odd jobs for the parish down in Regál. I heard that. And once in a while, he'd show up at the Spur. I mean,

I don't spend much time there, but sure enough, I mean, once or twice I seen him there.'

'He would have known Johnny Rabke, you think?'

Jake fumbled another cigarette, the butane lighter turned up so high that it scorched a third of the cigarette before he got it turned down. 'Sure, he woulda. I mean, how could he not? It was his brother that Johnny tangled with last year, am I right? I don't know why he woulda picked the guy up like that. Don't make much sense to me that they'd be friends now, after what happened. Unless maybe he just didn't recognize him, in the dark and all.'

'And since then . . . did you ever see Rabke and the Mexican fellow exchange words? Any argument between them?'

'See, I don't spend much time down there, Sheriff. I mean at the bar.' He held up his left hand, pushing what might be an onyx engagement ring out toward her. 'See, when the day's done, I like to head on home.' He grinned shyly. 'I got a girl at home, now.'

'I heard that you did. Marcy Gabaldon.'

'Yup.'

'Sweet girl. Congratulations.' Estelle knew that Marcy had landed a job teaching second grade at Posadas Elementary, and now had landed herself her cowboy.

'Yes, ma'am.'

'So one more time, Jake. You had Johnny Rabke out there with you building that fence. Who else is on your crew?'

'I guess you'll find that out anyways,' he said. 'Just the five of us. Keenan Clark? You know him.'

'I do.'

'And then EJ Stance and his little brother. Howie? They're camping out at the site, cause it's a lot easier than driving in every day from Deming. We're all workin' with the Boyd ranch.'

'The Stance boys used to live in Posadas.'

'Yes, ma'am. They did. Then here a while back, they got hired on by the state Highway Department, I mean EJ did, and he and his brother both, they ended up in Deming. I guess that didn't last too long.' He tried a weak smile. 'Seems like there aren't too many folks who want to tangle with wire and drivin' posts these days, but maybe it beats spreading hot asphalt.'

'If they're camping at the site, who's driving in right now? The deputy says *two* men are wanting to pass through our roadblock on Fourteen right now.'

'That'd be Keenan Clark, and he said he was going to pick up Ricky Boyd. The Boyd kid's dad wants him to work a little. We'll see how that's going to work out.'

For a moment Estelle regarded the young man. 'When did you load up all the supplies?'

'Yesterday, after work. I stopped off at the mercantile. That way I didn't have to fuss around this morning early.'

'And you're telling me that you didn't spend time at the Spur last night?'

'I didn't go there. I really didn't, Sheriff,' he insisted. 'I was home right after work. Walked through the door to home at five forty-five.' He said it as if coming home promptly was a grand accomplishment. Maybe it was. He puffed up a little more. 'I ain't been to the Spur since last week. You can ask Marcy.'

'But you worked with Rabke all day yesterday?'

'Yes, ma'am. He was loading up his truck when I took off for home. See, he's got the two ATVs in his trailer, and tools and stuff. He was going to head into town and fuel everything up. I mean, he lives right there, south of town. He was also worried some about his truck. Wheel bearing going bad or something like that.'

'He was carrying his gun yesterday?'

Palmer hesitated, his eyes growing wide at the surprise question. 'Yes, ma'am. Always does.'

'The gun you saw him carrying while he worked . . . tell me about that.' She watched Palmer as he ran the thoughts through his head. The last time *she* had seen Rabke had been weeks before, in the parking lot of the Broken Spur Saloon, the young man's home away from home. As she swung her county car into that parking lot, she'd caught sight of him taking the pistol off his belt, ready to shove it under the front seat of his pickup.

Palmer dug out yet another cigarette. 'He liked to practice, you know what I mean? When we'd take a spell from work, he'd practice on his fast draw, like a damn cowboy in the movies. He didn't use no tie-down holster rig like the movies, though. He called it workin' on his *tactical* skills. And you know, he could get it out in a hurry. He always wore one of those shorty plastic holster things, with no spring latch or safety. He was always looking for snakes to kill, and he'd say things like, "I'll get him before he gets me." Stuff like that.'

'What was the gun, Jake? You saw it often enough.'

'Oh, yeah. Nice piece. A custom something or other. Kimber. That's what it was. Kimber Custom. Heavy thing in forty-five, I'm pretty sure that's what it was. He spent some money on that puppy, that's for sure.'

'What about you?'

'About me what?'

'You carry when you're working?'

His expression was just a touch wistful. 'Dang, I can't afford one of those things. Anyways, Marcy won't allow a gun in the house.' He re-seated his battered, sweat-stained hat more firmly on his head. 'But sheriff, Johnny must have been taken by surprise, you know what I mean? Fast as he was, somebody still beat him to it and stuck him with that butcher knife. How's he going to move much after that? That's my guess.'

'How did you ascertain that he was deceased?'

He almost laughed, then looked pained. 'Look, I could tell, just lookin'. His eyes were open and all dried out like, his mouth is hangin' open, and . . . and . . .' He stopped and looked away. 'And he smelled like shit, ma'am. You know . . . like what you'd think he'd smell like, spending the night all dead and everything.'

'And just a couple other . . .'

'Three ten, three zero eight.'

Interrupted by her hand-held, Estelle touched the mike. 'Go ahead, three zero eight.' She turned and walked a pace or two back down the road.

'Estelle, Deputy Sutherland has a truck stopped with two workers wanting to head south for a fencing site just north of you.' Sheriff Taber's voice was soft and unexcited. She could have just as easily shouted the distance between her and Estelle. 'They won't be a problem for us, but Sutherland also has a delivery semi headed for the Zone, waiting on us. We can walk 'em through?'

'That's affirmative for the semi. No pass for the fencers. We'll be wanting to talk with each one of them back in town, so have Sutherland put a hold on 'em. And tell Sutherland to contact us before he lets anyone else through. Just the semi for now.'

'Ten four. Sergeant Pasquale is on scene. And Bob Patchett just pulled up. He says anything we need, he'll do.'

'Perfect.' She glanced back down the road and saw Patchett's black-and-white state SUV pulling in behind the sheriff's. 'Jake, this is what needs to happen now,' Estelle said. 'We need a formal deposition from you – a statement of what you did, what you saw, when you saw it. Everything you can think of since you turned on to this road earlier this morning. Include everything you just told me, and then anything else you can think of. All right?'

'Sure, I guess. I mean, sure.'

'Good. You were the first one here, so what you saw is important to us. When you and I are finished here, you're going to drive back to the Sheriff's Department in Posadas with Sergeant Pasquale. I think you know him.'

Palmer grinned. 'Oh, yeah.'

Estelle didn't ask for amplification. 'Sergeant Pasquale will follow you back to the county building, and then talk you through the preliminary procedure for the deposition.'

'But then . . . I mean all this stuff,' and he waved a hand at the fencing inventory behind him in the bed of the truck. 'They'll need it out to the fence.'

'Today's a morning off for you, Jake. You and the crew both. They'll be following you in to town as well.'

'So, we're in trouble, am I right?'

Estelle smiled. 'Not a bit. It's just what we do. We talk to anyone and everyone who was anywhere near the area of the attack.' She nodded at Rabke's truck. 'We could all stand around out here in the sun, or we could pay you all a visit at home, or we could all be comfortable at the office.'

'Mr Boyd's going to be pissed, us not gettin' the job done.'

Estelle slipped one of her business cards from her left breast pocket. 'If he complains, give him this. Have him call me. But I know Wallace pretty well, Jake. There won't be a problem.'

He read the card as if there were five hundred words on it instead of eight and contact numbers.

'Just sit tight until I have a chance to brief Sergeant Pasquale. Then he'll swing by here and you can follow him in.'

'He don't need to do that. I know the way.'

'Wait for him before you move this truck.' She looked hard at him to make sure she had his attention and that he had understood. 'That's just the way we do things. The others all drive their own rigs?'

'Well, sure.'

'Good. Just daisy chain with the others. We need to talk with anyone who was with Rabke yesterday, but we do that one at a time.'

The young man shrugged. 'Well, OK, I guess. Whatever you say.'

'And for now the ATVs can stay in the trailer. Both Rabke's truck and trailer will be at the SO boneyard until we process them. You know where that is, down at the county complex?'

'Yes, ma'am.'

'One last little thing, Jake. You've seen Johnny Rabke wearing his gun, correct? Not just heard him talk about it. You've *seen* it while he works.'

He nodded. 'Yes, ma'am. Lots of times.'

'Was he right or lefty?'

Palmer frowned as his hand drifted to his waist. He touched his heavy leather belt. 'Lefty. All the time. I mean, yeah. He was.' He jerked an imaginary gun out of an imaginary holster on his left hip. 'Just like that.'

'Make sure you mention that in your deposition, Jake.'

'But see, he could shoot that thing just about as well with either hand. I've seen him do it. He had that ambi thing set up.'

'The ambidextrous safety?' He nodded. 'Include that, too.'

He looked rueful. 'Jeez, the way I write, it'll take me all day.'

'That's all right. We're open twenty-four seven, Jake. Don't forget to give your Marcy a call before she heads off to school.' She reached out and tapped the business card Jake still held. 'Have her call me if there's a problem. Just tell her that nobody on your crew is in trouble. It's just something we have to do, and do it right, and do it now.'

'It looks to me like they did each other, am I right? To my way of thinkin', that's what I'd say.'

She didn't reply, but instead said, 'Sergeant Pasquale will be here in just a few minutes.' As she walked back down the road, she mused that Jake Palmer had taken his good sweet time to ask the question that most folks would blurt out in the first thirty seconds of conversation.

SIX

'What are you thinking?' Sheriff Jackie Taber had stepped away from the roadway to give the ambulance room to maneuver. With Linda Pasquale once again filming video of the process, Dr Guzman, the two EMTs, and State Officer Robert Patchett worked to remove Johnny Rabke's body from the pickup, sliding the stiff, jack-knifed corpse sideways so that the knife's handle wouldn't snag on the steering wheel. Arturo Ramirez's corpse, sprawled across the ditch, was an easier matter.

Sheriff Taber's question was prompted by Estelle's expression. Frowning hard, the undersheriff stood with fists on her hips, turning like a compass needle out of whack. 'I'm trying to piece together how this went down,' she said. 'Did Johnny pick up Arturo Ramirez at the Spur? I'm curious about why he would do that? We don't know anything about the history between these two, other than the obvious.'

Taber looked skeptical. 'Maybe it's this simple, Estelle. Arturo Ramirez and his brother Pablo didn't look much alike. They weren't together that night last year when Pablo was killed at the Spur. I remember him as being stocky, kind of longish hair. Arturo was on the slender side, but a little more heavy featured. I can understand Johnny Rabke not recognizing him in the dim light of the saloon . . . or out in the parking lot, if that's where they met.'

'But then,' Estelle added, 'assuming Johnny didn't recognize Arturo, just picked him up because picking up a hitchhiker is a natural cowboy thing to do, was that just a case of Arturo baiting the trap? He waits until they've driven out into the boonies, where he could attack without witnesses and then stand a good chance of slipping away?'

'If that's the case, Arturo didn't count on one thing.'

'A forty-five within handy reach.'

'Exactly. And it looks to me like he was traveling with a definite purpose in mind. Traveling light. Not much carry-on luggage,' Sheriff Taber said. 'Some water, phone, a change of underwear and socks . . . and a big knife.'

'And here we go again,' Estelle said. 'There's that leather knife scabbard on his belt, so we can guess that he was carrying that knife. I mean, it makes sense that he was, but . . .' She paused. 'I know that when he was in this country, Arturo often stayed with Benny and Concha Aguilar down in Regál. They bought Betty Contreras's place after she had her stroke and moved over to that senior center in Silver City. If some of his stuff was left at the Aguilars', that gives us something. That maybe tells us something. They might have noticed that he carried the knife. Maybe.'

'So when he left the Spur, Ramirez normally would have headed south, toward Regál. If that's where he was shacking up. Or back across the border, on farther south to Janos, to home.' Taber held up both hands a basketball apart. 'Rabke lives in that old trailer behind Wayne Feed, south of town. The place that looks abandoned.' Estelle nodded. 'So when *he* left the Spur, whenever that was before the bar's two a.m. closing, why wouldn't he have headed *east*, to home?'

'And yet here they both are, northbound on County Road Fourteen,' Estelle said.

'We'll want a simple answer for that,' the sheriff said. 'I mean, traffic *can* get back to Posadas heading north to State Seventy-Eight and then heading in past the airport. But that's the long way around.'

'It may just be that with a heavy trailer load, Rabke wanted to drop it off at the fencing site first, and not have to haul the trailer back to town,' Estelle said. 'And the other half of the equation? Arturo Ramirez wasn't concerned with heading back to Regál. At least not yet. Not until he finished his business with Johnny Rabke. I can imagine that, after a few too many beers, Johnny Rabke had no idea who was climbing into his truck with him. He never saw it coming.'

'That leaves us a question. Why did Arturo wait a year to avenge his brother? Where's that volatile Latin temperament I've heard so much about?'

'Some of us like to ponder and think and brew and plan. Give things time to fester.' She smiled. 'Or a simpler explanation. He didn't know where Johnny Rabke lived, or where he was working. Circumstances weren't right. The stars weren't aligned.'

Linda Pasquale joined them as the ambulance maneuvered to a spot of prairie flat enough that they could turn around. 'Everything,' she said. 'Both still and video.' Linda nodded with satisfaction as she zipped the last of her cameras into the duffel bag.

'We're particularly interested in the pattern of the forty-five shell casings,' Jackie Taber said.

Linda nodded vigorously. 'I checked to make sure they're all exactly what we need. The images are all sharp and clear. Every which way.' She held up the fingers of one hand, spread wide. 'Five cases located and recovered, with three live rounds still in the gun. One round still chambered, the last two in the magazine. Close-ups of each case in situ, and panorama showing everything. Details of the truck's interior. You can even read the radio legend, telling us what station he was listening to at the moment the truck stalled.'

'Then we're good to go. I'm disappointed that there are no tracks on the roadway itself. Rabke never exited the truck. And Ramirez? He was apparently *blown* out the door. No other prints.' The sheriff looked across at Dr Guzman. 'You're good?'

'For now,' Dr Guzman said. 'I have a couple other things hanging fire on my calendar. Can we shoot for one o'clock today?'

'Oh, what fun,' Linda quipped, knowing exactly what was coming.

'You want to flip for it?' the sheriff asked.

'You win,' Estelle replied. 'We have Tom working the interviews with the fence crew, and we'll see how that shakes out. He may want to bring Lieutenant Mears in on that. You two are at the autopsy at one o'clock today. More big questions coming with that. I want to run down to Regál to talk with the Aguilars, and then we'll see about going on down to Janos. I need to understand more about Ramirez's movements last night.'

'I'll give the family the official call,' Taber said. 'But you're right. A visit by one of us is better.'

'Definitely. And then today, if there's some daylight left, I want to meet with Wallace Boyd. He owns the land where the fencing crew is working . . . where Johnny Rabke was working last.'

'You're going to want us to give Bobby Torrez a heads-up?' Taber asked. 'I'd like to hear what he has to say about the ballistics involved here.'

Estelle nodded. 'We don't want him to get too comfortable with this retirement business.' Despite Torrez's taciturn, monosyllabic nature, Estelle had always been able to pry keen insights out of the former sheriff.

'I was just thinking,' Taber added, 'which is a good thing to do.

This is country where Bobby spends a lot of time hunting, and he knows Wallace Boyd as well as anyone. He's going to be interested. On top of that, we all know the man can't resist a tidy ballistics puzzle, and we for sure have one of those dropped in our laps.'

Linda Pasquale held a pistol grip index finger pointed south, and Estelle turned to see the Suburban easing off the gravel road to the narrow shoulder behind Jackie Taber's unit. 'The boss is here.' The big SUV's headlights winked a couple of times.

'*Ay*,' Estelle said. 'This isn't a social call.' She knew that despite his age, Bill Gastner's habits could put him anywhere in the county, at any time of day or night. But she also knew that he was loath to show up at a crime scene like this one, running the risk of finding himself as extra baggage that no one had the need or inclination to talk to. He could have called Estelle on the phone, or in an emergency reached her via county radio. But here he was.

As she approached, she saw the driver's window of the Suburban roll down, but Gastner did not make the effort to get out. This time, he was traveling alone.

'*Padrino*,' Estelle greeted Gastner, using the Spanish for 'godfather'. But she recognized the solemn set of his old bulldog face. He didn't do distractions well, didn't like to clutter his thoughts with small talk.

'This is one of those "better late than never" deals.'

She reached out and rested a hand on his left elbow, but said nothing.

'Oh, yeah. Now, I have to get my times straight.' He glanced at the enormous Rolex on his left wrist. 'The other morning, when Carlos and I went joyriding?'

'That would be yesterday, *Padrino*.'

'So it would. Now don't embarrass me, sweetheart.' He pointed ahead. 'That truck – I don't know about the trailer – that truck belongs to the Rabke kid. What's his name?'

'Johnny.'

'Johnny Rabke. Right. And I think the trailer belongs to Wallace Boyd. I think. Yesterday morning, then, and I recall it was about five thirty or so, Deputy Thompson stopped that rig down on Fifty-Six. Right at mile marker twenty-two.'

'All right.' She smiled at his wonderfully selective memory. And the memory of the dispatcher's logbook no doubt would agree with Gastner's.

'We drove by, Carlos and I – and chalk it up to busybody me. Both parties were out of their vehicles, having a chat over behind the truck, on the offside of the shoulder. Pretty much out of view of the highway.' He held up his left index finger. 'This is my concern. Your son, whose quick wit and keen vision are both in a different league from my own, mentioned that he saw,' and Gastner tapped the left lens of his glasses, 'that he *saw* young Rabke standing with his hand on Deputy Thompson's shoulder.'

He paused. 'That's it. None of my business. For all I know, they could have been standing there discussing a flat tire or something. Or something. But that was enough for me to think, "Well, now." So I slowed, took my time, and turned around, which with the Queen Victoria here is no mean feat. And as we passed them again, coming back the other way, Deputy Thompson walked along the roadway side of the two vehicles, headed for her unit. I rolled down my window and asked her if everything was all right. I remember maybe offering another bumper jack or something if they needed it. She agreed that all was well, they didn't need a thing. And I got no tips from her expression.' He looked at Estelle and grinned. 'I mean, we remember what it's like when we'd stop to check on a couple of teenagers parked somewhere necking, and maybe their behavior is not quite as what, *discreet?* as maybe they should be, and we look hard at their faces during the encounter, especially at the girl's face, for the tells?'

'What I recall is that you are a master at that, sir.'

'Yeah, well, *was* maybe. But that was decades ago. Still, all appears well, Deputy Thompson reports, and she's as collected and cool as she can be. So with a "stay safe", off we go. That was yesterday at five thirty a.m. or thereabouts. Life goes on. And today, twenty-four hours later, the world finds Johnny Rabke, never to see his twenty-fourth birthday. That's what I'm told by Ernie Wheeler in dispatch.'

'I'm going to have to talk with that young man,' Estelle chided gently.

He turned and looked hard at Estelle. 'I can be persuasive,' Gastner said. 'More important, you know what I believe about coincidences, sweetheart.'

'Yes, I do.'

'I'd sure as hell want to talk with Deputy Thompson. Sure as hell would. But I didn't want you to discover later that Carlos and

I had had that brief encounter – with what we both saw yesterday morning, and then never made the connection after the events today. Might be nothing, might be something. That's all. The hand on the shoulder might seem trifling, but there it is. If Carlos saw what he saw, then it needs to be checked out.'

'I appreciate the info, sir.'

'Well, see, I could have mentioned it to you last night, when I was over for dinner. But I didn't, because there was maybe no reason to, maybe because I had a hell of a case of food focus. But now, I think there's reason to.' He shrugged. 'Or if I'm way off base, tell me to shut up and go away.'

'That'll never happen, sir.'

'Again, none of my business, but is Deputy Thompson on scene right now?'

'No.'

He laughed. 'What a fine, descriptive answer.'

'She's up in Albuquerque at a child custody hearing.'

'Oh, those are ugly. Not hers, I hope.'

'No, sir. But believe it, I'll have a talk with her as soon as she comes back.' She reached out and punched Gastner gently on the shoulder. 'And I will have a chat with your ride-along companion. I want to hear his version of the hand-on-the-shoulder thing.'

'Because you never know.'

'That's absolutely correct, *Padrino*. You never know.'

'Then I'm out of here.' He reached down and triggered the ignition.

'You're welcome to a crime-scene tour, as long as you're here, sir.'

'No.' He smiled at his imitation of Estelle's own answer.

SEVEN

B etty Contreras had lived in Regál for decades before fate handed her a new challenge. A turn, a trip over essentially nothing, and the resulting broken hip marked the beginning of her decline at age eighty-three. The busted hip was followed shortly by a stroke, and with her husband Emilio long passed, she was left with only neighbors in Regál and a single daughter in Albuquerque. She made her decision quickly. Several neighbors had helped her move to Silver City, and almost before she knew it, she was settled in Days' Care Senior Living. It was as if she'd never lived in Regál at all.

She hung on for a year being coddled by the nursing home, then decided that assisted living was not her idea of living. She promptly died on a warm spring morning a year after her initial stumble. When her estate offered for sale her tidy, picturesque adobe in Regál, the first one after the long downhill approach to the village, it sold promptly, thanks to a blitz of advertising on the internet.

Estelle Reyes-Guzman had driven south through the San Cristóbals hundreds of times on State Fifty-Six, always mindful of the deer population that appreciated the hedge of grass along the highway's shoulder. This time, as she crested Regál Pass and started down the switchbacks into the tiny village, she could see the flat roof of Betty Contreras's former home, just an easy walk across to the mission and its parking lot behind the newly expanded border crossing.

Initially ecstatic about their purchase of Betty's former home, Californians Ralph and Marie Harris discovered that they didn't enjoy the forty-mile drive to the one grocery store in Posadas, nor the hundred-plus miles to the vast shoppers' heaven in Tucson. They were even less than enthusiastic when they discovered that most of their new neighbors spoke – at least to them – only the ancient, idiomatic border Mexican lingo. The first time that a surprise winter snow blocked Regál Pass, clogged the dirt streets and lanes through Regál, and marooned them at home for a few minutes, the Harrises panicked. The snow-packed paths through the village then thawed to mud the consistency of chocolate pudding. That put the cap on it.

Realtor Kevin Parks, who had brokered the initial deal between Betty Contreras's estate and the Harrises, convinced Ralph and Marie to keep the adobe as a sure-fire investment. He convinced them that renters were easy to find . . . and they were. Benny and Concha Aguilar were delighted to move from Janos, Mexico, to Regál. They knew Kevin, they knew at least half of the twenty-three residents of Regál.

A plus for all involved, since seventeen of the twenty-three residents were seventy years old or better, was that Benny Aguilar had a strong, tireless and willing back. What fireplace construction, car port, irrigation ditch, or winter firewood cordage that he couldn't handle by himself, he knew who to call. That his frequent helpers, the Ramirez brothers down the road in Janos, Mexico, were undocumented didn't bother him a bit. Neither Benny nor Concha had ever bothered with the paperwork either.

Estelle had known Benny Aguilar for decades, since the night that young Benny and Estelle's uncle Reuben had stolen a sagging pickup truckload of railroad ties from the highway boneyard near the intersection of County Road Fourteen and State Fifty-Six. It had taken then Posadas Undersheriff Bill Gastner about fifteen minutes to figure out who the perpetrators were, and another ten minutes to apprehend them, sweaty and enjoying a beer at Reuben's cabin.

He'd then watched impassively as Reuben and his less-than-eager cohort had returned the load of purloined railroad ties. He didn't let the pair just dump the ties back in the state yard. He wasn't satisfied until the heavy ties were stacked perfectly in the very spots from which they'd been taken.

Braking hard, Estelle made the tight turn from pavement to the dirt neighborhood lane. She nosed the Charger into the Aguilars' driveway, parking behind Benny's sun-bleached, turquoise '65 Chevrolet pickup. The last time she'd seen it, the Chihuahuan license plate was wired to the tailgate. When the tailgate was lowered, the plate would be conveniently out of sight.

She let the car idle as she radioed dispatch and logged her location. Ernie Wheeler confirmed and then added, 'Three-ten, the sheriff wanted to confirm with you that she has contacted both victims' relatives. She said that you'd want to know, and that they'd welcome a visit from you. At your convenience.'

'Ten-four.' Finding Johnny Rabke's family, now just a stepmother and two older sisters in Las Cruces, wouldn't be difficult, either.

And after Johnny's barroom escapade a year ago, with his scalp laid open with a knife slash, stepmother and sisters might not have been rocked with surprise at the young man's current fate.

The trip south to Janos, Mexico, though, would have to wait until she could drive one of the unmarked department cars, leaving all of her personal hardware on the US side of the border. Mexican authorities had no patience with firearms crossing into their turf, even when worn by cops. A telephone call from the sheriff was a distant second best behind a personal visit, but Estelle had no desire to struggle this day with the Mexican bureaucracy. She or the sheriff, or both, would plan a visit to Janos as civilians when they could.

Benny Aguilar pushed open the screen door and stepped out on to the porch. Thick through the shoulders and high-waisted, his full-cut jeans and denim shirt made him appear more bulky than he was. He regarded Estelle through an unruly thatch of salt and pepper hair as she got out of the Charger.

'I'm late getting going this morning,' he said by way of greeting. 'You ever have a morning like that?'

'More often than not,' Estelle replied. 'Benny, how are you?'

He took his time thinking of an answer. 'You know, I'm OK.'

'And Concha? I haven't seen her in months.'

'You got to rise and shine first thing to catch her,' Benny said. 'Look, I have coffee on.' He reached out for the screen-door latch. 'You content out here, or inside?' Estelle had half expected Benny to greet her in Mexican, but his English was fluent and easy. The nearest neighboring residence was a hundred yards diagonally across the narrow lane, half hidden behind a struggling grove of aging peach trees, far enough away that their conversation wouldn't be overheard.

'This is fine. May Concha join us?'

'She walked over to the Roybals' for a few minutes. They have a baby on the way. You know what *that* means. Lots of long hours.'

'Ah. It's good that Concha can help.'

He nodded his agreement 'So what brings the law here?' He offered an easy smile. 'How come you missed out on that sheriff's job when Bobby retired?'

'No miss,' Estelle said. 'You have to be careful what you wish for, Benny. Politics wasn't on my wish list.'

'That Taber woman is doing all right, then?'

'She's doing fine.' Estelle took a deep breath. 'Benny, I need to talk to you and Concha about Arturo Ramirez.'

Benny's left eyebrow drifted upward, perhaps surprised at the sudden cessation of neighborly chitchat. 'We haven't seen him in a while.'

'What's "a while"?'

'Well, you know. He's in and out. You know how it works.' He pointed southeast toward the Iglesia de Nuestra Madre and the new border crossing headquarters just to the south of the mission. If such unrest of spirits actually happened, Estelle had always thought Betty Contreras's husband Emilio would be turning in his grave whenever he looked at the ugly new building that squatted beside the church. The *iglesia* had been built in 1826, whitewashed until it hurt the eyes, a simple mission style with a traditional carved wooden door that – until the year previous – had never been locked. Emilio had lavished his time and talents on the church's maintenance.

Nothing in the neighboring INS building's design complemented it. A portion of the towering border fence had approached the village from the east, but its construction had halted a hundred yards from the border crossing and the mission. For now, the official border crossing made do with barbed wire and chain-link. Farther to the west, the border fence ran up through the craggy foothills of the San Cristóbals, making do with four strands of barbed wire.

Estelle knew that, years ago, Benny Aguilar had made regular use of the various deer trails that led across the border. Travelers on foot easily hopped the border fence and hiked to the back doors of willing and cooperative Regál residents. No one made an issue of it. The Border Patrol ignored the few folks who labored on either side of the border but who chose to avoid the formalities of the Port of Entry. Trying to apprehend them just made the cops look foolish.

'Arturo's working with you now?'

Benny shook his head. 'Not today, no.'

'Was Arturo here last night?'

Benny hesitated. 'He left some of his stuff here. Then he walked over the pass. Or maybe he caught a ride, I don't know.' He turned and pointed his upper lip toward the church. 'You know, Father Anselmo was here earlier yesterday. It's possible that Arturo caught a ride with him.'

It's more than possible, Estelle thought. Father Bertram Anselmo, even as he approached doddering old age, was always quick with the taxi service – especially for weary travelers with potential border problems.

'They were talking about what it would take to build the new steps for the mission.' He looked quizzically at Estelle. 'Maybe he'll be back later today. Maybe tomorrow. He's always careful, that one. You know, the way we live,' and he grinned coyly, 'we got to keep close watch over the *federales* on that side, and the Border Patrol over here. They can sure make life miserable.'

'Keep your tailgate down, Benny.'

He brightened. 'Hey, let me just show you.' He was off the porch in an instant, rounding the pickup. He lifted the tailgate and beckoned Estelle. 'Look at that, now!' Sure enough, the sun glinted off the shiny New Mexico license plate, complete with a current registration sticker.

'Nice. Now I don't have to shut my eyes whenever I pass you on the highway.'

'Now that we have a permanent New Mexico address, *no problema*. And don't be thinking that I stole that plate off some tourist's car up in the grocery store parking lot.'

'I would never think such a thing, Benny.'

'Straight from the MVD.' He lowered the tailgate. 'If I see Arturo later on, you want me to have him call you?'

'I wish that were possible, Benny.' She waited until he had stepped away from the truck. 'The bad news is that Arturo Ramirez was murdered sometime last night or early this morning. That's what I came down to tell you.'

His frown was so intense that his bushy eyebrows nearly met in the middle.

'That is not possible, *agente*. He was just here . . .'

'Last night, you said earlier. And then Father Anselmo probably gave him a ride over the pass. Maybe he intended to go to town. We don't know.'

'I don't know that either. But he might have. What happened?'

'We're not certain yet, Benny.'

'But where?'

'North of here.'

'You mean at the Spur?'

'No, not there.'

'The brother last year, now this,' Benny whispered. 'Do his parents know?'

'The sheriff has contacted them by phone. I'll go down to talk to them, when I know more.'

'He was robbed?'

'It's too early to know, Benny. I came down right away to talk with you because we're trying to trace Arturo's route north. Where he went, who he talked to.'

'I understand . . . but I *don't* understand, if you know what I mean.'

'I do. And I'm sorry I can't tell you more.'

'Is there anything you wish me to do?'

'Not at this moment, Benny. If you would show me whatever effects Arturo left with you, I'd appreciate that.'

'It is not much, but of course.' He beckoned toward the front door.

'I'll be with you in a moment.' Estelle returned to the Charger and drew the digital camera out of the center console.

'He would stay in the small room off the kitchen,' Benny said when she returned. 'It is not much . . . just the one bed, and he would use the bathroom down the hall. He would come and go through the kitchen door. Sometimes, we would not even know he was here, or that he had *been* here. I get busy, Concha is busy. The kitchen door is never locked.'

'Did he ever travel with companions?'

'Not to my knowledge. Before last year, he would sometimes travel with his brother. But not since. Not that we know. And I think he would tell me if he was accompanied. As a courtesy, you know.'

He led her through the house, the first time she'd been in it since Betty Contreras had lived there. The kitchen was painted several shades of bright yellow and blue, the front of each drawer bordered with white. As soon as it cleared the San Cristóbals, the morning sun would blast through the kitchen window and turn the place into a rainbow.

'Right here.' Benny opened the door to the bedroom. He pointed to the bed. The room was not much larger than a generous closet. 'You remember Betty?'

'Of course.'

'This was her pantry at one time. We asked the new owners if we could remove . . . if we could *renovate* a little. That *armario*?

Hernán Duran made that. With that and the bed, there isn't much
room, no?' He reached for the burlap sack that rested in the corner
by Hernán Duran's handcrafted wardrobe, but Estelle stopped him.

'Give me a moment, Benny,' she said. The camera clicked a dozen
times as she moved around the room. She snapped on a pair of thin
Latex gloves, and opened the burlap sack. A change of underwear, a
single pair of socks. A half-package of soft tortillas, curled around
two energy bars. Tucked in was a plastic zip bag with a toothbrush
and a tightly curled tube of toothpaste. No razor. Estelle took a deep
breath, drawing in the traces of Arturo Ramirez's scent.

After more photos, she returned the items to the bag and closed
it. 'Will you show me the bathroom that he used?'

'Of course. It is just the one.'

'Benny?' A woman's voice interrupted them, and quick, light
footsteps brought her to the bedroom door. Concha Aguilar was
petite and dark, just about half Benny's size. She was dressed in
blue jeans and a white smock. 'I do not mean to interrupt. But I
saw the police car outside.'

'Estelle Reyes-Guzman,' Estelle offered, and Concha's handshake
was warm and quick. 'We've met several times.'

'Of course. Your husband owns the clinic, blessings on him,'
Concha said.

'Yes.'

'Conchita, there is terrible news. That's why the sheriff is here.
It is about Arturo.'

'What has he done?' She looked first to Estelle, then back to her
husband.

'Concha, Arturo was killed sometime during the early morning
hours today,' Estelle said. 'I'm afraid that's all I can tell you at this
time. We are trying to establish his movements yesterday and early
this morning.'

'He's dead? But I mean, where?'

'Farther north in the county. That's all we know. We don't know
where he was going, or why. But I need to know from you . . . he
was here during the day yesterday?'

'Yes. Of course he was.'

'And what time did he leave?'

'Just after noon. I offered him lunch, but he had seen Father
Anselmo's car over at the church, and he was eager to talk with
him.'

'That's the last time you saw him, then? Shortly after noon?'

She nodded. 'But this is impossible,' she said. 'He was just here . . .'

'The sheriff needs to inspect the bathroom,' Benny said. 'Where Arturo was.'

'I don't think he ever used it, Sheriff Guzman. He was here such a short time.' She turned and gestured down a narrow hallway.

The tidy bathroom included the usual trio of commode, tub with shower and sink, with the same riot of colors dancing in the light.

'When he stopped by – he never intruded. I mean all the other times. We would offer the shower, but he made no use of it.'

'To be clear, Benny . . . he stayed the night? Last night, I mean.'

'No. He arrived during the day yesterday. I was working on the *acequia* with the neighbors. As Concha said, she offered him lunch, but no. He was eager to meet with Father Anselmo at the mission. I think Father was planning work for him there. When I returned home, he was not here.' He lifted his hands helplessly. 'I did not see him again after that.'

'But he left his belongings here. At least some of them,' Estelle said. 'So we assume he was planning to return before long.' She looked once more at the modest sack of Arturo's belongings. 'He took his knife with him?'

'Always, he had that,' Benny replied promptly.

Even if the murder weapon was a cheap copy of a Ka-Bar, Estelle thought it unlikely that Arturo had meant to leave the heavy blade buried in Johnny Rabke's chest.

'When you know . . . would you tell us what happened?'

'Of course.' She handed them a business card. 'It's certain that I'll need to speak with you again, Benny and Concha. In the meantime, if you think of anything I should know, you can reach me twenty-four seven. I would appreciate it.'

She returned to her car, leaving the couple on the porch, both looking stunned and, she thought, more than a little guilty, even though it wasn't their charge to protect Arturo Ramirez from himself. That task might fall, in part, to Father Bertram Anselmo. His aging and battered Oldsmobile was not at the mission, but Estelle knew that Father Anselmo would have heard about Arturo Ramirez's confrontation with Johnny Rabke via the efficient neighborhood grapevine.

EIGHT

The Iglesia de Nuestra Madre may have been the heart and soul of the rumor grapevine that grew strong in Regál, but it was clearly rivaled by the Broken Spur Saloon, on State Route Fifty-Six, twenty-seven miles southwest of Posadas, and a quarter-mile from the intersection with County Road Fourteen. That county road, thanks to hundreds of belly-dumps of gravel and deft grader and culvert work, now sped tourist traffic north to NightZone, the gigantic astronomical center that capped Torrance Mesa. It had also sped Johnny Rabke north to his destiny with Arturo Ramirez.

Estelle had been seventeen years old when the Broken Spur Saloon opened. Forty years later, not much had changed. The original owner, Victor Sanchez, had been short tempered, belligerent, and unforgiving. It had often been joked that Victor could not be accused of being prejudiced – he hated every one equally. He especially saved a practiced snarl for minions of the law, politicians, tourists with noisy children, and vegetarians. What guaranteed the Spur's success despite its owner's foul manners were two of Victor's habits. First, he rarely left the kitchen. He didn't appear in the saloon proper to chat with customers. He didn't trade jokes with vendors. He didn't greet people warmly. He stayed behind the heavy swinging kitchen door and worked.

Second, customers could count on his gluttonously huge burgers to be served piping hot, with perfectly finished fries or onion rings that would blister lips if the patron wasn't a little circumspect. He never deigned to enter one of those annual 'Best Burger' contests that newspapers loved to run. He knew his were the best, and to hell with the rest. The accompanying beer was so cold the frosty glass would make the fingers ache.

The Broken Spur found space for a pool table but no juke box. Victor hated the noise of blaring cowboy music. There was seating for seven at the bar, and seating for another twenty-four people if the four-tops in the separate 'community room' were added to the mix. No service club had ever met for lunch in the community room.

Predictions were ripe about what the saloon's future would be when Victor finally drank and smoked himself to death. His son, Victor Junior, had spent twenty-five years cowering in his father's shadow, somehow content to be treated as if he were a perpetual eight-year-old with no apparent ambition to break away.

After Victor's death, it was expected that Victor Junior miraculously would either turn a new leaf and blossom of his own accord with the saloon growing and prospering, or slam and lock the door and walk away, to bury himself in the obscurity of the nearest large city.

He had done neither. He didn't change or improve the menu. He didn't extend or shorten the saloon's hours. His onion rings were neither better nor worse than they had been. If anything, he spent more time in the kitchen, rarely venturing out into the saloon. He did install a wide screen television behind the bar, locked to one of the sports channels, with the volume control on zero and the remote hidden on the shelf behind the clock.

And, for the last four years, he had hired Maggie Archuleta as his bartender/waitress. Maggie apparently didn't object to her six-and-a-half-day work week, with the Spur open from eleven a.m. to two a.m. each day, including a somewhat shorter day on Sunday. Unlike Victor, she was charming and affable. She lived in a single-wide mobile home immediately beside Victor's, between the saloon and the arroyo behind it. Some folks assumed a relationship, others seriously doubted it.

The Broken Spur was not open for business when Estelle arrived that morning, but both Victor's fancy pickup truck and Maggie's long-of-tooth Saturn compact sedan were parked between the trailers.

The back kitchen door was open, with only the screen door preventing the files from enjoying the food. Estelle rapped the door frame. 'Victor?' She heard a clank as if he'd dropped a stainless steel bowl in the sink. He appeared, wiping his hands on a veteran apron.

'Undersheriff Reyes-Guzman,' Estelle said, and he nodded.

'Yeah, I see you.' No belligerence, no greeting beyond the simple, unadorned announcement. 'Just a sec. The screen is latched.'

No taller than Estelle's five foot seven, Victor was going to fat, his middle ballooning so that his aproned belly habitually rubbed against the greasy stove, the wet stainless steel sink, or the well-worn laminated prep table.

'Victor, was Johnny Rabke here last night?' It wasn't a question that she could have asked Victor Senior without earning a stinging, short-tempered rebuke, and then a refusal to say anything more. His son, however, was more pudding than starch. Estelle opened the screen door after Victor unlatched it.

A mound of ground beef spread out on a stainless tray, brown juice creeping from the mountain's sides like thin lava. Victor had been molding the lean beef into generous patties, individually wrapped in cling plastic. The untouched portion of the mound indicated that he had a long way to go.

'Victor, I need to know what time Johnny was here last night.'

'Who?'

'Johnny Rabke.'

'Why is that?'

'Do you know?'

'Well, I don't think I do. I mean, I don't notice who's what or where or when.'

'What about Arturo Ramirez?' She saw an eyebrow lift a little.

'Why would I see him?'

'Because he was here?'

'I don't know. Look, *Maggie* would know. I mean, *she* works out front. I don't.'

'She'll be here shortly?'

'Well, sure.' He nodded at the ground beef. 'I certainly hope so.' He offered a tentative smile, almost fetching, and certainly more welcoming than any expression she might have earned back in the day from Victor Senior 'I don't mean to be unhelpful, Sheriff. But I really don't pay attention to who comes in.' He tapped the stainless spatula against the edge of the prep table. 'Unless there's a fight or something . . . then we call you guys.'

'No fight last night?'

'No.'

'No loud arguments?'

'No. Well, not that I heard.'

She looked at Victor Junior long enough that he started to retreat back toward the hamburger.

'I'll check Maggie's trailer, then.'

'She should be up by now, yes. When she comes in, she always walks around and unlocks the padlock on the front door. She doesn't come through this way.'

'I'll find her. Victor, thanks for the help.'

'Not much help,' he said affably. He didn't ask why the curiosity about Johnny Rabke or Arturo Ramirez – doubly interesting since he would have been sure to remember the incidents of the previous year resulting in the knifing of Rabke and the death of Arturo's brother, Pablo, his skull cracked by a hurled billiard ball.

NINE

What a tiny world, Estelle thought as she approached Maggie Archuleta's single-wide mobile home. The young woman worked long hours every week, without a full day off. There were a zillion things that she would not be free to do with that schedule. Yet, as far as Estelle knew, Maggie had been the solo bartender at the Spur for two years, taking the job when she turned twenty-one two years before that. The only silver lining would be that she didn't have to share her tips.

An enormous tabby cat waited by the trailer front door. It offered no comment as Estelle approached, but almost sat up. An enormous belly provided the anchor. Its ears twitched in response to sounds inside the trailer, and in a moment Maggie Archuleta opened the door.

'Hi?' she greeted, the single word sounding like a question. She stood in the doorway, one hand holding the screen door, the other on the jamb. Her large body made an effective block. More burly than fat, Maggie looked capable if the need arose with rowdy patrons. Her wide, flat face was far from beautiful, with smallish eyes, pug nose and heavy lips. But the smile she offered was pleasant. 'Sheriff Guzman. Do I remember right?' Like most people with whom Estelle conversed, Maggie made no distinction between 'sheriff' and 'undersheriff', the latter being the department's second in command. Estelle had stopped bothering with the correction long ago.

'You do.'

'I heard you drive in. And I'm thinking maybe you wanted to talk with Victor? He's over in the kitchen by now.'

'Actually I wanted to talk with you, Maggie.'

'Oh, well, then, here I am. Come on in out of the sun. Don't trip over the cat.'

Estelle sidestepped the cat, which played it safe by not bolting at the last minute. The trailer's interior was cool, thanks to a single-window air-conditioner unit set on 'low'. The living room was crowded with heavy, low-slung furniture. Most of the chairs, including a purple bean-bag, were aimed toward the sixty-inch television that dominated one corner of the room. Only the pumpkin orange fake leather sofa favored the large picture window that faced the arroyo and the eastern prairie beyond.

'Can I offer you something to drink?' As Maggie said that, she motioned toward the sofa.

'I'm good,' Estelle said. 'Maggie, I need to talk with you about a couple of customers.'

'Sure,' Maggie said with a cheery nod. 'I mean, I'm not a priest or anything.'

'And I'm sure you have some regulars who unload their worries on you over a few long necks.'

Maggie laughed, a musical burst that started high and trickled down to an easy chuckle. 'Oh, boy, don't we ever.' She shrugged. 'I guess that's part of the fun.'

'How about Arturo Ramirez?' Estelle settled on the inviting orange sofa. It was thick and soft, the kind of place the old fat cat would favor.

'Oh, him?'

'Oh, him.'

'And he was going to stay here last night, too. But he didn't,' she added quickly. 'Is he in trouble with you guys? I mean, I know he's an illegal and all, but he's such a hard worker. And you know,' and she swept her hand across the chair's vinyl upholstery beside her thigh as if removing a speck of dust. 'He was just here for a little while.'

'Last night, you mean.'

'Well, late afternoon. Probably around five thirty or so. Padre Bertram dropped him off. You've known the padre for a long time, I bet.'

'A *long* time. You saw Father Anselmo drop Arturo off?'

'No, I didn't actually *see* that. I mean I didn't happen to notice Padre's car pull into the parking lot. I mean I was busy. No, Arturo told me that's how he got the ride up. After he dodged the crossing.' Maggie touched two fingers to her thick bottom lip as if to say, 'Oops.'

'But he wasn't here for long?'

'No. Just long enough to use the phone.'

'Do you know who he called?'

'No, 'cause whoever it was didn't answer.'

'Ah.' Estelle looked around the living room. 'But he didn't mention to you who he was talking to?'

'No. You know. It was dinner time, and I was bouncing off the walls. So I didn't ask.'

'Lots of traffic yesterday?'

'Well,' and she shrugged. 'It comes in spurts, you know. We had a school bus stop for burgers and stuff. We put them in the community room, away from the bar, and don't I wish that Victor would hurry up and hire some help for me. They were an eighth grade summer activities class from Las Cruces, heading home. I guess what they serve up at NightZone was maybe beyond their budget. Or maybe just too fancy. I don't know.'

'Maggie,' Estelle began, then paused. 'I guess I have to ask. Did Arturo stop by here regularly? He would stay with you here, from time to time?'

Maggie blushed. 'Now and then.'

'What does that mean?'

'I know that sometimes he would stay with the Aguilars in Regál, and sometimes, once in a while, he would . . . he would stay here. Not often enough. But once in a while, here with me. I've got the room.' She jutted out her wide chin in defiance. 'But look, Mrs Guzman. As far as I'm concerned, Arturo can come and go as he pleases. I know he doesn't carry paperwork. That's *his* business. Where he works, what he does . . . that's *his* business.' Her tone became pleading. 'Do you understand me? I listen to him rant about the Border Patrol and their dumb fence. About how they check this and check that. But they have their own job to do. I try to tell Arturo that, but he'd rather scramble over a barbed-wire fence and hike the mountain trails than deal with the Border Patrol. He's stubborn that way. I mean, he could get a work visa if he wanted to.'

'Maggie, I do understand.' She sat up a little straighter on the sofa and reached out to cover Maggie's left hand with both of hers. 'I want you to know that I have to ask all these questions, Maggie. I'm not just being nosy. I have to bring you this bad news. I have to tell you that sometime during the early hours of this morning, Arturo was shot and killed, up on the county road, not too far from here.'

Maggie's jaw dropped. She said something unintelligible as her other hand flew to her cheek. 'You would not make up a story such as this.'

'No, I would not.'

'He is dead, then? That's what you're saying?'

'Yes. I'm sorry.'

Maggie slumped backward, drawing both of her hands free. She reached up and covered her face as she let her head tilt back and sink into the soft cushion behind her. Estelle remained silent. Finally Maggie said, 'I have never forgotten the fight here last year, when Arturo's brother, Pablo, was killed. After he cut young Rabke with a knife over some silly argument. You were there after that.' She lowered her hands to her lap. 'You remember.'

'I do.'

'And now Arturo.' Her gaze swiveled back to Estelle. 'Can you tell me what happened? Who was involved?'

'Not in any detail, Maggie. We're working as fast as we can to trace Arturo's route yesterday – last evening and during the early hours of this morning. But I can tell you this much, and I hope you will keep the confidence. It appears to us now that Arturo died somehow after a confrontation with Johnny Rabke.'

'The same? No.'

'Yes. That's the way it appears.'

'But he was at the saloon last evening. Johnny Rabke was.'

'How long did he stay?'

Maggie frowned and gazed out the picture window toward the empty prairie. 'He arrived shortly after eight yesterday evening.' She nodded quickly. 'Yes. I'm sure. Just a few minutes after eight. He always flirts with me, you know. And then he played pool with several others. I'm trying to think, now.' She squinted into the distance. 'I get so busy, sometimes I don't pay attention.' She held up a finger. 'One of them was EJ Stance and his little brother, Howie. Howie can't buy beer yet, but EJ takes care of that.'

'How long was Johnny here?'

'He stayed long after the others left. He played pool with another rancher until closing, and then he left. *Ay.* Johnny is all right?'

'He is not. Both he and Arturo are dead, Maggie.'

'Oh.' She put such desolation in that one syllable that it made Estelle's heart ache.

'We have to know, Maggie. During any of that time that Johnny Rabke was here, did Arturo Ramirez enter the bar? Was there any confrontation that took place here, or, as far as you know, out in the parking lot?'

'No. I'm sure of that. Because I remember from last year.' She held two fingers twined together. 'The two Ramirez brothers, you know. There is never any forgive and forget there.'

Estelle fell silent, staring at the floral-patterned linoleum.

'What can I do to help you?' Maggie asked.

Even though there was no choice for Maggie Archuleta in the matter, the undersheriff felt the need to make it sound as if there were. 'I know you work long hours, Maggie, and right now you're short of help. But would you agree to come in to the Sheriff's Department tomorrow morning as early as you can? We need a written deposition from you about what you saw, what you heard. If necessary, I can have one of the deputies pick you up and then bring you back.'

'I can do that. I will drive there.'

'Can we meet at eight?'

Maggie closed her eyes and groaned, but nevertheless sounded cheerful when she replied, 'Eight? Of course. I have to go to town anyway to visit the pharmacy.'

Estelle extended her hands for a double handshake. 'Maggie, thank you. I'm sorry about all of this, but I appreciate you understanding that what we've discussed today must remain confidential. Do not discuss this with anyone else.' She smiled gently. 'Not even the old cat.'

'Ah, I'm sorry, but I have no secrets from him,' Maggie said.

TEN

Her patrol car was parked near the east corner of the saloon, and to her surprise, Father Bertram Anselmo's barge-like Oldsmobile 98 was tucked in close beside her Charger. A tall man with a pronounced dowager's hump and a spine curved by arthritis, Father Anselmo's craggy face was untouched by the ministrations of modern cosmetics. His complexion was dark and heavily lined, blotched with age spots. His bushy beard and mustache were now pure white like the few tufts of hair that stuck out from under his LA Dodgers baseball cap. A thin black linen shirt provided the background for the large wooden crucifix that hung high on his chest.

'Hello, my favorite one,' he said. 'I think you become younger every time I see you.'

'Flattery will get you everywhere, Father.' Estelle rounded the front of her car and returned the powerful hug. Without the padding of an ounce of fat on his bones, hugging Bertram Anselmo was like hugging a badly warped railroad tie. His clothing was strongly scented by wood smoke and the effluvia of old age.

Relinquishing the hug, Anselmo stood with a hand gripping each of Estelle's shoulders. 'Tell me that your family is well.'

'My family is well.'

'Good, good.' His smile revealed far fewer teeth than the originals. 'You include Carlos in that assessment?'

'He is healing, Father. It's a long slow process.'

'I should think so. His godfather has filled me in a little.' His hazel eyes twinkled. 'Just a little.' He glanced up at the sun, then at the front door of the Spur. 'I would hope that you could take a few minutes to join me for a late breakfast or an early lunch, wherever we are on the clock at the moment.' Characteristically, Anselmo was not wearing a watch. It was one of the continuing mysteries that his Mass celebrations at any of his three parishes were never early nor late.

'Father, I can't this morning. I wish I could, but I can't.'

He held up a hand to counter her explanation. 'I know. I know.

This is why I stopped when I saw that . . . that hot rod that you drive. I spoke with Hernán Duran a bit earlier. I was in Tres Santos, at the mission there, when he caught up with me. He tells me the tragic news. Apparently he had received a call from Benny Aguilar? And moments before or after, I'm not sure which, he was notified by Esmeralda Ramirez that her second son had been somehow caught up in tragedy. She received a phone call from Sheriff Taber.'

'Correct.' The grapevine was flourishing, Estelle mused. No one had let a moment slip by, no *Mañana Rule* invoked. 'Father, I'm told that yesterday, you offered a ride over the mountain to Arturo Ramirez. When he visited you at the *iglesia*.'

'Yes.'

'And that you dropped him off here.'

'That is also true.'

'Father, it would be helpful to know what the two of you discussed. We're trying to trace his movements during his last few hours.'

He frowned at Estelle, the corners of his mouth pulling his mustache so that he looked vexed. 'Like so many in his position, he was looking for work.'

'Were you able to help him with that?'

'My suggestion was that he arrange to speak with Mr Waddell up on the mesa. I know Miles to be an approachable man. Arturo was under the impression that there would be no chance of employment there, but I suggested otherwise. I suggested that Arturo was welcome to use my name as a reference, if he so wished. And in addition, I suggested that Arturo check the message board that is so thoughtfully posted just inside the door here at the saloon. I browse that myself from time to time, so I can pass the word to parishioners.' He huffed a deep sigh. 'So tragic, this. So very tragic.'

'Did you happen to mention to Arturo about the major fencing job that Wallace Boyd has started? That would be the sort of work that would suit him.'

'I did, as a matter of fact. And then, *mea culpa*. After I told him, I remembered that the wild one – Johnny Rabke? That he was working for Mr Boyd. Believe me, I had no intention of putting Johnny Rabke and Arturo Ramirez on the same job site.'

Estelle's pulse jumped a peg or two, but she kept her expression blank. 'I appreciate the information, Father.'

'But I must know. What actually *happened*, Estelle? What can you tell me?'

'At this point, I wish I knew. All I know for sure is that two fatalities are involved, most likely occurring sometime during the early morning hours, out in the country north of here. Arturo was involved, as was Johnny Rabke.' She held up both hands helplessly. 'We know there was bad blood between the two of them from the incident last year.'

'With the death of the elder brother, you mean.'

'Yes. But beyond that, we don't know.'

'But you're telling me now that both Arturo and young Rabke are dead.'

'Yes.'

'Knowing what I know, I'm assuming that they somehow managed to kill each other?'

'That's possible. At this point, we just don't know, Father.'

'You've spoken here with both Victor and Maggie, I presume?'

'Yes.'

'Nevertheless, I would think that tracing Arturo's movements might be something of a challenge.'

'It is indeed.'

'His is . . . *was* . . . not a lifestyle that fits any modern mold. My prayers are with him. You know, and this is no secret for you, I'm sure . . . there are a significant number of the needy for whom the border restrictions are more than a challenge. And it's no secret that I help in any way I can – as do you, as does your husband. A simple car ride for a hiker out in the wilderness, for instance. Whatever.'

He frowned and wiped the corner of his mouth. 'Arturo was an unsettled young man, Estelle. It was my hope that he could find permanent employment, that someone like Miles Waddell could help him find a direction.'

'I understand all of that, Father. But now the issues are more immediate. We've had two lives lost, and we do not know why. It's easy to assume, but that's not the way the law works. A case of two young hotheads, caught up in revenge prompted by a stupid bar fight a year ago? Maybe. Both are dead now, instead of looking forward to growing old in peace.'

'I could speak some platitude like "it is God's will", but I don't think that's the case here. We humans have a lot of latitude to make our lives miserable. Or in this case, short.'

'I'll know more after today, Father.'

He nodded, and to her surprise pulled an iPhone from his back pocket. 'As you see, I am dipping my toe in the twenty-first century. This was given to me by someone who sincerely thinks that I need it, given along with a – what do you call it? – a subscription for service? Unfortunately . . . well, perhaps fortunately, I don't know how to use it.' He smiled. 'I'm told that if I would sit down with the average child, I could be taught in minutes. One of these days, I may do that. In the meantime . . .' He shrugged helplessly. 'You know that if you need anything from me, it is yours.'

'I'll always be able to find you, Father.' She stroked the sun-bleached fender of the Oldsmobile. 'Not easy to hide this old guy.'

'If nothing else, remember that you're welcome on any Sunday morning. Or Wednesday evening in María, or Saturday evening in Tres Santos.' He brightened. 'I have a gathering in Tres Santos of eight youngsters each Saturday evening. Perhaps I can ask one of them for instruction with this gadget.'

'Resist that temptation, Father,' Estelle laughed. 'We love you just the way you are.'

ELEVEN

'I was hoping this was a date for lunch,' Miles Waddell said. 'But I bet I'm out of luck.' His voice sounded mechanical issuing from the speaker of her car's radio.

'Unfortunately that's the case,' Estelle replied. She had just passed the entrance to NightZone's parking complex, and was continuing northward on County Road Fourteen, beyond where only a few tracks recorded the story of Johnny Rabke and Arturo Ramirez's death. Rabke's truck and trailer were gone, with only some scuff marks remaining.

'You sound as if you're right in the middle of something.'

'I am. A quick question. Did a young Mexican man, Arturo Ramirez, contact you recently?'

'Who?'

'A young Mexican national. Arturo Ramirez.'

'He's the one who—'

The grapevine tendrils had reached Miles Waddell. Estelle interrupted him. 'Yes. We're investigating his death out here on the county road.'

'That's where you are now?' If he'd turned to look out the north window of his office suite, he would be able to see the dust cloud billowing behind her Charger.

'Northbound. I'm told that Arturo was thinking of talking to you about a possible job. I spoke earlier with Father Bertram Anselmo. He was the one who gave Arturo a ride north from the church, down in Regál. He's the one who suggested to Arturo that he should talk with you.'

'Nope. It's unusual to have a day go by without someone trying to join the payroll, but no. Nothing yesterday. I guess I should say *no one* yesterday. Or today. And I'd remember if he had mentioned the good Father's name as a reference.'

'You heard about the incident, though.'

'A delivery truck driver said that he passed by something going on up the road a mile or so. He said he saw one victim covered up in the ditch, and another inside a stalled truck. And lots of you guys buzzing around. You can see a lot from the cab of a semi, I suppose.'

'Apparently so. Thanks for the info, Miles.'

'Lunch sometime. And bring that son and his fiancée along. They're such a treat to talk to. And your husband. You know how often I get to chat with him?'

'Almost never, I'm guessing. Not much serenity in his life right now.'

'Well, let's find some. But I won't keep you. Don't be a stranger.'

She switched off, doubly sorry that Arturo Ramirez hadn't taken the turn-off at NightZone, hadn't sought out Miles Waddell, hadn't been able to avoid Johnny Rabke.

She was able to cover five miles of gravel road before her phone intruded into her thoughts. The dash display indicated Sheriff Jackie Taber on line.

'You out of traffic?' the sheriff asked, and Estelle laughed.

'About as out of it as I can get, Jackie.' She toggled the volume up to counter the roar of tires on gravel.

'That's good, because two things. Number one, Dr Guzman wants Linda, either me or you or both, and he makes a suggestion that if we're going to bring in Bobby Torrez, now would be a good time. He's done some clean-up and external, but he doesn't want to start the autopsy until the gang's all there.'

'I'm on my way. I'll be coming in by way of the airport and train station. ETA about forty.'

'Productive morning?'

'We have a lot to talk about.'

'Your husband says we'll have a lot more after our session with him. And before I forget it, number two, Carlos needs to speak with you. He says it's in reference to his ride-along with Bill, whenever that was.' She laughed. 'This day already seems as if it's a week long.'

'He didn't call me.'

'Knowing him, he didn't want to interrupt you in the middle of something.'

'I'll add it to the list,' Estelle said. 'See you at the hospital in a bit.'

The northern stretch of County Road Fourteen was an invitation to play dirt-track race driver, with its sweeping curves around mesa bottoms and ducking down to cross unbridged arroyos. It rose sharply to cross over the interstate, and then flattened out in the run north to NM78. Not including routine service and vendor vehicles headed for NightZone, she counted seven others raising dust south-bound on CR14 as she passed, and every one of them would have welcomed the chance to park for a private gab session.

One of the vehicles was Wallace Boyd, and the rancher slowed to a near-stop as he saw her approaching, opened his window and waved a hand. It might have been just a friendly greeting, but Estelle doubted that. The two killings had set the rural folks on edge. She braked hard, pulled close to his pickup's door, and looked up toward his window.

'Taber said you'd be wanting to talk with me.' He jarred his truck to a full stop and graciously shut off the engine so she could hear.

'I'll be in touch a little later today. You'll be around home?'

'Probably so. Or you got my cell.'

'I do. We'll talk.' He nodded his satisfaction with that, and Estelle accelerated away. As she watched in her rearview, she noticed that Boyd took his time resuming his trip down CR14. Like everyone else touched by the events of the past twenty-four hours, he had a lot to think about.

Once on the patched and potholed pavement of NM78, she pushed the Charger hard, thankful for the light traffic. A mile west of the newly expanded Posadas Municipal Airport, now referred to simple as the ATS, or Airport/Train Station, she overtook the eastbound NightZone train, the hi-tech propane/electric locomotive that plied the forty-eight-mile round trip of scenic rails out to the astronomical facility on Torrance Mesa and return. The train ran twenty-four seven, its service a continuing maintenance challenge for the loco-motive crew. But Estelle knew that its ambitious schedule was paying off for Miles Waddell's venture. 'Convenient access to a remote spot,' Waddell often said when explaining his vision.

Her Charger joined the fleet of county cars that had gathered in the back of Posadas General Hospital's parking lot, the fleet including one that didn't share the polished black of the county's livery. Former sheriff Robert Torrez's 'bailing wire special', a mostly forest green '72 Chevrolet three-quarter-ton pickup whose bed looked like a small version of the county landfill, suited Torrez's habits. 'Never need to lock it,' he had said more than once. 'Who'd want to steal it?'

Estelle entered the hospital through the Emergency Room access, and was greeted by Paul Escobar, one of the ER staff. The traditional stethoscope hung around his neck, and his light blue scrubs looked as if he might have had a busy, long night.

'They're all down below, Sheriff,' he said cheerfully. 'Even my cousin, the big ugly guy.'

'Thanks, Paul. Is everything going great with Erlynda?'

He held his arms out, indicating an enormous belly. 'Any day now. The sonogram says it's twins.'

'*Ay*, what an amazing time for you two. Please give her my best.'

'I'll do that.'

Down the hall beyond radiology, she took the stairs to the ground floor instead of waiting on the elevator. Sheriff Jackie Taber and retired lawman Robert Torrez waited outside the first morgue doorway. Torrez offered a curt nod, about as close to an ebullient greeting as he ever came.

''Bout time.' Torrez managed to offer a faint smile as a supplement to the nod. Easily topping six-four, and even in his grubbies – which he was – Robert 'Bobby' Torrez could be mistaken as a movie star, with his massive build and handsome face. His unparted curly black hair was cut short. Estelle shook hands with both Taber and Torrez, noticing that the former sheriff offered the wafting aroma of Hoppe's #9 gun solvent. Perhaps he favored it as an aftershave, or soaked his hands in it to remove warts.

'How's Gayle putting up with you at home all day?' Estelle asked.

Torrez offered the hint of a shrug. 'Been out and about, so I ain't home much.'

'We're waiting on Linda to finish the first round of photos,' Jackie said. 'Dr Guzman didn't want the crowd in the room while she does that. Too many shadows to confuse things.'

'Did Jackie fill you in about what we have going?' Estelle asked. 'Yup.'

'As I told Bobby,' Jackie said, 'we know what this all *looks* like. But, we know how that goes. We want to be sure.'

At a time like this, Estelle was delighted that her already hyper-busy husband had accepted the post as medical examiner, filling in for the now-retired Alan Perrone. Dr Francis Guzman brought a forensic investigator's mindset to his job. Knowing that a careless scalpel or bone saw could just as easily destroy never-to-be-replaced evidence, he worked with care and precision – and careful advanced planning. Estelle and the others in the Sheriff's Department, as well as the other local law enforcement officers who on occasion needed the medical examiner's expertise, had come to appreciate Dr Guzman's insights. On top of everything else, the physician had been able to organize his time so that medical examinations were prompt.

The door cracked. 'Folks, come in and suit up.' Lola Marino, Dr Guzman's assistant, held the door ajar for them. 'Booties, suit, gloves, hairnets. Everything is organized by size in the white cabinet on your right. Bobby, there's a triple-X giant size on the bottom shelf. And folks, when we're all done, everything goes in the yellow hamper for disposables over there in the corner.'

With one hand holding the inner door, she watched with a continuing nod as the group suited up. 'Good. Now you all look just like me. We won't be able to tell you all apart.' She winked at Torrez. 'Well, sort of.'

The impeccable organization of the Posadas County morgue made it seem larger than it really was, but it was still a challenge to find a convenient spot to observe without knocking elbows. Dr Francis Guzman reached up and pulled the slender boom of the microphone down a bit lower. Unlike his guests, his attire showed signs of being in the war zone.

'Folks, I wanted you here from the get-go, because I see some things that need your explanation, and that might – might – influence how you go about this investigation. Linda,' and he nodded toward the suited Linda Pasquale, who was perched on one of the lab stools, camera in hand, 'already has compiled a fair photographic record, and of course that will grow as we dig into this.'

He touched the corner of one of the white sheets that completely covered the body on his left. The body was contorted on its side, twisted at the waist so that the left knee tented the sheet.

'I want to give you a little tour before you barrage me with questions. Then we'll go from there. The cause of death in either instance is not in question, although great questions are prompted by the *manner* of insult to the body.' He looked up. 'Have I been obscure enough for you? The fundamental question here is, "What the hell happened?"'

With great care, he peeled the first sheet back, exposing the first corpse from head to toe. The corpse's hands were bagged with clear plastic, and tagged, but nothing else was covered for modesty's sake. 'What we have here is a twenty-three-year-old male. The body shows several prior injuries and wounds, all entirely healed, none of which have any immediate bearing on the present circumstances. Blood work has not been received, but I can tell you with reasonable confidence that the victim was intoxicated, or nearly so, at the time of his death.'

He touched the corpse with his gloved hand. 'The wound on the anterior surface of the upper right thigh is consistent with fine bird shot, the sort we'd expect from a small shotgun, or a handgun loaded with snake shot. It's clearly a grazing wound, and appears that the tissue damage suggests that the wound was inflicted from left to right, relative to the victim. I'm confident that we'll discover several of the pellets *in situ*, along with fibers torn from the victim's clothing by the shot pattern. The large bruise near the center of the wound is likely caused by the plastic over-shot wad that those kinds of cartridges use.

'As you can see here,' he continued, 'the body is fully rigored, and remains in what would be a seated position, as found . . . as if twisted at the waist and slumped over to his right in that truck seat. Special notice. It appears from the wound track that the weapon was held low, almost as if lying on the victim's *left* thigh, the shot pattern angling across his lap to graze the right thigh.' Francis Guzman straightened up. 'By the way, now is a good time to catch you up on the photo library. Linda is going to use the printer in my office to make copies of the photos she's taken thus far. You can add to that inventory as we go.'

He pointed toward a locker to his left where the victims' clothing was bagged and stored. 'The fabric of the trouser pant leg clearly shows a close-range grazing pattern, around the torn fabric. Lots of powder burns. As I said, Linda will provide us a clear photo of that here in a few moments.'

Dr Guzman moved upward. 'Now, I wanted you to look closely at this before the knife is removed, or the wound disturbed.' He beckoned to Torrez. 'Bobby, a hand please. We want to roll the body flat on his back, so he'll end up in a reclined but seated position, knees high.' That accomplished, he touched the handle of the protruding knife.

'A large, heavy hunting knife, or even what, an assault blade? We'll have measurements when it's recovered. But for now, this is what is most important. The blade was not just driven straight in and left there. Driven in, yes. And with violent force. Driven in all the way to the hilt. But what's interesting to me is that the wound around the blade indicates that it was then rocked from side to side, with the entry wound enlarged well beyond the width of the blade.'

He held his fist clenched beside the hilt of the knife without actually touching it, and then rocked his hand from side to side. 'Rocked from side to side *hard*. Notice that the wound is two full centimeters *wider* than the width of the blade. Notice also that there is significant bruising in the immediate area around the hilt, where it appears that the blade was initially driven in hard, until the knife's hilt bruised the skin around the wound.'

The room was silent as Dr Guzman paused in his narrative. 'I wanted this little demonstration *before* I continue with the autopsy, since this site will be disturbed as we continue. We'll have clear photos detailing the whole procedure, but I wanted you all to see this. This is what you need to consider. That knife is hefty. And it's a lever of sorts. Driven in straight is one thing, driven in all the way to the hilt. I would have to guess that the blade's point, if it's present, if it didn't break off, would have to be lodged close to the spine itself, maybe just to the victim's right of it. The initial bruising from the forceful knife blow is just slightly right of center, through the sternum.

'The perpendicular position of the knife's handle lets me guess fairly accurately the orientation of the blade, *when it was first driven in*. But, when the knife is wrenched sideways, imagine the track of that knife blade. I'm confident that the blade will slice the heart's right atrium when the blade rocks this way, to the victim's left, and the tip may impact the spine when the blade is rocked to the victim's right.'

He stepped back. 'I know I'm going out on a limb here, but the full autopsy will say yea or nay. It'll give us absolute details. But I can conjecture this: if this young man had been lying on an operating room table in a large metro hospital when the knife was plunged into his chest, he *might* have been able to survive if there was a surgical team standing by to save him. Standing by right then. No ambulance ride. No chopper flight. It's my guess that initially the knife stab came close to missing the heart, but sliced the pericardium, no doubt cutting veins and arteries along the way. Without *immediate* surgical intervention, and I mean immediate, the wound would not be survivable. He'd bleed to death in minutes. But, in this case, when the knife was then wrenched from side to side, with massive damage to the heart, the wound becomes immediately fatal. Survival counted in seconds.'

Guzman looked from face to face. 'You can probably see where I'm going with this. That blade is wide across the back, and it's even serrated. Imagine the force it would take to rock that blade from side to side when it's clamped in place by muscle and bone. Rocking it nearly an inch side to side.'

He once more sheeted Johnny Rabke's corpse, and turned to Arturo Ramirez.

TWELVE

'Let's start the same way, with the bird shot . . . with the pellets. Here you can see a pattern that struck the victim as if he was turning away from the shot, turning to the right so that the pellets struck him under the posterior margin of the left armpit. We have the entire group of pellets here, and I suspect that Bobby's forensic talents can produce an identical pattern so we can judge the distance between gun muzzle and wound. It was close up, I can guarantee that. Next, there's a partial pattern, a group of only ten pellets that grazed Ramirez's cheek just above the jawbone, traveling from back to front. I think several of the pellets are still *in situ,* so we may be able to see what we have for size. Once again, it appears that Ramirez was turning away from Rabke when the shooting started. As if he was trying to put some distance between him and that gun.'

Dr Guzman nodded as Linda Pasquale returned. She carried a thick manila folder. 'You'll have lots of photos to study,' he said. 'But onward. The pellet wounds did not kill Ramirez. They might have provided some impetus for him to dive out of the truck if that's where this ruckus started, which to me seems likely. What I *do* know is that a heavy caliber bullet – not a shotgun pellet – struck Ramirez just posterior to the left mastoid. Just behind the left ear. I'm getting ahead of myself here, but I'll go with this narrative based on examination of the external wounds. The bullet traveled through the brain, exiting through the victim's right eyebrow. Through and through.' He looked up at the silent group. 'He would have been dead when he hit the ground outside the truck. Details to come after the full autopsy.'

He took a deep breath. 'There's no doubt in my mind that the head wound is catastrophic, and would have resulted in instant death. Because it's through and through, it would be only luck if the bullet were ever recovered.' He shrugged. 'It's out on the prairie somewhere.'

Dr Guzman straightened and spread his hands. 'Now, questions?' The room remained so silent that Estelle could hear the digital wall clock.

'Awesome. It's going to be a long afternoon, folks. I want to request some overtime for Linda. I'd like her to remain and continue the photo documentation. There's no one better.'

'Aw, shucks,' Linda said.

'Aw, shucks is right,' the physician agreed. 'In that folder is a photo of the pellet wounds. If I were to be presumptuous, I'd suggest that Bobby needs to duplicate those patterns to give us an idea of distance . . . from the muzzle of the gun to the wound. I think we all can guess what we're looking at, but actual photo and measurement documentation will help.' He reached out a hand and touched Johnny Rabke's now sheeted shoulder. 'And the knife and its wound will be carefully documented. I think one of you should be here for that dissection.'

He fell silent, looking at the two sheeted corpses for several moments. 'What's obvious? If Mr Ramirez had been shot first, including that head wound, he never would have been able to stab Johnny Rabke. If Ramirez climbed into that pickup truck and then, with maybe no hesitation, stabbed Rabke, I could understand Rabke managing to draw a handgun somehow, and almost out of reflex, pull the trigger – maybe even half a dozen times. Ramirez falls out of the truck, and Rabke collapses without moving from his seat behind the wheel.'

Again, he held up both hands in surrender. 'But I'm having trouble with the rest of the scenario. If Rabke is stabbed, and then the knife yanked back and forth while buried in his chest, to the point of actually cutting into the heart? I don't see him being able to aim and fire a handgun multiple times with that sort of injury.'

'You're suggesting what?' Torrez asked bluntly.

'I'm saying that's maybe our question. Let me extend this show-and-tell just a little bit.' He pulled the sheet clear of Rabke's corpse, and held thumb and forefinger on either side of the thigh wound. 'I'll repeat myself. This is a grazing wound. It's messy, sure enough. There's some what I would call minor tearing of the skin. A good bit of powder burn. Likely a deep bruise from the over-shot wad. It would have been a messy bleed. Not an artery pumper, but bloody nevertheless.'

Dr Guzman straightened up. 'Had Rabke been walking when that happened, with no other wound involved, he would have been able to limp along without assistance. But.' He walked to one of the locked closets and opened it, removing two evidence bags. 'First, let's take a more critical look at the victim's T-shirt.'

He opened the bag and removed the blood-soaked garment. 'What we see here is a *mass* of blood from the chest wound. It's exactly what I would expect to see knowing that the murder weapon was jerked back and forth, cutting and tearing the chest tissue. It's much *more* than I would expect from a wound where the knife is driven in cleanly. Lots of blood drains into the chest cavity itself with a clean, forceful blow, but not so much leaking outside the body.' He outlined the bloodstain on the shirt. 'Folks, this is a lot of blood.'

'What am I missing?' Estelle asked, and her husband nodded emphatically.

'Good question.' He carefully spread the T-shirt out so that it covered Rabke's chest, then opened the evidence bag containing Rabke's blue jeans. 'This is what you need to see.' He spread out the jeans and laid them out to cover the corpse from the waist down, adjusting each pant leg as best he could to cover Rabke's awkward rigored anatomy. 'This is the tear in the thigh from the bird shot . . . the snake shot.' He waited until they had all stepped closer.

'Not much, is it? But what I see is this: the wash of blood – and that's what it is, a *wash* – flows heavily down the victim's chest, the river favoring his right side, since that's the way he's leaning.' His gloved hand followed the heavy flow of dried blood.

'Now this. It flows downward toward Rabke's lap, across his belt line, between his legs, with some heavy flow over his right thigh. *Over* the relatively minor wound in his thigh. Soaking everything in sight.' He looked at Linda. 'There is a good, clear photo of the victim sitting slumped in the pickup seat. His thigh is blood-soaked. The seat is blood-soaked. The floor . . . and so on. All that from a relatively minor, grazing thigh wound from a round of snake shot? I don't think so.'

'If I'm hearing you right,' Sheriff Taber said, 'the massive bleed happened *after* the thigh wound. And following that notion, the massive bleed would also be *after* the other shots. The rounds that peppered the cab as Ramirez was turning away, and the final hard ball round that exploded his head.'

Dr Guzman remained silent, watching the group process that.

'The knife was plunged in,' Estelle said, '*then* the five shots. Rabke could have remained conscious enough to do that, almost out of reflex.'

'But he had to do that *before* the added insult of the larger wound . . . when the knife was yanked back and forth,' Jackie added. 'Ramirez was dead by then.'

Dr Guzman held up both hands. 'If Rabke was stabbed, and then the knife was yanked back and forth to the point of actually cutting deep into the heart? I don't see him being able to react and fire a handgun multiple times with that sort of injury.'

Bobby Torrez's eyes locked on the physician's. 'You're saying somebody else was at the scene.'

'That's our question, isn't it. And that's why I wanted you folks in on this. If that's the case . . . *if* . . . then this wasn't just another version of the Rabke-Ramirez feud.'

'Someone else was there,' Sheriff Taber repeated softly. 'If that's the way it happened.' She looked at the others. 'Let's get at it.'

Dr Guzman turned and beckoned to Lola Marino. 'Lola will be here, of course, along with Linda. I need one officer from the Sheriff's Department here to participate and guide questions.' He looked up expectantly. 'Take that folder of photos with you. And we'll have lots more.'

Sheriff Jackie Taber waggled a finger. 'I need to do that. I know that Estelle is in the middle of interviews, and it'll be more productive use of her time rather than spending the afternoon in here. I'll keep everyone apprised of our progress.'

'Lieutenant Mears is working fingerprints along with Sergeant Pasquale,' Estelle added. 'They'll need to pick up the knife when it's released into evidence. They already have the firearm that we think was involved.'

'The well-oiled machine,' Dr Guzman quipped. 'Then if there are no questions at the moment,' and he smiled, 'thanks for dropping by, and you can give us room to work now.'

Once shucked of paper hygiene suits and standing outside the morgue, it was Bobby Torrez who voiced his concern first. 'Who's workin' the truck?'

'Mears, Pasquale and Sutherland.'

'Did they find all the casings?'

'They found five. All inside the cab of Rabke's truck. Linda documented the placement of each.'

'Gonna want to see those,' Torrez said.

THIRTEEN

'*H*ijo, you know that I have some questions for you.' She beckoned her son and then pointed at the chair nearest her desk.

'Not guilty,' Carlos offered.

'I certainly hope not. Would you like coffee or tea or something?'

'I'm good.'

She tapped the small pocket recorder on her desk. 'This has to be on, *hijo*, because what we generate through our discussion may end up in a formal deposition. All right?'

'Sure. I've never taken a lie detector test before.' That earned the young man a mock glare from the undersheriff.

Estelle spoke both their names, the date and the location into the record, then leaned back as if she were finished.

'*Padrino* – Bill Gastner – mentioned that he and you saw one of the Posadas deputies involved in a traffic stop on New Mexico Fifty-Six earlier this morning.'

'Yesterday morning,' Carlos corrected. 'Thursday.'

'Yesterday. Excuse me. It's been a busy morning. What time was that?'

'Just coming up on five thirty . . . *a.m.*'

'Why were the two of you out and about at that hour, and in that particular place?'

'We were just crusing. *Padrino* . . . and since we're being formal, let me call him William K. Gastner, former sheriff of Posadas County. Mr Gastner invited me along. We were headed to NightZone for breakfast.'

'Were either of you involved in any way with official business on behalf of the county? On behalf of the Sheriff's Department?'

'No.'

'Did you recognize the deputy involved in the traffic stop?'

'Not at that moment. I've met her just a time or two in the past, so I don't know her well. Mr Gastner recognized her, I think. I learned a little later that it was Deputy Lydia Thompson.'

'Did you recognize the truck that was stopped?'

'Truck and trailer. I did not. I learned later from *Padrino* that the driver was a young rancher named Johnny Rabke. The name was familiar to me because I'd heard about the bar fight a year ago that occurred in the Broken Spur Saloon here in Posadas County. That was, by rude coincidence, the same time that Tasha – Tasha Qarshe, my fiancée – and I were injured in a bike crash out in California. You initially responded to that bar fight, but then had to break away to fly out to California.'

'As you drove by the scene early yesterday, what did you see?'

Carlos folded his hands in his lap. 'Both the driver of the truck and the deputy were out of their vehicles. They appeared to be in conversation, standing on the shoulder side of the pickup truck, about at the front passenger door. They were obscured by the truck and the poor light. But the truck's cab lights were on, and both the deputy and Rabke were just in the halo of light.'

'What kind of vehicle was the truck?'

'A several years old Dodge Ram 2500 crew cab dually. They all kinda look alike, and I couldn't guess what year it was. And I didn't see the license plate.'

'And then?'

'As we drove by, and Mr Gastner had slowed the pace considerably, I looked across and saw the young man had lifted his left hand and rested it on the deputy's shoulder.'

'Would you describe that as an aggressive gesture? Or an affectionate gesture? Or simply friendly?'

'I didn't see enough to draw any conclusion. It was dark, the truck was in the way. I would describe what I saw as just an *impression.*'

'Did there come a time when you learned the rancher's name?'

Carlos grinned at the repeat question. 'A few minutes later. Mr Gastner mentioned that it was Johnny Rabke.'

'Did either you or Mr Gastner speak with the deputy?'

'Mr Gastner did. He had pulled off the road on the wide shoulder, then turned around in a shoulder-to-shoulder U-turn. I had mentioned the contact between the two people, and I think that alerted Mr Gastner. Because of the contact between the two – what I said I saw as contact – he wanted to make sure that all was well. By that time, Deputy Thompson had walked back around the truck to the highway side, and we exchanged brief pleasantries.'

Carlos held his hands flat together. 'By that time, she was standing right at Mr Gastner's driver's door. I could see her clearly. She spoke in what I considered to be a normal conversational voice. She reported that all was well, and that no additional help was needed. Mr Gastner had offered a spare jack if one was needed. They didn't need it.'

'Did you actually see anything wrong with the pickup truck that had been stopped by the deputy? Any reason for that stop that was obvious?'

'No. But remember that our view of the incident was limited by the vague lighting and the positions of the two participants.'

'And then you left?'

'Yes. A few minutes later we heard Deputy Thompson clear ten-eight with dispatch.'

Estelle smiled. 'That's very precise, *hijo*.'

'What can I say. I'm a cop's kid.'

'Indeed.' She reached over and turned off the recorder. 'The reason that this is important is that your brief observation places one of the victims from a dual homicide with great accuracy, Carlos. Twenty-four hours later or so, Johnny Rabke and another young man are dead. Why? We'll find out.'

'You'll also talk with Deputy Thompson, I assume?'

'I will.'

'Is she in trouble?'

She gazed at her son for a moment. 'The answer to that makes me uneasy, *hijo*, because at this point, I'd have to say, "I don't know." But I'll quote something Mr William K. Gastner has said to me probably a hundred times over the years. I don't like coincidence.'

'I mean, there's nothing wrong with what she did, right?'

'The only accurate answer to that is, "it depends."'

'From what's been said, she apparently has been through a lot over the years.'

'Yes, she has.'

'So a friendly pat on the shoulder . . . even if he's a new boyfriend, what's the big deal?'

'The big deal is when the new boyfriend – if that's what he is – ends up murdered twenty-four hours later. Then we have to ask questions.'

Carlos shrugged philosophically. 'I suppose. You'll talk with her?'

'Of course.'

'Maybe she doesn't even know about the homicides yet.'

'She knows, Carlos. She was up in Albuquerque all day at a child custody hearing, but trust me, she knows.' Estelle glanced at the clock above the wall map of Posadas County. 'She comes on duty at midnight, but she'll be in long before that.' She nodded at the tape recorder. 'It's always interesting to compare story versions.'

FOURTEEN

't's the only thing that makes sense.' Robert Torrez held the large .45 automatic pistol, slide back, magazine out. 'This ain't the Kimber that Rabke had. It's my own Kimber, and it works just the same. Same model, same everything.' Perhaps leaving the Sheriff's Department had relieved a quantum of stress from Torrez. Estelle found him easier to talk to now than when he'd been at the helm.

He sat down in the straight-backed chair to the right of Estelle's desk. 'So he's sittin' in the truck. Without no warning, he's suddenly got this big-ass knife buried in his own chest. If he'd seen it comin', if something tipped him off, he'd have done something about it. But he didn't. No defense wounds. Never lifted a hand.'

He held up the automatic and turned it this way and that. 'Nothin' to feed it,' he said, indicating the missing magazine, and then turning the gun so that Estelle had a clear view of the chamber, 'nothin' in its mouth.' Torrez thumbed the release and let the slide slam forward. The hammer remained cocked.

'Anybody scared that a rattlesnake is going to jump in his back pocket is going to carry the gun like this. Bullet in the chamber, cocked, locked. So all he has to do is thumb the safety, and he's ready to go.'

'When Rabke went inside some place where firearms aren't allowed, like at the Spur saloon, he'd shove it in the door pocket and then lock the truck,' Estelle said. 'I've personally known him to do that. He and I even talked about that in the past.'

'Yeah, well, maybe he did. There's wear scuffs on the door panel that says that's true. But he's a lefty, we're told. So even if he's belted up and carryin' it, the gun's on the left side of his belt. So in the door pocket or holster, maybe it don't matter much. He pulls the gun out, and he can't be thinkin' straight, not when he's got that Ka-Bar stuck in his chest. He tries to lift the gun, and the first round goes off when it's right here, in his lap. He wouldn't mean to do that, so it's a good guess that he's already been hurt bad.'

Torrez reached across and sorted through the photos from Linda

Pasquale's efforts. He chose one of Rabke's corpse, slumped in the driver's seat. He pointed at the leg wound. 'That's when the first one goes off. Ignore what the doc said about the blood all over everything. We ain't talkin' about that yet.' He held up the automatic. 'These automatics eject the empty casing up, back and to the right. And pretty hard.'

'So it's a good chance the empty would have bounced off Rabke himself.'

'Yup. Mears found one empty down beside the right side of the driver's seat.' He selected another photo, this one an eight-by-ten close-up of an empty casing. 'Recently fired case, powder burns on Rabke's jeans and residue embedded in the skin of his thigh.'

'All of that can be easily matched,' Estelle said.

'Yup. The shape of the shell casing guarantees that it's a bird shot cartridge, or snake shot, or whatever you want to call 'em. They're aluminum, and they're not reloadable. You can see on the headstamp.'

Estelle turned the photo so she could see the image clearly. 'CCI, NR, .45 Auto.'

'CCI is the manufacturer. The NR means "not reloadable".'

'So the first round grazed Rabke across his own thigh. No doubt accidental.'

'Well,' Torrez almost laughed. 'Accidental in that he didn't mean to shoot himself. And yeah, close range. The bird shot, the wad, they both tore him up pretty bad. Woulda hurt like hell.'

'Then?'

'We've got a shot pattern in the passenger door, just under the electric window switch. Pattern shows a hundred and twenty-seven pellet marks. The pellets are pretty small, about like a grain of sand. Not all of 'em hit the door. About enough to make a rattler really angry, unless you hit him at close range, right in the head.'

'We're told that Rabke always carried when he was working, in the hope that he'd find a snake.'

'Yeah, well,' Torrez shrugged, unimpressed.

'That second shot likely would have missed Ramirez,' Estelle said. 'Like maybe it went under his arm without hitting him and struck the door.'

Bobby shrugged. 'And the gun's still sorta sideways, and pitches the case so it hits the center console and bounces on the floor.'

'So that's two. Thigh and door.'

Torrez rummaged through the eight-by-tens. 'A handful of pellets struck Ramirez high in the right chest, and also the door window frame. Grazed him. Woulda stung like shit, but not much damage. I'd guess that at that point, Ramirez is turnin' away. Turning from the crazy man with the gun. Wants to vamoose out of there.' He selected a companion photo. 'This group was maybe fired with the muzzle four feet away or so. Ramirez is turning to scramble out of that truck cab, and the fourth round catches him under the armpit. Doc will have all the pellets, or most of them. About a hundred and fifty or so. Empty casing ends up on the cab floor.' He pantomimed the action. 'Boom, boom, boom, boom. Rabke's workin' that trigger pretty good for a dead man. Gonna be dead, anyway. Likely by then he ain't thinkin' much about shooting stance or shit like that. He ain't thinkin' about what kind of loads he's carryin' in that gun. He's just jerkin' the trigger, more out of reflex than anything else.'

'And then?' Estelle prompted.

Torrez held up the automatic. 'Rabke's Kimber had eight rounds in it. One in the pipe,' and he poked the slide with his finger, 'and seven in the magazine. One through four were snake shot. The last four in the magazine were Speer Gold Dots. Those are hollow point rounds that do the real business with rabid dogs or bad-ass humans. I've carried 'em myself for years.'

Linda's photo lineup of the gun's cartridges showed all eight in a neat row . . . four empty, aluminum casings, along with four shiny brass casings, only one of them empty. 'We know where that last one went,' Torrez said. 'A lucky shot, if you ask me. Rabke wasn't aimin' by then. Like I said, I can't believe he's thinkin' about what he's got loaded in that gun, snake shot or hollow points. He's just in reflex, squeezin' the trigger. Just boom. That last shot blows Ramirez right out of that truck and into the ditch. Only he don't know it, 'cause most of his brain ain't in his skull any more.'

'And Rabke drops the gun, unable to hang on to it any longer.'

'Yup. There's enough blood smeared on it, plenty of fingerprints. All that plus NAA tests for the powder residue. Ain't going to be no question.'

Estelle leaned back and regarded Torrez thoughtfully. 'Just a little bit of a problem, Bobby.'

'Yup. Only it ain't a little bit of one.'

'You're going to pattern those shot shells for us? For the record?'

'Yup. I don't think there'll be any surprises. Any report from Dr Guzman?'

'Not yet.' She glanced at the clock again. 'I'm expecting something by six. Maybe a little after. It depends on what he finds. In the meantime, we're waiting on prints off the truck, and now that we have the knife, Mears will take a close look at it. If my husband is right, that might give us an answer.'

Torrez almost smiled. 'Or more questions.'

FIFTEEN

'What I'd really like is a nap,' Linda Pasquale said. 'Staring at a computer screen is enough to drive me bonkers. I also need to pick up the twins at day-care, if Thomas is going to spend his day with all this cop business.' The department photographer's normal bouncy, driven pace had slowed a little, and Estelle's expression was sympathetic.

'Nevertheless,' she said, 'Before you take your nap, just one more thing.' Estelle felt guilty saying it, since the day was stretching into evening . . . and no one had yet to make an appearance at home.

'I wasn't assuming that I'd *get* one,' Linda said. 'Nap, I mean. I just *want* one. You know, like I could want a new Cadillac, or a vacation in Northern Scotland. That doesn't mean I'll get either one.'

'Northern Scotland?'

'Can't you imagine Tom and me and the twins in kilts?'

'*Ay.* I'll buy you outfits for Christmas. Then you can wear them around here, all you want.'

Linda laughed. 'I don't think so. What's the one more thing?'

'And as always, feel *more* than free to bring the twins here. It's a lift for us to see them.'

'Shut the suspect in a room with them, and in fifteen minutes, you'll get a confession to anything.'

'There is that. But Linda, if you haven't already, I really need a photo documentation of the knife now that it's been turned over to evidence.'

'I can do that. Is the lieutenant finished mining it for prints?'

'Yes.'

'Surprises?'

'Oh, *sí.*' She held up a letter opener that had been on her desk. 'When you're set up, I'd like to meddle and supervise. As you'll see, the lighting is going to be a challenge. I want to see how you do it.'

'This sounds serious.'

'It is.' The expression on her face turned delighted. '*Padrino.*'

'And here I am,' Bill Gastner announced. He folded his walker and leaned it against the wall beside the door. 'Mrs Pasquale, how's your nonstop day been?'

Linda stepped across the room and offered the old man a hug. 'Just duckie, sir. The photo industry loves me. The county manager will have a conniption when she sees the bill for toner, paper, folders, labels, and on and on.'

'I've never witnessed Leona Spears having a conniption. Sounds like fun.' He turned in time to intercept Estelle's hug. 'Lydia's on the way?'

'She is. She left Albuquerque a little after one, so she should be rolling in any minute.'

'You ought to rope Carlos in on this, sweetheart. I never saw anything. He's the one that caught all the action.'

'He and I had a good session,' Estelle replied. 'I have the transcript, but if it turns out that we need him, I know where he is.'

The 'any minute' lasted just a few seconds. They both looked up as Lydia Thompson appeared in the doorway, dressed neatly in her regular deputy's uniform that she'd worn to the hearing in Albuquerque, but still looking a little road weary. 'We're glad you're back, Lydia,' Estelle said. 'Good trip?'

'Way too long, ma'am. The sheriff reached me earlier and said you'd want to talk to me. I got back as quickly as I could.'

'The sheriff no doubt explained that we have a bizarre double homicide on our hands.'

'She did.' She crossed to where Gastner had eased himself into a chair. 'Sir, it's always good to see you. And by the way, I stopped to talk with Sheriff Torrez for a moment out in the parking lot.' She nodded. 'He seems to be doing OK.'

'For one of those retiree people,' Linda quipped.

'Careful there,' Gastner added.

Linda beamed a farewell. 'I'm gone now. Sheriff, I'll have the photos ASAP.'

Estelle rose and crossed to the door. She closed it, and turned to Lydia. The deputy had doffed her Stetson, and she sat on the edge of the chair seat, as if ready to spring away.

'My questions concern the day before that incident – the early morning of June sixth. The dispatch log records that you made a traffic stop on southbound State Fifty-Six that involved the pickup and horse trailer operated by Johnny Rabke.'

For a moment, Lydia Thompson said nothing. Perhaps it was because she hadn't yet been asked a question. Then she nodded and said only, 'That's correct.'

Estelle sat back behind her desk, sliding a yellow legal pad so that it was convenient to her pencil.

'When you initiated the traffic stop, did you know the vehicle belonged to Johnny Rabke?'

'Sure . . .' She just as quickly changed her answer to the more formal deposition response. 'Yes, I did.'

'What was the purpose of the traffic stop?'

'I stopped because he was parked in such a way that the left rear of his livestock trailer was impinging on the pavement. Not much, but enough to pose a potential hazard. I parked in such a way that my unit would offer some protection from southbound traffic.'

'The full inventory of your unit's emergency lights was operative?'

'They were.'

'When you engaged Mr Rabke in conversation, the two of you stood on the off-road side of the vehicle. Is that correct?'

'Yes.'

'How did he explain his parking the truck-trailer unit where it was?'

'Mr Rabke told me that he thought his right front wheel bearing was going bad. I accompanied him to the front of his vehicle. I used my flashlight to illuminate the wheel while he gripped it and rocked it hard against the suspension to check for play.'

'What conclusion did he reach about that?'

'He decided that the right front wheel bearing was indeed loose. I agreed.'

'At that point, what did he decide to do?'

'He said that he'd drive carefully up to the fencing project site approximately two miles north of NightZone. He'd be able to unload the truck and trailer there, and perhaps be able to jury-rig a repair for a trip back to town the next day.'

'You understand what happened the next day, during the early morning hours.'

Lydia closed her eyes for a moment. 'So sad,' she said.

'He was found in the truck with the stock trailer still hitched, so apparently he decided against dropping it off somewhere.'

'I don't know about that.'

Estelle let the silence hang for a moment. 'How well did you know him?'

Lydia took her time, looking down at her hands, clasped in her lap. 'Although last year I was not the officer who responded, I was in the area, you know, when he was hurt in that bar fight at the Spur.' She drew an imaginary line under the hairline across her forehead. 'And the other boy was killed by what, a billiard ball? And then there was the grand jury session that cleared Rabke of any culpability. I had seen him now and then after that.'

'Ever socially, after that?'

Lydia Thompson looked puzzled. 'No, ma'am.'

'Lydia, do you recall Mr Gastner stopping by the other night, offering assistance?'

'Of course.' She glanced in Gastner's direction. 'He asked if everything was all right. If I might need a jack or some other assistance.'

'There was a passenger in his vehicle?'

'Yes. Your younger son, Carlos. He said that they were headed up to NightZone for breakfast.'

'And you declined assistance?'

'Yes. None was needed. I told him to be careful out there, and off they went, to turn around and head up to the Zone.'

'You have a good memory for detail, Lydia,' Estelle said.

'Well, that's what we do, isn't it. Short and to the point, get the motorist back on their way, wish them well. Tell 'em to be safe. We've said it many times.' She smiled at Gastner. 'I'm willing to bet that an officer of Sheriff Gastner's long career has said it *thousands* of times over the years.'

'After clearing ten-eight, what did you do?'

'I made sure that Mr Rabke's unit was safely back on the highway. I drove behind him for a short distance before overtaking and heading on down south toward Regál.'

'Did you see Mr Rabke again that evening?'

'No, I did not.'

'During the stop, was your dashcam operative?'

'It was, but that big stock trailer was parked in such a way that the image toward the front of the pickup truck's cab was blocked from view.' She frowned a little, but her tone was simply curious, rather than provocative. 'Did I miss something? As far as I was concerned, the only thing that was out of the ordinary was that the driver – Mr Rabke – was outside of the truck, on the passenger side, and met me as I walked the length of the trailer toward him.'

'At any time during the encounter, did Mr Rabke touch you?'

'I beg your pardon?'

'Did he touch you?'

'That's an interesting question, Sheriff Guzman.' When Estelle did not reply or comment, Lydia Thompson sighed and refolded her hands. Her body language, her facial expression said, 'cool, calm, collected'.

'How many times has it happened when a motorist has been rubber-necking the scene of an incident, and ends up colliding his own vehicle with someone or something. When the oncoming vehicle slowed, and it turns out that it was Mr Gastner's Suburban, both of our reactions – Mr Rabke's and mine – was to step a bit farther away from the parked truck-trailer rig. It's just second nature. Perhaps especially this time since I'd mentioned to Rabke that a portion of his trailer was on the highway.'

'And so . . .'

'We both looked up at the traffic, and we both stepped back from the truck. As we did so, Rabke's hand reached up and touched my shoulder, as if maybe steering me away from the truck. I interpreted it as a polite, natural reaction on his part. At the same time, he raised his off-hand in sort of an informal salute to the driver. Maybe he recognized Mr Gastner or his vehicle. I don't know, and Rabke did not comment on it, until the Suburban slowed, signaled, and pulled a wide U-turn to return.'

'What did Rabke say at that point?'

'I remember his exact words as, "We got company."'

'Were you relieved?'

She frowned. 'No, "relieved" isn't the right word, Sheriff. My first concern was to make sure that the temporary roadblock caused by Mr Gastner's Suburban promptly moved on in an appropriate manner without further impinging the traffic flow.' Her fetching smile was immediate. 'Not that there was any traffic flow out there to impinge. That's one quiet stretch of prairie.'

'Did Rabke leave promptly after that?'

'He did. He remarked that there wasn't anything he could do about the growling wheel bearing other than hope it would give him a few more miles. I agreed, checked back with dispatch and we went on our way. I went on to Regál, and Johnny Rabke turned north on County Road Fourteen.'

'Lydia, I have one last question. At any time during your conversation with Johnny Rabke did he mention any issues he was having with anyone? With coworkers on the fencing crew, with other customers at the Broken Spur? Just anywhere. With folks at the Rancher's Feed and Supply? With anyone . . . just *anyone* . . . in the neighborhood?'

She shook her head. 'From my perspective, no. He was concerned about his truck, about getting his load of fencing supplies to the job site along with a couple of ATVs he had on board. That doesn't mean that there weren't issues, obviously. We didn't talk about them, if there were.

'I didn't know the other boy who was killed, the Mexican national? I met him once, I believe, in Regál, in the early fall. He was picking an armload of apples from the Martinezes' apple tree, the one right by the two-track through the village. I slowed, then stopped. We chatted for a couple minutes. He offered me an apple, which I took.'

'Did you ask where he was from?'

'No. I saw no reason to. As far as I'm concerned, he can pick all the apples he wants. I did not know him at the time. I found out later who he was when I happened to be in conversation with the Aguilars, there at the corner of the village by the main highway. She was doing laundry, he was working on repairing a trailer. I saw it as an opportunity for a little community outreach. And then this.'

'It can all turn on you, can't it,' Estelle said.

'Sadly, yes, it can.' Lydia Thompson turned and looked at Bill Gastner, who had not uttered a word during the deposition. 'What do you think, sir?'

The old man puffed out his cheeks. 'I'm sure a huge organization like the New York State Police doesn't know enough to miss you, but I'm glad you somehow ended up out here.'

SIXTEEN

The darkroom downstairs in the county building had once housed the central heating plant before renovations had made the old furnace obsolete. The advent of digital photography had consigned the original darkroom, with its noxious chemicals and red lights, to the dark ages of film photography.

Linda Pasquale now worked with a spread of three computers and a large, state-of-the-art color printer. A selection of measuring devices hung from a peg near the table. A clever camera support, the descendant of old-fashioned tripods, allowed her to mount her digital camera on free-turning gimbals that eliminated the error of shaky human fingers. The evidence photos that she produced were huge, with the curious jurors in mind. If a five-by-seven photo was good, an eight-by-ten was better, and a fourteen-by-twenty was better yet.

On the table in front of them lay the Chinese copy of the Ka-Bar military knife that had ended Johnny Rabke's life, covered carefully in clear plastic wrap. It once had been shiny stainless steel with a brown leather handle. Now it was coated with dried blood, no shine left.

Estelle took a moment to read the evidence tag. 'Seven inches of blade, five inches or so of hard leather handle. The wound clearly showed the results of that serrated blade edge.'

Lieutenant Tom Mears watched Linda as she fussed with the camera. He was of slight build, agile and graceful of movement, and he stayed out of her way, not kibitzing as she then adjusted the knife in its magnetic rack. When she was satisfied, the knife hung as if suspended in mid-air in front of a flat-black background, allowing photographs from any direction.

Mears drew a slender stylus from his shirt pocket. 'Ramirez was not wearing gloves,' he explained. 'It's not surprising that we would find his prints on the knife, especially since it appears that he never had time to wipe anything down after the attack. Also interesting is that there is no trace of Rabke's blood on Ramirez's hands, his shirtsleeves or trousers.'

'And you explain that how, LT?' Estelle asked.

'One hard knife blow, but he doesn't stay there to wallow around in Rabke's blood. My guess is he stabs, maybe sees Rabke's gun coming up, and makes every effort to dive for cover, out of that cab. What blood is on Ramirez is Ramirez's own.

'Now for sure, there's a lot of residue on the blade that was buried in Rabke's chest, so what we have is quantities of blood. But . . . when we get to the hilt and the handle, that's a different story.'

He touched the knife handle with the stylus. 'Here, here and here. A clear partial, right beside the hilt, or the *haft*, if you will. The print is intensified by the surrounding blood. It's printed in the blood, like leaving a boot track in wet cement. It's clear enough that I'm going to make an educated guess that that partial is from Rabke's right little finger.'

'How can you possibly tell?' Linda Real said with amused sarcasm. 'You've only examined a million and a half fingerprints in your career.'

'Two point one six nine.' Mears offered a reptilian grin. 'Rabke could have been trying to hold that handle with his right hand, like so.' Mears held his own right hand up against his chest. 'By now, there's some bleeding, all around the blade, the hilt, and even out on to the handle. Maybe not profuse, with the knife still in place to act as a dam, but some. What's interesting to me is that there are no other readable prints on that knife. Nothing other than smudges.

'Then, a *lot* of blood, for sure. The knife is yanked from side to side, and sure enough, *lots* of blood. The dam is broken, so to speak. All down the front of the victim's shirt, soaked the crotch of his jeans, soaked the truck seat. There's even a puddle on the floor in front of his seat.' He tapped the stylus on the counter. 'He didn't move from that seat after being stabbed, that's for sure.'

'Dang close to being pinned in place like an unlucky insect,' Linda offered.

'True. But some of the preliminary autopsy results are showing that he was stabbed once, hard, right through the sternum back to the vertebrae, and then the blade was jerked hard from side to side, hard enough that the serrated spine of the knife tore the wound first to the victim's right, and then the cutting edge sliced across to the victim's left, with the blade actually slicing open the heart.'

'We have two interesting things to ponder, then,' Estelle said.

She had been standing behind the table, out of Linda's way, and was content to listen to Mears's recitation. 'Evidence shows that Rabke somehow managed to pull his gun from the driver's door pocket, where he habitually carried it when it was not on his person. He was left-handed, and he fired the weapon five times. *Five* times.'

'Correct. And there are no fingerprints on that weapon other than Rabke's,' Mears said. 'Nor on any of the shell casings. His and his alone. NAA tests say that he fired the gun.'

'Theory number one. Rabke pulled the gun and fired *before* being stabbed.'

'Unlikely,' Mears said immediately. 'First of all, there was no sign of a tussle in the truck cab. The knife strike came from out of the blue, so to speak. No prior tussle, no defensive knife wounds. Second, the pattern of the snake shot tells us that Rabke hit himself with his own first shot, whether from pain or panic we don't know. But the first shot, fired left-handed, grazed his own thigh. The subsequent shots sort of walked across the cab, with Ramirez moving away and turning to escape. The patterns track as if the gun's recoil is forcing the muzzle upward. The final shot, a jacketed hollow point, strikes Ramirez in the head. Period. *Punto.* That's the end of his story. After that final shot, whether from the gun's recoil or not, we don't know, it's clear that Rabke drops the gun.'

'Any knife work Ramirez did happened before the shooting,' Estelle said.

'I think so. Absolutely. I can't see it happening any other way. Because as the shots are fired, Ramirez is turning *away* from Rabke . . . as most people would do when facing the threat of a loaded gun.'

'The trouble with Theory Number One is that it doesn't account for the savagery of the final knife wound. Yanking the knife from side to side like that,' Estelle said. 'Stabbing once – even as forceful as that strike must have been – stabbing once is one thing. Grabbing the knife handle and yanking the blade from side to side? That's hard work. That's dedication to the task, LT. Somebody *really* wanted to make sure that Johnny Rabke never left that truck alive.'

Mears looked skeptical. 'Yeah, but.' He fell silent, thinking hard. 'Yeah, I can see the attacker doing that, yanking the blade from side to side. And in the process Rabke manages to pull the gun. Maybe he's already started to do that.'

'Started before the strike?'

'It's possible.'

'But,' Estelle said, and watched attentively as Linda focused with great care and then shot a series of photos of the knife's blood-caked handle. 'Theory Number Two accounts for a couple of things, LT.'

'Let's hope so.'

'Ramirez at some point climbs into Rabke's truck. There's no sign of a fight prior to the stabbing. Evidence so far says it happened without warning. The initial strike drives into Rabke's chest, but he is able to react – maybe because the knife doesn't strike the heart. His off-hand – his right – clutches the knife handle. His *left* hand finds the gun. That makes sense to me. He wore that gun all the time. If he didn't actually wear it, it was within reach. And reacting that way makes sense to me. A year ago, when he fought Ramirez's brother at the saloon, he didn't have the gun. It was out in his truck. When he is struck with a painful knife wound to the forehead, he still reacts instantly, first with a pool cue, and then with the billiard ball. I mean, in an *instant*.'

'I'm with you so far,' Mears acknowledged.

'Even stabbed – probably fatally stabbed – Rabke manages the gun. That's an instinctive thing for him to do, even hurt as he is. It's in the door pocket, and as Bobby tells us, it's in condition three, cocked, locked, and ready to go. Rabke doesn't have to think. He yanks the gun out and more out of instinct than anything else, manages to fire five times, killing Ramirez. I say *instinct*, because of the way his five shots made a pattern around the cab. He damages himself in the process, but probably doesn't even know it. I doubt whether he knew that he actually managed to hit Ramirez.'

'And there he's left sitting,' Linda observed.

'Yes. There he is, knife in place, afraid to move. Hurting beyond his wildest dreams. An incapacitating hurt, a deep, awful hurt. The last thing he wants to do is move that big knife even a fraction.'

Mears nodded. 'You're thinking someone else is involved. That's what Bobby thinks.'

'Yes. Because consider that. None of that gusher of blood from Rabke's wound got on Ramirez. None. His own blood, yes. Whoever handled that knife for what we could call the second attack, wore some blood afterward. Had to. That makes sense to me. Someone else arrives, we don't know how soon. Rabke is still conscious, maybe, maybe not. Third party reaches in and grabs the knife handle, which is large and handy to the driver's side window. That same someone gives the handle a series of sideways yanks, finishing the job that Ramirez started. The killer, other than Ramirez, never entered the cab.'

Estelle used her own ballpoint pen as her pointer. 'That explains to me why the handle prints are smudged. Whoever did it wore gloves, for sure. Yank, yank, maybe shifts his grip because of all the blood. Yanks some more. The autopsy prelim talks about half a dozen cuts sideways to the heart tissue. If the killer stood at the door, with one hand bracing on the open window frame, the other hand is free to put tremendous force on that knife handle.' She grasped the edge of the table with her left hand, and jerked her free right hand from side to side. 'Rabke can't defend himself.'

'What if this bad guy was a backseat passenger?' Linda asked.

'Unlikely. Look at the close-up portraits you took of the knife wounds, Linda. If the killer reached around the headrest, and then reached around Rabke's body to grab the knife, that would be really awkward. And the cuts that the knife inflicted were directly to the side, right and left. No upward torsion that we'd expect if the killer was reaching around from behind.'

'More or less,' Linda said, 'that's exactly what Doctor Guzman said. He could count the cuts, and fit them to the damage.'

'Someone finished Ramirez's job for him,' Mears said.

'That's what makes sense to me at the moment,' Estelle said. 'It's a crime of perfect opportunity. The killer saw his chance and took it.'

SEVENTEEN

An arc light out in the parking lot shone through Estelle's office window, and she snapped the blind closed. With a dozen things she should have been doing, and that many more already done in a whirlwind day, it felt good just to sit, letting the leather swivel chair cradle her weariness. She had been about to go home. It had been fifteen hours since the discovery of the murders on County Road Fourteen, and now, as the clock swept the final minutes until nine p.m. on this unending Friday, Estelle felt as if all their best efforts had uncovered only one slim thread that wasn't painfully obvious.

Someone else had assaulted the already stricken Johnny Rabke, someone after Arturo Ramirez's violent, focused attack, someone after Ramirez's lifeless body collapsed into the bar ditch. That someone could have stopped, peered in the window of the pickup truck at the dying young man, and simply driven away, leaving Rabke alone to suffer through his final moments. What had the killer gained by reaching through the truck window and finishing what Arturo Ramirez had started?

While Estelle had talked first with Jake Palmer at the crime scene, then with the Aguilars in Regál, with Maggie and Victor at the Spur, with Father Anselmo, with Bill Gastner, and finally with her own son Carlos – even with the disturbing images from the morgue, no clear picture of *who* and *why* had started to coalesce in her mind. She needed a few moments to let things digest and ferment, and sought the quiet solitude of her office, closing the door so she didn't have to listen to the occasional jabbering of dispatch.

She'd read them a dozen times already, but Estelle once again picked up the scant pile of depositions from Rabke's coworkers. They were brief and particularly uninformative. To Estelle, they read much like the excuses uttered by a kid caught with his hand in the cookie jar. *Who, me?* The men building the four-strand barbed-wire fence across the prairie not many miles from where Johnny Rabke had been murdered knew Rabke as just another laborer who talked too much, didn't take enough baths, and tended to be sloppy

when it came to fence post placement . . . and was the sworn
enemy of any rattlesnake he could find.

Richard 'Ricky' Boyd, Wallace Boyd's oldest son and grandson
of the late and legendary rancher Johnny Boyd, was a surprise for
a rancher's kid. Ricky was tubby, in his late teens, and not likely
to revel in hiking the endless New Mexico prairie, lugging posts,
post drivers, wire, stays and clips. He appointed himself chief driver
of one of the ATVs. He told interviewing deputies that he'd been
impressed with Johnny Rabke's skill with the Kimber .45 semiau-
tomatic. He mentioned that the shredded snake corpses hung on the
newly built barb-wire fence surely attested to Rabke's skill.

Keenan Clark, the elder fence contractor, was a veteran at thirty-
one. He hadn't known Rabke well, but acknowledged that the young
man arrived at the job site early, worked hard, and willingly stayed
until the sun set. Clark had wished that the young snake hunter had
announced his intentions a bit before he 'cleared leather' and popped
off a round or two. Still, Clark admitted that he felt better with
Rabke working on ahead, clearing a path. He made it sound as if
the mesas and foothills through which the fence line passed were
literally crawling with feisty, poisonous reptiles. In truth, in the two
weeks of fence work, it appeared that Johnny Rabke had killed only
four rattlers.

Clark expressed surprise that anyone would be able to get the
jump on Rabke with a mere knife – despite the evidence of the faint
white scar across Rabke's forehead to the contrary.

Elliot 'EJ' Stance, twenty-two, and his brother Howie, seventeen,
lived on a ten-acre, hard scrabble 'ranchette' just west of Newton,
the 'census-designated community' just outside of the Posadas
County northern border. Enough population to earn a post office
but not much else, Newton was one of those communities that tourists passed through without stopping, maybe wishing that the place
could support a gas station. Orrin Stance, with the occasional help
of his two boys, raised and trained mules and built custom wagons
for his mules to proudly pull. The business was a good fit for
Newton, but Estelle knew that Orrin was impatient for more income
. . . and a little more than miffed with Miles Waddell, who refused
Orrin's scheme to run a mule and saddlehorse outfit on NightZone
property.

The Stance family had known Rabke for most of their lives, and
EJ, at least, didn't take much stock in any tale the young man chose

to tell. Those stories were legion, apparently. Rabke's claimed success with women rivaled his success at decimating the rattlesnake population.

Estelle read that observation and wondered once again if Rabke had more in mind than pedestrian safety when he palmed Deputy Lydia Thompson's shoulder.

Young Howie Stance didn't wonder about much of anything that wasn't loaded on his iPhone, but his older brother was mature enough to wonder about where Johnny Rabke got his money. Fancy late-model truck, long and frequent hours spent at the Broken Spur, a fancy handgun that must have cost 'close on to a thousand bucks'; EJ Stance had grown curious about Rabke's source of income, which didn't come from schlepping barbed-wire supplies across the prairie.

And Jason 'Jake' Palmer, whom Estelle had interviewed as he sat in the morning sun on the tailgate of his truck – the young man who'd been first on the scene of the Rabke-Ramirez murders, who hadn't hesitated to call Posadas dispatch on his cell phone, and then waited patiently for the deputies to respond. Twenty-seven years old, he'd been unnerved by the whole episode, unable to control the shake in his hands as he sat in the sun or the need for chain-smoking his cigarettes as he spoke with the undersheriff.

Estelle shuffled the depositions and glanced through them again, filing away a few mental notes. She turned and looked at the Seth Thomas clock beside the county wall map, wondering not about the time, now growing late in the day, but about Arturo Ramirez. She wasn't surprised that Arturo had waited almost a full year to avenge his brother's death. Like a volcano festering under the earth's crust, Arturo's rage had grown and deepened until some circumstance had triggered the fatal confrontation with Rabke.

Apparently Arturo hadn't just festered. It wouldn't be hard to discover exactly where Johnny Rabke called home – the aging single-wide mobile home just south of Posadas, behind the now-defunct Wayne Feeds. An aging, sometimes-functional windmill pumped enough water from the well behind the mobile home to suit Johnny's needs. He had often joked that he preferred alcohol to water anyway.

Arturo hadn't sought out his target there, even though Johnny's residence was no secret to anybody. It was no secret that Johnny spent hours at the Broken Spur, savoring his beer and flirting with Maggie Archuleta – or perhaps even with Posadas County Deputy

Sheriff Lydia Thompson. There was no secret about where Rabke worked, either. The fencing project, now underway for a full two weeks, kept him occupied and paid. Estelle frowned. The fencing job kept Johnny Rabke within a handful of miles from the border, an easy enough trip for Arturo Ramirez.

Estelle tapped the depositions into a neat pile and flipped them into the folder. She stood up and stretched. After his frenetic day, if Dr Guzman was home, he'd be asleep. *If* he was home. The hospital now employed a squad of EMTs for Emergency Room duties, one per shift. For anything more serious than a sprained ankle, Dr Francis Guzman would be called. If Estelle went home, she'd join him in bed, but would lie there restless, staring at the ceiling . . . unless he woke up.

Dispatcher Ernie Wheeler looked up from his textbook as Estelle approached. He closed the book, keeping a finger in place, and she could see the tome's cover. Going on fifty years out of print, the fourth edition of O'Hara's *Fundamentals of Criminal Investigation* was neither light reading nor apt to keep Wheeler awake through the finish of his swing shift.

'You're welcome to browse the bookshelf behind my office door,' Estelle offered. 'If there are Post-its stuck all over the pages, please don't remove them from the book.'

He patted the heavy book. 'Just historical perspective. It's interesting how things are changing over the years.'

'Indeed.'

'You're homeward bound?'

'No, actually I'm headed down to the Broken Spur, among other places. If you need something urgent, I'll be ten-eight, but I want to stay off the air. Phone's all right. It'll be on vibrate if I'm out of the car.'

'It's been a quiet night, Sheriff. A couple of domestics, but other than that, things seem to have settled down some.'

'We hope it stays that way.' She looked at the duty board and saw Sergeant Pasquale's on-duty magnet, along with Deputy Brent Sutherland's. Two officers was standard for a Friday swing shift, with Deputies Lydia Thompson and Dwayne Bishop coming on at midnight. The State Police would be working the interstate hard, but they seldom dropped into the quiet, dark reaches of the rural byways, and never kicked up dust on the two-tracks. Who knew where the Border Patrol would be. Father Anselmo might know.

Once upon a time, Arturo Ramirez would certainly have known. The knowing hadn't done him any good.

'We'll keep backup close by.'

'I appreciate that.' She smiled. 'Close by, but not lurking in the parking lot.'

EIGHTEEN

The stink of spilled beer and hot hamburger grease reminded Estelle why her stops at the Broken Spur Saloon were usually only in response to bar fights, or complaints about penniless vagrants. Pushing overloaded shopping carts or fat-tired bicycles carrying all their worldly possessions, the travelers sometimes stopped in the Spur parking lot to camp overnight. Local ranchers ignored them. No one locally filed complaints about border-dodging, undocumented Mexicans, either. Once he clambered over the barbed wire out of sight and west of the border crossing, Arturo Ramirez was free to travel at will.

Light-fingered folks being as ubiquitous along the highway as they were anywhere else, Estelle parked the Charger directly in front of the window outside the Spur's community room where she could keep an eye on the sleek sedan. She locked the doors and set the alarm. In this case, the alarm had been rigged to the raucous air horn, a tool normally used to chase deer and elk off the highway right-of-way.

The saloon was in energy-saver mode, with the four bulbs in each of the two deer antler chandeliers coping with about 40 watts apiece, the rheostat dialed low. One of the antlers haloed the pool table's less than tournament-grade surface. A double shop light with thin LED bulbs illuminated the bar. A modest sconce added just enough light to each booth along the wall that customers could read the large print on the menu headings.

The swinging door that led to the kitchen had the added attraction of a piece of raw plywood covering where the glass once might have been. Victor Junior could work in peace without customers ogling him or his kitchen.

As soon as she entered the saloon, Estelle veered to the right, through the accordion door leading to the community room, a simple space large enough for five four-top tables, an empty buffet steam table that hadn't seen steam in several years, and a rack of folding metal chairs. Families – or school-busloads of traveling underage customers – could seat themselves in the dining room, away from the rowdy influence of the saloon traffic.

Maggie Archuleta appeared in the first thirty seconds of Estelle's arrival, carrying a tall glass of iced tea, heavy on the ice. She beamed at the undersheriff as she placed the tea near Estelle's right hand.

'Do you need to talk to me?'

Estelle pointed with her upper lip as she gently moved the tea a little farther from the table edge. 'Actually, I need to talk with those two.' Those two were Elliot and Howie Stance, sitting at the two bar stools closest to the kitchen door. EJ was turned just enough to see Estelle's entrance, and now he shifted a bit to improve his view. 'If I could ask you to tell them that I'm here?'

'I think they know,' Maggie said. 'But I'll make sure. Anything to go with the tea? Fries? Carrot sticks? Celery and peanut butter? A nice juicy cheeseburger?'

'I'm set, Maggie. Thanks.'

'No wonder you don't weigh nothing. Do I need to move Howie into the community room?'

'Not as long as he's not drinking alcohol, Maggie.'

'He's heavy into Dr Pepper.'

'Then he's OK.'

Sure enough, in a couple of minutes, long enough to demonstrate little interest, EJ Stance pushed himself away from the bar and sauntered across the room, stopping long enough to whisper in the ear of a patron whom Estelle knew to be a resident of Tres Santos, down in Old Mexico. Whatever he said prompted a round of loud snarky laughter, and both men looked across toward Estelle. Emiliano Casteñon broke eye contact immediately and ducked his head. EJ left Casteñon in the company of the young woman seated with him at the two-top.

'Did you want to ask me something?' EJ asked. His breath was easily aviation fuel octane.

'If you have a few minutes.'

'Well, what if I don't?' He looked quizzically at Estelle, and his eyes followed the contour of her body downward, despite the professional modesty of her tan pants suit.

'Then I'll catch you tomorrow, out at the fence job.'

His laugh was harsh and unattractive, which was unfortunate, since the rest of his image was too attractive for his own good. Estelle gave him a return survey, then pointed at the chair opposite.

'We don't work on Sundays,' he said. 'Although we're kinda short-handed now, so maybe we will.'

'It's going on Saturday, EJ.'

He squinted into the distance. 'Yeah, I guess it still is. I lost me a day somehow.'

'Or I can catch you at home. On a Friday night, I'm sure you're perfectly content to be here. But one way or another.'

'Not at home too often.'

'Then I'll arrest your young ass and we'll do it that way.'

'Come on,' he said, offering up a wide grin, dimples, white teeth, and enough tan skin to prove that the relentless New Mexico sun was working hard to catch up with him. 'I'm just givin' you a hard time, Sheriff.'

'Believe me, after today, I don't need a hard time from any of you guys.'

He frowned down at the table, suddenly serious. 'I'm sorry, ma'am. You know that I talked with Sergeant Pasquale earlier today. We got called down to the station to make statements.'

'Yes. I'm following up on a few things.'

'What else can I tell you? I don't know much about what happened.'

'Who had it in for Rabke, EJ? Who was after him?'

'After him?' EJ shuffled the straight-backed chair around and sat sideways, left forearm on the table as if making ready for a quick escape. 'You know, he's just . . .'

Estelle waited, then prompted, 'Just what?'

'Well, it probably ain't for me to say, Sheriff.'

'So say it anyway.'

'He was just . . . just Johnny, you know? He'd say the damnedest things to just anybody. Kind of a king-sized asshole, if you know what I mean. Everybody knows that Mexican that got killed yesterday was kin to the guy that Rabke killed last year, right here in this barroom. Maybe Rabke shot off his mouth once too often. To the wrong person.'

'Did you see them together recently?'

'You mean Rabke and the Mexican?' Estelle nodded, and EJ continued, 'No, not me.' EJ leaned forward, tone confidential. 'You know, that thing last year? When Rabke got cut in that fight? He never talked much about that. Talked about lots of other things, but not much about that. Even though he carried that knife scar for all to see.'

'Maybe the experience hit a little close to home.'

'Maybe. Maybe that and the jury thing afterward. His court troubles.'

'You heard all about that, I imagine.'

'Everybody knows all about it. I think that kind of scared him. Or maybe embarrassed him some. I don't know.'

'I can imagine that it would.' She fell silent for a moment, then asked, 'You all got along all right with him at work?'

'Yeah, I guess. He was a good worker most times.'

'Most times?'

'Well, you know. He's all about him, if you know what I mean. Everything he says is all about him.'

'Kind of all wrapped up in himself, maybe.'

EJ nodded vehemently. 'You got that right.'

Estelle hard-wired a tiny, growing suspicion she had harbored since Gastner's report of the traffic stop between Rabke and the deputy. 'Rabke have any women friends? Did he talk about that?' When EJ hesitated, Estelle added, 'I mean, some time he's bound to go beyond just hanging snake carcasses on a fence for kicks.'

EJ snorted a laugh. 'That's one way to put it, I guess. He'd talk to anybody who'd listen.' He gestured toward the bar. 'He'd play pool a lot, and the time or two I watched, I don't think he ever stopped talkin'.'

'Saying what, for instance?'

'Just stuff. You know. Blah, blah, blah.'

'He had family?'

'You know, I don't know. He never talked about 'em if he did.'

'Who did he hang out with?'

'I know . . . I know that he liked it here.' He ducked his head, as if embarrassed. 'I mean, he usually had a pretty good audience here, small as the place is. Even, you know, like,' and he turned to wave a hand at the Mexican customer that he'd spoken to a few minutes before.

'Folks like Emiliano Casteñon.'

EJ looked startled. 'Oh, you know that guy?'

'Yes, I know that guy.'

He shook his head and glanced back across the barroom toward his brother, still deep into his Dr Pepper and his iPhone.

'So tell me, EJ, the last time you talked with Johnny Rabke. When was that?'

He scrunched up his face and turned toward the door as four men entered. One of them was Benny Aguilar, and he raised a hand in salute to Estelle.

'You know him too?' EJ asked.

'Yes.' With a straight face, she added, 'They're all members of the Regál Rotary Club. Again . . . Johnny Rabke. When was the last time you spoke with him?'

'Sorry. I'm tryin' to think. I guess it would be yesterday. Out at the fencing job.'

'What was the big topic of conversation?'

'Same old, same old. You know.' He shrugged.

'Rabke was upset about anything? He seem off his feed about anything?'

'He talked about his truck. He was sure he had a front wheel bearing going out on him, and he was thinking about heading into town to get it fixed. Or find a bearing and fix it himself. He's handy.' The smile that followed that was sly. 'Leastwise, he claimed that he was.'

'At least he knew enough to check it before the wheel fell off,' Estelle said.

'Well, yeah. He said he got stopped by the cops down on Fifty-Six. He pulled over to check things out with the noisy wheel, and a cop stopped by to check. Johnny said it was one of your guys.' He looked up at the ceiling. 'And *that* got him going. I guess the cop was on the upside of good looking? I think he went on for an hour about how he was going to follow up on *her*, if you know what I mean.' He snarked at the same time as Emiliano Casteñon and his girlfriend joined the 'Regál Rotary Club' in a raucous round of laughter.

'What did you say about that?'

'About dating the deputy? I told him that her husband would probably cut his nuts off. Maybe she ain't married. I don't know. Johnny said she wasn't, but hey. What can you believe from him, right?'

'Who's the boss of your fencing crew, EJ? Who's in charge?' He frowned so hard that Estelle laughed. 'It's not a trick question, EJ.'

'No, I know. I just thinkin'. Mr Boyd, he comes out to ride along the line pretty regular.'

'That would be Wallace Boyd?'

'Yup. I guess money for the fence is comin' out of his pocket, so he's the boss. He barks at the boy about every time. His son?

Ricky? That kid ain't worth much, if you ask me. But they don't ask, so there you are. Anyway, Mr Boyd comes out regular, but I guess the actual job boss is Keenan Clark. He don't take any crap from nobody, but he's a good guy to work for.'

'Did Rabke have any problems with the boss man? With Mr Clark?'

'Not so's I'd notice. I mean, Keenan was a cool dude, long as we got the work done.'

Estelle took a small sip of the ice tea, its bitterness now diluted a bit by the ice. 'Do your parents know that you bring Howie down here? Mom doesn't mind?'

The sudden shift startled EJ, and Estelle saw the color rise in his tanned cheeks.

'She's moved to Albuquerque. She don't care.'

'I'm sorry to hear that. How about your dad?'

EJ shrugged. 'He was going to come, but then decided to stay home.'

'He's not camping out with you boys?'

'No. Campin' out ain't his first choice. Anyway, somebody's got to stay home and take care of the livestock.'

'I'd like to talk with your brother for a bit.'

'Now?'

'Yes. That'd be easiest. Just him and me.'

'He's not in trouble, is he? I mean, *we're* not?'

'Not as long as it's Dr Pepper, EJ.'

NINETEEN

I f it was Dr Pepper, it likely had been fortified, and Estelle was amused to see Howie grab a large handful of peanuts from the bar bowl and chomp them all the way across the room as he made his way toward her table. He clutched his iPhone as if it were his lifeline, but his pace was steady.

Estelle gestured toward the vacant chair. The peanut-breath was powerful, especially lubricated with whatever was in the Dr Pepper. He wouldn't meet her gaze.

'It's a tough day for you boys.' She stood and reached out a hand, and after a moment of thought about which one, Howie took it and offered a dead-fish grip.

'Hi,' he said, and his voice cracked. He repeated himself, with a bit more volume. Not as tall as his brother, Howie wore the ubiquitous rancher's uniform of Wrangler blue jeans, dark green work shirt that had lost a round or two with barbed wire, and a John Deere ball cap that had seen its share of grease. He was working on a mustache, but wasn't making much progress beyond the blond fuzz stage.

'Good reception in here?'

He nodded but didn't offer to hand over the device.

'Howie, I don't know as we've ever formally met. I know your brother and dad. I'm Undersheriff Estelle Reyes-Guzman.' His eyes flicked back to meet hers in brief recognition, then as quickly snapped away. 'I know you were interviewed this morning down at the Sheriff's Office, but I wanted to follow up on a couple things with you.'

This time his nod was a little guarded, and he turned to look back toward his brother as if needing support from him.

'I understand from EJ that you two are camping up on the fence line north of here. Where you're working.' When he didn't answer, she added, 'Is that right?'

'Yes. Him and me and Jake. The three of us. And sometimes Ricky Boyd.'

'You have great weather for it.'

He nodded.

'That new super tower north of here? Up west of Newton? Do you get good reception out in the field with your iPhone off that?' The tower that Bill Gastner had called the 'new abomination' just topped 400 feet. Eventually, Estelle knew, some local ranch kid would find a way to climb it, hopefully not with a thunderstorm brewing.

'It's OK, yeah.' This time he actually looked directly at her, as if her curiosity about his iPhone was suspect.

'So tell me about Johnny Rabke.' His eyes opened wider. He obviously didn't know what to say, so she added an easier challenge. 'When was the last time you saw him?'

It took a moment for him to figure out which answer might be safe. 'Yesterday.' It was more of a whisper.

'Were you down here last night as well?'

'Yeah, I guess. For a while.'

'When you left to go back to camp, Rabke was still here?'

'Yeah. He was playin' pool. He stays late.'

'Sometimes even closes the place.'

'Yeah. He does.'

'But you didn't see him after that.'

'No. He lives in that trailer back towards town. He doesn't camp out.'

'The incident happened just down the county road from where you guys are working. What, a couple of miles or so?'

'Yeah, I guess.'

'You heard gunshots?'

'No.' He looked a little vexed as he met Estelle's gaze. 'I told the deputy that I didn't.'

'Can you tell me why Johnny Rabke would be driving his rig north on County Road Fourteen that late at night? As you said, he lives in that mobile home behind the old Wayne Feed Store in Moore.'

'My brother might know about that. All I know is that he had the stock trailer hooked up, carrying a lot of stuff. He wanted to leave the trailer at the work camp so he could drive into town to get some wheel fixed. On his truck.'

'That makes sense, I suppose.' Empty stock trailers behind pickup trucks were a badge of status for some ranch hands, rattling down the highway with the pickup's big diesel spewing smoke. Johnny

Rabke wouldn't think twice about driving into Posadas pulling the cumbersome trailer, empty or loaded, but it would get in the way if he wanted to stop at a repair shop.

'He had the wire mule with him, all fueled and stuff,' Howie volunteered. 'That and the flatbed Mahindra and about a ton of posts. He didn't want all that in town.'

'Sure. I saw that Jake Palmer had another load in his truck.'

'Yup. We figured that we're doing about nine miles of fencing, so that's a *lot* of posts and wire. We're just comin' up on that section of rimrock north of the new railroad. There's a couple of cuts in the rock where the cows find their way down and wander on to the tracks.'

'That wouldn't be good.'

'Happens all the time, but the train goes slow enough. Good thing.'

'Dangerous in the middle of the night, though.'

'Well, yeah.'

'So tell me, Howie. All the time you've worked on this project – what, we're going on a couple weeks now? Did you ever see Johnny Rabke arguing with anyone? That ever get your attention?'

He worked a peanut fragment out of his teeth while he thought. 'Not more'n usual.'

'What's usual?'

'Well, you know. Just stuff. He'd pick on Ricky, 'cause Ricky was always gettin' in the way. I mean, the little fat kid always wanted to be driving one of the rigs, 'cause he's got something against walking. And then half the time, he'd park it right in the way. You know, little stuff like that. Just like Rabke was always after me if I wanted to check out the phone, or got messages and stuff.' He made a face. 'I mean, it was all right for him to go off shootin' rattlesnakes all the time. Not that I minded that. Those things scare the shit out of me.'

'Who else visited the fence line?'

'Nobody. I mean, who cares about a dumb fence? It ain't exactly a tourist attraction. Mr Boyd comes out about once a day. He's fussy about how tight the wire is. He says if it's too loose, the cattle will just push through it, or under it, or some dumb thing. If it's too tight, it'll break in the winter if the weather gets cold enough. Keenan keeps it just right, most of the time.'

'Keenan Clark?'

'Yep. Workin' on the flat, it ain't too bad, except for the rocks. But when we have to cross a water cut, and the fence line has to go down and up,' and he drew a deep V in the air with his hand, 'then that takes some work. We got to make a good solid deadman or two to hold the wire down snug. Otherwise the cows will just slip under. Especially the calves.'

'Hard work,' Estelle said.

He smiled for the first time. 'Yeah. But I like what Keenan says: *It's hard work, but at least it don't pay good.*' He actually laughed.

'Are you going to run your own ranch someday?'

'No, ma'am.' The immediacy of the reply amused her. 'I got accepted at U of A, so in a month or two, I'm gone to Tucson.'

'Good for you. Studying what?'

'Don't know. Not barbed-wire, though.'

'I'd picture you as a computer pro. Maybe one of those . . . what do you call them? An "influencer"?'

'Oh, jeez . . .' But Howie's face lit up. *Howie the Influencer.* He obviously liked the sound of that.

'Aim high, Howie.' Estelle pushed her chair back. 'It's late and it's been a long day. I'll get out of your face now. Thanks for talking with me. You two be careful going back to camp. I don't want a call saying you guys are in the ditch somewhere.'

'Yes, ma'am.'

She detoured past Emiliano Casteñon's table and touched his shoulder, just a touch to let him know she was there. Estelle didn't know the girl with him, but read the young lady's smile as one of innocence . . . and over twenty-one. She offered a fleeting smile to Benny Aguilar, but not enough that he'd feel it necessary to explain to his friends about his earlier conversation with her down in Regál. Estelle stepped to the bar and leaned against it, waiting a moment for Maggie to acknowledge her. She nodded sideways toward EJ, whose beer bottle was nearly empty.

'*No más,*' she whispered, and Maggie nodded. Turning to EJ, Estelle added, 'Stay safe, Elliot. Pay attention driving back up the mesa.'

Outside, the air was within a degree or two of the inside temperature, but sweeter with the aroma of chamisa, creosote bush and juniper. She was amused to see Sergeant Tom Pasquale leaning against his department SUV, parked beside the Stances's stake-bed truck.

'*Hola, vato.*'

'What's new in your world?' Pasquale said. 'I figured much longer and I'd have to run a breathalyzer on you.'

She frowned in mock panic. 'But I've only had two!' It was the stock excuse 95 percent of intoxicated drivers gave to deputies when fortunately stopped before they killed someone.

'You haven't been monitoring your radio?'

'Switched off inside,' she said. 'I was talking with the Stance brothers. They're about to head back up to their camp.'

'And almost sober, I hope.'

'Almost.'

'You'll enjoy this, Sheriff. We have a report of a civilian running on the railroad service road.' The narrow, well-groomed gravel two-track immediately paralleled the narrow-gage NightZone line, extending the entire twenty-four miles from the Posadas Municipal Airport to NightZone's terminal. 'Well, not exactly *running*,' he amended.

'You spoke with him or her?'

'No. I thought that if you're going back to town that way, I'd leave that chore up to you.' He patted the fender of his unit. 'It's usually not a problem, but we don't get a lot of wheelchair traffic on that route.'

'Oh, come on.' She looked at him in disbelief. Late at night, out in the boonies in a wheelchair . . . who else could it be. 'Gastner?'

'Himself. He's parked his Suburban at the airport, and gained access through the service gate. Apparently he has a key.'

'He does. That's true.' Thanks to his long-time friendship with Miles Waddell, Gastner had easy access to anything NightZone. If he so chose, he could wander into the elegant gourmet kitchen any time 24/7 to make himself a peanut butter and jelly sandwich.

She glanced at her watch. 'Eleven fifteen. Maybe that's better than his usual insomnia attack at two or three in the morning.' She immediately thought of Gastner's daughter, Camille, who would be sure to have something to say about this latest escapade. 'Who called it in?'

'Monty Schaffer, the engineer. He recognized Gastner. Didn't stop, but thought someone running a wheelchair along the railroad frontage was a little strange.'

'Ya think? *Padrino, Padrino, Padrino.*' She looked up at Pasquale.

'As time goes by, this is going to become a challenge for all concerned, I suspect.'

'Without a doubt. But you know his moods best. You'll talk with him?'

'Yes. Whether or not it will do any good is another question. At least I can find out what's on his mind.'

'Well, as long as he doesn't start playing in traffic on the Interstate.'

TWENTY

During the twenty-five minutes on the flight back up State Fifty-Six to Posadas, while the Charger pounded out the miles, Estelle had time to think of all kinds of scenarios. They all returned to a basic theme about William K. Gastner's characteristic behavior: time of day was not a determining factor for his actions.

Years ago, he had embraced his deep-rooted insomnia without complaint, without resorting to drugs, without fighting what to him was an obvious solution: be out and about. He roamed 'his' county now just as he had forty years before, when he retired from a twenty-year career with the Marine Corps and joined the Posadas County Sheriff's Department.

During her own tenure with the department, Estelle had accompanied then-Undersheriff Gastner on innumerable adventures, long after the sun had set and long before dawn broke in the east, their way lighted only by the low-wattage bulb of the 'perpetrator light' wired under the front fender. The little bulb cast just enough light that the roadway's shoulder was faintly illuminated, but not glaring enough to be noticeable to anyone else.

Gastner had not let the notion of an assisting walker, or now even a wheelchair, change his habits. She smiled when she recalled Gastner's delight when his 'wounded warriors' four-wheel drive, all-terrain wheelchair had shipped to his house. Her prediction about its use was correct – it became a high-mileage chariot that allowed the old man to be out and about in some of the most outrageous places. Not a conventional chair in any sense, its four electric motors, one powering each large, soft, knobby tire, allowed impressive battery range between charges.

His modified Suburban with its hydraulic lift was the muscle to carry the 320-pound chair to his departure point. From there, he could meander ten or twelve miles through the fragrant prairie – always remembering that it would be five miles out and five back if he didn't want to end up limping along with his walker when the chair's batteries were exhausted. Estelle knew that, predictably, *Padrino* spent time researching bigger and better models with longer-range capabilities.

The village was quiet as she swung north on Grande and then pulled into the Public Safety Building's parking lot. A couple of minutes later, she had the keys for 304, the 4x4 Tahoe that civil deputy Dwayne Bishop usually drove. It took only moments to check Gastner's home on Guadalupe Terrace to make sure that his Suburban hadn't yet returned. If his Sheriff's Department radio was turned on, he wasn't answering.

The once pastoral Posadas County Airport, seven miles out of town on NM78, had changed as dramatically as the rest of Miles Waddell's venture. Originally built almost a century before, with a single 2,500-foot east–west runway to handle the occasional Piper J-3 Cub or Cessna 120, circumstances had changed the airport's face. Now, with the original runway extended to 7,500 feet, with wide taxiways and abundant parking near the FBO, the past two years had added a crosswind runway and helipad.

The guiding hand of Miles Waddell was evident. His beloved train terminal was just west of the runway, with an attractive barn for machine maintenance.

The night-roaming Bill Gastner had made no attempt to hide his Suburban. It was parked just to one side of the barn's main door. The yard office was well lighted, and a lanky young man with an engineer's cap peered out the window, then headed for the door. Ronnie Holland's smile of greeting was huge.

'Engine will be here in about seven minutes,' he announced. 'You coming to ride, or to arrest me?' He jerked his hands as if he were on stage, working a fever-pitch audience with mike in hand. He'd been twelve years old when he performed an Elvis lip-sync routine in a Posadas High School talent show, and Estelle had been in the audience . . . not to watch him, necessarily. The grand piano that her son, eight-year-old Francisco, would play later in the show had been nestled in the corner of the stage.

'Ron, how are you doing? How's Myra? And Julie? And Benji? And Becky?'

His face went blank with astonishment. 'Sheriff Guzman, how . . . do . . . you . . . remember . . . all that?'

'You saying you and your family are not memorable, Ronnie? Anyway, I'm just reading the cue cards.'

Ronnie beamed and struck the pose again, holding the mike toward his audience and rocking his hips. 'You make me feel so good, baby.'

'Relax before you blow a hip socket,' Estelle laughed. 'Actually, I'm looking for the owner of that Suburban.'

'Sheriff Gastner went—' and he pointed an expressive forefinger westward. 'He said he had to check something out.'

'Did he say what?'

'He did not. I asked him, but he said he was just havin' fun and that he'd be back in an hour or two. Havin' fun in the middle of the night.'

She looked at her watch. 'Less than an hour ago. OK. Do me a favor, Ronnie. Pop the access gate for me?'

'You going after him?'

'For a ways.'

He managed a passable Clint Eastwood imitation as he said, 'You need backup?'

'I hope not.' She gestured toward the gate. 'Let me get going.'

'You got it.'

By the time she was back in the Tahoe, the access gate was rolling open. To her surprise, the railroad service road was smooth enough that she could have felt at home in the Charger, at least for the first mile or so. Then the speedy car would have chuddered itself to a halt in the prairie sand.

With the Tahoe's odometer set, she cruised southwest, keeping a steady fifteen miles an hour, with the windows open, headlights off, and the parking lights ample. In several spots, she saw the narrow tracks of what was likely the wheelchair's passing. She could picture Bill Gastner's delight as his amazing chair whispered along through the prairie night. The wind had died, and she could feel the warmth of the sun-heated sand rising and fragrant.

After leaving the airport mesa, the railroad route was far from straight. Miles Waddell had not been interested in a locomotive that charged across the prairie at eye-watering speeds. The tracks twisted and turned around the mesas and arroyo cuts, the route selected with two basic criteria: spectacular desert scenery, and availability of easement from landowners.

Estelle had marked only a mile before the locomotive appeared, a low rumble of steel on steel, but the propane-electric system barely a bass whisper. Most of the route was open range. Cattle, what few there were now, were free to wander along and across the tracks. On occasion they'd be found standing in the middle of the rails, and they'd stare stupidly as the locomotive approached.

Waddell didn't want the strident locomotive whistles shattering the peace of the prairie. Instead, engineers remained watchful enough, operating at a slow enough pace that they could brake to a sedate walking speed, nudging the puzzled bovines out of the way.

Although she couldn't see the locomotive cab's interior with its cabin lights off, she guessed that Monty Schaffer himself was at the helm of this night run, and the dark shape would be him sitting with his arm out the window, in company with Mark Eberhardt, his fireman – a historic title that had little to do with the demands of the modern engine. The locomotive's low-intensity wobble light bounced off the Tahoe's paintwork, and Estelle offered a wave and a single tick of the emergency light bar.

The train might have been slow, but electronics were speed of light. The engine and its four cars had glided past and its single dim taillight already faded out of sight when Estelle's radio broke the prairie serenity.

'Three ten, PCS. Ten twenty?'

Estelle pushed the lever into park and found the radio mike in the near dark. 'PCS, three ten is two point eight miles west of the train terminal on the railroad frontage road, westbound.'

Dispatcher Ernie Wheeler was silent at that, perhaps peering up at the map over his desk. 'Uh, ten four, three ten. Be advised that the NightZone folks are reporting a possible pedestrian accident on that route, just beyond rail mile marker four. No injuries reported, status unknown.'

'Three ten is responding. ETA six minutes.' She had already pulled the Tahoe into gear when Wheeler added, 'Three ten, the locomotive crew reports that they were going to stop, but the subject waved them on.'

'Ten four.'

Four miles from the airport, the route crossed the Salinas arroyo, the first of several spans along the route built to accommodate the locomotive's weight, and the first of four spans that would repeat crossings of the Salinas as the arroyo wandered at various times through all points of the compass, but generally working its way southward.

As she neared the looming silhouette of the bridge, Estelle turned on the Tahoe's lights as well as the high-intensity spot. The beam lanced forward, making harsh shadows of each prairie bush. Waddell wouldn't have approved of the light show, but there were times, Estelle knew.

Perhaps because of yet another fanciful notion by NightZone owner Miles Waddell, the arroyo bridges were built in an old-fashioned, frontier design, grounded by massive twelve-by-twelve wooden beams that he had located at a saw mill in New Mexico's Jemez mountains. He had proudly showed a historic photo he'd found in a logging operations coffee table book that illustrated one of the massive bridge spans that had been built over a gorge near Cloudcroft, New Mexico.

'That's what I want,' he had declared. 'Touched up to modern standards to be safe, but otherwise, just like that.'

At this moment, of more interest to her was the figure sitting in the dirt by the roadway, forearms relaxed on his knees. He held up a hand in salute as she rolled to a stop.

'PCS, three ten is ten ninety-seven.'

'Ten four.' Ernie Wheeler's tone was flat, devoid of any tinge of curiosity.

She doused all of the lights and got out of the Tahoe.

'Isn't this a gorgeous night?' Bill Gastner offered as she approached, flashlight in hand.

'Spectacular.' And it was. The canopy of stars arched down to all four horizons with the moon still in hiding. The Salinas arroyo was a jagged black accent across the prairie, its sheer sides crumbling here and there.

'Perhaps you've wondered why I called this meeting,' Gastner chuckled.

She stepped close and knelt down. 'I'm sure you have a good reason, *Padrino*. Did your batteries run flat?'

'Mine, or the chair's? How about a hand,' he said, and held out an elbow. 'As long as you're handy.'

With his right hand grasping the handle of his walker, and with Estelle heaving on his left elbow, they managed to hoist him upright, all with dramatic creaking and groaning on his part.

'Now to just stand still for a minute,' Gastner said. 'Who ratted on me?'

'The train crew, sir. Monty recognized you.'

'How could they see me in the dark?'

'The wheelchair was the giveaway, *Padrino*.'

'At least it wasn't Camille. Anyway, take a short walk with me, and I'll explain all.' He slipped one of those incredibly bright mini-flashlights out of his pocket, turned it on, and pulled the cylinder in to widen the beam. With her arm linked through his elbow, they walked the few steps to the point where the road swung into its approach curve to the arroyo. He stopped and focused the beam on the wheelchair – thankfully upright, but now parked in the center bottom of the arroyo. 'Not a good time for a flash flood,' he observed.

'And you drove down in there, why?'

'The honest reason?'

'Sure. That would be entertaining, sir.'

'It *looked* all right. The other side of the arroyo looks hard-packed.' He narrowed the beam of the flashlight and swept the beam across to the far roadside. 'You can see tracks there on the other side from recent traffic. So I thought, "what the hell?" I started down and right away felt the treachery of the sandy slope.'

'That's almost poetic, sir.'

'Yes, well. I realized that the only *safe* route was to continue down to the flat bottom. Trying to go backward was risking a capsize. So that's what I did. Safe and sound, down on the bottom. But returning the way I came? I don't think so.'

'What had you decided to do?'

'I hadn't. Not yet, anyway. Then the train came along, first one way and then the other. About every hour and a half, it comes by, one way or another. A perfect night, and I knew I wasn't going to sit out here all night, anyway. If worse comes to worse, come dawn I'd be able to examine the service road and plan out a route that would take me up and out without landing on my head.'

'I see.'

'Sort of a live-and-learn moment, sweetheart.'

'I'm sure. I have a couple of sons who lived by those rules when they were growing up.'

'And it worked for them, in spades. My only worry is going to be the acid tongue of my eldest daughter when she hears about all this.'

'I can offer blackmail with easy terms, *Padrino*.'

He laughed. 'Anyway, now that you're here. On to the important stuff.' He swung the flashlight beam across to the trestle and narrowed the beam to its fullest extent. 'Climbing up out of this damn arroyo is a one-time event for me at the moment. But you, my dear, can slide down there in a blink of an eye. I want you to go into the arroyo, staying out of any other tracks that you might find, and go over to the trestle. I assume you have a good flashlight. Look at the supports and tell me what you see.'

TWENTY-ONE

After a day soaking up sunshine, the trestle was fragrant, even this many hours after sunset. The creosote-impregnated beams were still pungent. Sidling closer, Estelle kept a vigilant eye and ear tuned to the denizens of the desert who sought shade in the structure during the day, and took their time exiting with the cool of the night.

From five feet away, she stopped and played the light on the nearest beam. From up on the bank, Gastner didn't offer guidance, but waited patiently, leaning on his bird-foot walker. Estelle estimated the trestle's length at close to a hundred feet, with the smooth road bed offering three feet of walking space on either side of the iron rails. From where she stood, the trestle soared more than a dozen feet above the arroyo bottom.

She surveyed the beamed supports over her head, and drifted the light downward. Several swallows burst out with noisy squeaks, vanishing into the night. They'd been busy nesting, their messy constructions tucked into half of the joints between beams. The vertical supports of the trestle angled in from the side buttresses, allowing space in the middle of the span for seasonal flooding. Waddell's engineers had chosen this spot where the Salinas ran straight, so that no side turbulence would chew away the bank, threatening the supports.

'All right,' she said.

'See 'em?'

'The swallows? Yes.' She looked down again, at a spot just below the eastern concrete buttress. 'And the bull snake is dozing over there on the east side.'

'I saw him. Actually, I think it's likely a "her", looking for a nice sheltered spot to deposit her eggs. No matter. Focus in on the trestle.'

'Lots of pressure-treated, creosoted spruce.' She methodically drifted the flashlight beam down each trestle member. 'It might help if I knew . . .' She stopped in mid-sentence and stepped close. With the flashlight in one hand, she drew out her knife from its pocket clip with the other. The blade snapped out with a sharp flip of the wrist. She knelt and gently probed the trestle girder with the blade tip, scooping out a pea-sized fragment. She rolled the substance between thumb and finger. 'Now why would that be?' she muttered to herself. The pea-sized ball of wood putty was just that, filler dabbed into the wound cut in the girder.

She bent close, flashlight nearly touching the wood. The cut was neat, almost precise, and extended around the square perimeter of the girder, leaving a scant half-inch of the girder uncut.

Standing up, she rested one hand on the nearest girder while she swept the flashlight beam around the ground. Footprints may have scuffed some of the evidence, but the chainsaw had fountained a stream of sawdust that would take a heavy rain to disburse.

'I found six spots,' Gastner said. 'Where you're standing is right in the middle of the six. There's three to your left, two to your right. They're all about three feet off the ground.' His flashlight beam arced here and there as he made his way along the arroyo edge, working toward the railbed. 'And an interesting thing, too.' He stopped, both hands on the walker. 'The cuts are not horizontal. They're at a good angle, starting high, angling down.'

'Meaning what?'

'I don't know what it means, except that the cut girder would tend to sheer under stress. I'm not a goddamn structural engineer, but that's the way it looks to me.'

'First things first,' Estelle said. 'Train traffic stops, right now. That's the first call. Second is to get an investigative crew out here. Right now. We'll start with our guys, then pull in whoever we have to.'

Her survey found all six cuts, all nearly sawed through the girders, all patched to make them invisible from a cursory inspection from either above or on the service roadway.

Dispatcher Lawrence Burke answered his phone on the first ring, full of energy this early in his graveyard shift. 'Sheriff, this is Burke.'

'Larry, Bill Gastner and I are at the railroad bridge at mile marker four, right at the Salinas arroyo. Call NightZone rail dispatch and tell them to halt all engine traffic on that line. If there's a locomotive rolling westbound, have them stop immediately. Tell Monty Schaffer that I want to see him out here ASAP. He needs to use the service road.'

'Sheriff, that's an emergency stop to all rail traffic. And send Monty Schaffer your way ASAP.'

'Correct. Then call Miles Waddell and tell him to meet us out here. ASAP.'

'Ten four.'

'Then we're going to need the team out here. I want Linda, Tom Mears, Tom Pasquale, Sheriff Taber, and whoever else you can find. I have a couple others I'm going to call from here.'

'Ten four. Regular shift right now is Deputies Thompson and Sutherland.'

'Send them both.'

'Ten four. Are you going to be requesting EMTs and ambulance?'

'No. Not as long as all rail traffic is stopped immediately. Call me if you have an issue with anyone.' She disconnected abruptly.

'The cavalry is coming, *Padrino*.'

'That's what I like to hear.' He chuckled. 'I mean, if I can't sleep, why should anyone else?'

'And since we have a few seconds of peace and quiet, tell me, *Padrino*. How did you happen to stumble on this mess?'

His flashlight snapped off. 'First of all, the darkness will hide my goddamn embarrassment.' He hobbled closer to the edge of the arroyo and waited while Estelle made her way up the slope of the service road. 'See, I only figured out how stupid my arroyo stunt was when I was about halfway down the grade. By then I didn't want to stop mid-slope and find myself all tipsy. And there was certainly no turn-around possible, at least at my skill level. I mean, Carlos would have just spun a brody and gone back up and out.

'For me, the only choice was to continue down to the flat arroyo bed. About crapped myself. And then, the worthless prostate kicked in. So I park where you see the beast parked now, and because human nature being what it is, I hobble over under the protection of the trestle, out of sight of all humanity.' He waggled the flashlight. 'And there I commence to do my business. "*Oy*, what's this?" I say. And I discover the first cut. Well, then, I find the next cut, and the next, and so on. Somebody's been damn busy with the chainsaw, haven't they?'

'Indeed they were. And you elected not to try assaulting the hill with the chair.'

'I may be old and stupid, but I'm not *that* stupid, sweetheart. It's a beautiful night, and what's the harm of taking time to think this whole mess out. Worse-case scenario is to climb up here on my hands and knees. Turns out I was able to work my way up sideways, little steps at a time, like someone on skis chopping sideways up a steep ski slope.'

She reached out and took him by the right arm, shaking it gently. 'I need to make some calls. You're welcome to a comfortable seat in the Tahoe while I do that.'

'As long as I don't have to sit in the back seat, behind the prisoner screen.'

Estelle laughed. 'You know, I was thinking about that.'

TWENTY-TWO

'Where's the body?' A fair enough question, Estelle Reyes-Guzman thought, considering the circumstances. Sheriff Jackie Taber had wasted no time prying herself out of bed, and had broken most of the speed limits enroute to Mile Marker Four along the NightZone narrow-gage tracks. The sheriff stood near the downgrade and looked at the wheelchair parked below. For a full minute she was silent, and then did a slow turn toward Bill Gastner. The old man had climbed carefully out of the Tahoe when the sheriff arrived, and walked around the front with one hand on his three-footed walker/cane and the other stroking the Tahoe's paint.

'So tell me, sir,' Taber said. 'I'm sure we'll hear the whole, unabridged story several times during this unending night, but . . . you're up here, the chair is down there. In twenty-five words or less, can you tell me what you might have learned from this escapade?'

Not the least bit embarrassed, Gastner patted the fender of the Tahoe as if it were somehow a co-conspirator. 'Absolutely. When you want to Evel Knievel an arroyo, get up *lots* of speed.'

The sheriff's laughter was loud and heartfelt but, like a stage comedian, she cut it off abruptly with a sober face. They all could hear vehicular traffic approaching, none of it sedate.

'Ah, good,' Estelle remarked when three Sheriff's Department units appeared out of the darkness, their dust cloud billowing. Sheriff Taber stood patiently, awaiting the crowd. She reached out and took Gastner by the shoulder at one point, as if they were old companions.

Sergeant Pasquale managed to bring his vehicle to a stop with a minimum hurricane of dust and gravel. He started talking before he was all the way out of the cab. 'Traffic is confirmed shut down. Monty Schaffer is not far behind us, and Miles Waddell is headed this way from the west.'

'Outstanding,' Estelle said, and watched Lydia Thompson park her unit behind Pasquale's, while Deputy Brent Sutherland found a spot behind hers. Estelle held up a hand and beckoned the three. 'First things first.' She turned and pointed down into the arroyo.

'We need that unit out of the arroyo. One of you drive it, the rest of us will push.'

'How'd . . .' Sergeant Pasquale started to ask, then shook his head. 'Forget it. Who's the lightest? Lydia, you are. You drive.' He turned to Gastner with a big grin. 'You get to watch, sir.'

'I can do that.'

'I'd love to have a video of how you did this.'

'No, you wouldn't.'

'Stay as far toward the south side of the road as you can,' Estelle suggested. 'Footing looks a little firmer, and we want to avoid compromising any track evidence near the trestle.'

'There's enough of us we could pick it up if we have to,' Pasquale added. 'Let's do it.'

With four pushing and the wheelchair's own effective four-wheel drive buzzing, little effort was needed. Once it was parked out of the way and shut down, Estelle said to Gastner, 'The battery life gauge says you have half power. Is that enough to make it back to your Suburban?'

'Should be. In a bit, sweetheart. As long as I'm here, I'd like to see the show.'

'Absolutely. All right, we're waiting on all the powers that be. But first, I want a team – that's Tom, Lydia and Brent – to survey the other five trestles between here and NightZone. Let me show you what you're looking for.'

They trooped down the hill into the arroyo, following the under-sheriff's tracks, and listened while Estelle explained what had been found. 'The putty – I think it's routine caulk filler like you can buy in a tube at the hardware store – is reasonably fresh.' She touched a small area and brought up a pea-sized sample. Rolling it between her fingers, it made a neat quarter-inch ball.

'You can see that the saw cut extends at least ninety percent of the way through the beam, and also notice that it's at a decided slant. The saw cut *downward* from start to finish. That's true of every cut we can see here.' She swept her flashlight from beam to beam. 'Here, here, here and so on. A total of six main girders have been cut.'

'But the train went by not long ago,' Deputy Thompson said. 'There was apparently no displacement then.' She laughed nervously. 'And we're standing under the structure right now.'

'We don't know why it didn't collapse, other than that luck was with them . . . and us,' Estelle said.

Pasquale ran a light finger along the caulked cut. 'Maybe they weren't ready to have it go. Not yet. You say there's five more spans in addition to this one?'

'Yes.'

'Then it makes sense to me that they would want every one of them to be ready to go. Maybe at one time. Maybe with a little help from explosives. Radio-controlled trigger somehow.'

'That would be complicated, but you may be right. A link makes sense to me,' Thompson said. 'What effects one span has no effect necessarily on the next one – unless there's a link, a signal of some kind. Let's call this one span one. How far are we from span two? How much solid track between the two?'

'I've ridden the train, and I never paid attention to that,' Pasquale admitted. He looked up at Gastner. 'Sir, you were here when these were built.'

'Yep. I don't want to guess, but there's a map on Waddell's office wall that shows the official engineering as-built. Right now, the most expedient thing to do is to drive along the service road here, and check 'em as you come to 'em. Five more after this one. In an hour or so you'll have part of the answer.'

Pasquale thumped the nearest girder with his fist. 'Disguised as they are, how'd you ever notice the damage, sir? I mean, in the dark and all?'

'That's a long and painful story.'

'I bet.' Pasquale pointed his flashlight toward the trucks, where Monty Schaffer's black Ram with the reflecting NightZone logos on the doors had pulled to a stop.

'This is what we need,' Estelle said. 'Two vehicles surveying west. Sergeant Pasquale, you're leading with your unit. Deputies Thompson and Sutherland in Thompson's. Monty will be behind you, hooking up with Mr Waddell when they meet up. That gives you five sets of eyes out there. We don't know if the cutter is still out there, still at work. No headlights. Use your perp lights, along with the spot if you need to, keep the windows down so you can hear, and stay alert. Check in with me and Sheriff Taber after each trestle.'

She paused as Monty Schaffer approached. 'Linda will be along sometime after dawn with a team to formally document the damages. For now, you all have cameras. I want digital photos of each cut. Nothing fancy. Just a simple, clear portrait of each cut, numbered one through however many there are. Watch where you step. There will be sawdust at the base of each cut, no matter how hard the cutter tried to clean things up . . . if he did. That sawdust can be analyzed, even the tiny residue of bar oil analyzed. So no size twelves tromping on the evidence.'

Sutherland looked confused. 'We don't have any idea who did this?'

'No.'

'None at all?'

'No.'

'And the other question that needs asking,' Lydia Thompson said. 'Is this all somehow related to the two killings yesterday down on the county road? Seems like it has to be, somehow. And another obvious question follows that. Are the guys out working on the fence in any danger? I mean, there's at least a couple of kids out there.'

'"Somehow related" is a fair question,' Estelle agreed. 'As you know, I'm not much of one for coincidence. So pay attention. Whoever did this is willing to commit mass murder, if one of those trains derailed and took a dive into the arroyo. So I'll say it again. Pay attention. Eyes, ears, nose, taste, touch, but work fast. As you complete the survey, tape off the scene.'

'Hard to close down a twenty-five-mile-long crime scene,' Pasquale said.

'At least they'll know we've seen their work. We can close off the service road at each end. We'll be working west to each site, coming along behind you. If someone has eyes out there, maybe they'll hesitate. You all keep us posted.'

She reached out to shake hands with Monty Shaffer as he made his way down the approach, taking care to keep the flashlight out of his eyes.

'Question,' Pasquale said. 'NightZone is full of tourists, all times of day and night. If we meet some of them out recording night bird sounds, what's our official line?'

'If they're on this service road, or anywhere close to it, or carrying a chain saw, arrest them. If they're just night birders or whatever, I'll be happy to apologize to them later if need be, but we'll want to know what they heard or saw.'

'And check their cuffs and socks for sawdust,' Lydia Thompson said.

'Exactly so.' She beckoned Monty. 'I'll take a moment to tour Monty around this damage so he knows what you're looking for.

In the meantime, saddle up the vehicles and stick to the service road, close to the tracks. When you're heading out, stay about a hundred yards apart, always within sight of each other.'

She turned to Monty. 'If you would, sir, try to step right where I step.'

Sheriff Taber stopped her. 'Estelle, I'll stay on top and play base station. I can catch folks as they arrive.'

'Perfect. Right now, we want as few sets of boots scuffing around here as we can manage.'

'What the hell is going on, Sheriff?' Monty Schaffer asked, clearly mystified.

'We don't know yet, sir.'

'Damage to the trestle somehow?'

'Yes.'

'Are we going to be able to resume train service tomorrow?'

'After you survey the damage, sir, I'll let you be the judge of that.' Staying to the small trail of footprints and gravel scuffs left by the deputies, she escorted Schaffer to the trestle. He stood with his hands on his hips, not saying a word as she stopped the flashlight beam on each cut. Finally, he shook his head in disgust.

'It ain't about to fall down standing like this,' he said. 'But get a hundred tons of locomotive and four cars loading her down, there just ain't no telling. And the train's been by now any number of times since the bastards cut this. I just don't know.' He let out a string of heartfelt curses. 'I can't even imagine what the hell it's going to cost to fix this.' He turned away, still shaking his head. 'Let me catch up with the others.'

She walked with him, back up the steep service road to his pickup, and Estelle watched his black Ram take the arroyo as if it were just a little dip in the road. She turned to the almost patient Bill Gastner.

'What now?' As the teams dispersed, Gastner's tone hinted that he wished he had something to do.

'First, we put you in protective custody,' Estelle said. 'Did you happen to tell anyone earlier in the evening – and I use *that* term loosely – did you tell anyone where you were headed for your nighttime prowling?'

'Ah, no.'

'So the first job is to get you home before your daughter sends out the sheriff's posse.'

'You are the undersheriff, and you and her nibs Sheriff Taber don't have a posse.'

'Perhaps we need one, sir.'

'If I'm not needed here, I need to get the chair home for a recharge. I can roll back to the airport parking. That's the easiest way. Take me an hour and fifteen minutes.'

'And I'll use that hour and fifteen minutes to do some thinking. I'll be right on your back bumper, sir.'

He grimaced. 'I don't need protection, and you don't need to waste your time escorting me, sweetheart.'

'No waste. I have a radio, I have a phone. I have a lot to do. On top of everything else, I don't want to have to worry about you out in the boonies if your chair quits.'

'Won't quit. Besides, the prairie is quiet. I don't need somebody tailgating me for four miles.'

'Humor me, *Padrino*.' Estelle smiled at him. 'And we have a handful of officers working out there who will testify that the prairie is *not* quiet at the moment, sir.'

She stopped short, looking hard at Gastner.

He tapped his own forehead. 'What? You're thinking again. I can see it.'

'If you went to all the trouble to do this damage, wouldn't you like to watch when a trestle crashed down with a train on top of it?'

He gazed at Estelle thoughtfully. 'There are six trestles, sweetheart. How do you pick one?'

'The biggest. The most spectacular.'

'That would be the one over Red Slade Gulch. Down the line a few miles.'

'The wood putty in the saw kerf tells me we have someone clever at work. I can imagine them setting up a trail cam, to film the event. A motion sensor, battery-powered digital. How difficult is that?'

'I couldn't tell you, being a Neanderthal with such things.'

'Bobby Torrez has used a trail cam. The more I think about that, the more it makes perfect sense.'

'That doesn't surprise me a bit.'

'That's something to pursue. With no rail traffic, the heat's off us a little. Now we take a closer look. A trail cam is small, but if we find the right vantage point, we find the cam.'

'If they used one. I agree, if some jerk wants to film a train crash, he'll be there with a camera.'

TWENTY-THREE

'It's one thing to puddle around with no particular destination in mind,' Bill Gastner said as he settled into his wheelchair. He fastened the seat belt securely. 'But I assume you want me out of your hair as efficiently as possible.'

'A nice, safe ride would suit me right now, sir.'

'What I was going to say was, this miracle chair has everything but decent headlights. So if you're going to escort me, give me lots of light, Miles Waddell be damned. Shoot the spot right past me so I'm not driving in my own shadow.'

She found that following within fifty feet gave the best compromise, and she settled into the three-mile-an-hour pace, working hard to keep heavy eyelids at bay.

'Three ten, PCS. Ten twenty.' The radio was startling.

'PCS, three ten is ten fourteen, coming up on mile marker three, NightZone rail service road.'

There was silence, and Estelle could imagine dispatcher Burke looking up at the card above the radio to refresh his memory about what 'ten fourteen' meant in the arcane ten code that the department preferred to use when not on cell service.

'Three ten, do you want to request a tow?'

'Negative. It would take as long to get someone out here as what we're doing. We'll be at the train station parking lot in an hour.'

'Ten four.'

'Three ten, three oh eight. Cell.'

'Three oh eight, ten four.' She racked the mike and slid her cell phone out of the center console holder, and speed-dialed the sheriff's number.

'Estelle, Pasquale was right,' Sheriff Jackie Taber said. 'A twenty-five-mile crime scene is a challenge. This is going to take the rest of the night, just surveying what the hell we've got on our hands so we don't miss anything.'

'I understand that,' Estelle replied. 'We've got what we've got. I'm about to talk to Waddell to try and organize our efforts a little bit. He has staff we can trust with this.'

'A *lot* bit.'

'That too.'

'I heard you say you're still an hour out?'

'More or less. Travel by wheelchair is leisurely. But he's doing a good job.'

'The deputies are coming up on the second trestle, that sort of short squatty one over the arroyo just east of one of the birding spots.'

The second of six, Estelle thought. A *long* night ahead for everyone. 'Someone's sitting somewhere, getting a laugh out of our efforts.' *Filming too?* she thought.

'I hope he, she or it sits there long enough for us to come up behind and tap them on the shoulder,' Jackie Taber said. 'I'm having everyone switch to cell to keep us off the air.'

'There goes half of the county's entertainment.'

'And given what we've got, that's a good thing. Let me know what Miles says.'

As if he had been listening in to their conversation, Estelle's phone displayed Miles Waddell's number.

'Estelle, Miles. I'd say good evening, but it obviously isn't.'

'It's only good in that no one was hurt, sir.'

'Yet. Where are you?'

'I'm escorting Bill Gastner back to the train station. We're about two miles out.'

'So you'll be there in a few minutes.'

'Well, make that going on thirty, sir. Our friend is driving his fancy new wheelchair, so we're hanging in there at about three miles an hour.'

Waddell fell silent for a long moment until he said, 'There's something in all this that I'm not understanding, Estelle. Monty tried to explain it, but he's talking gibberish.'

'Join the club, sir. The good news is that Bill discovered the damage before a major incident.'

'You mean like a derail?'

'Yes, sir.'

'That much damage to the Salinas trestle? That's one of the big ones.'

'I'd say so, sir. I'm not a structural engineer, but what I see is significant. But it would be helpful if you would bring an as-built with you of each trestle. Come daylight, we're going to have a lot of work to do. Documenting the damage, assessing the structures, collecting evidence.'

'If I'm understanding correctly, what evidence is there going to be besides sawdust?'

'We don't know that yet, sir. But making a hit on this scale, it's going to be impossible *not* to leave something behind.'

'Wow.' Waddell sounded resigned. 'I have to ask. Why the hell can't people just leave this project alone?'

'I have no answer for that, sir.'

'I know you don't, my friend. I know you don't. We're dealing with mysterious human beings here. Look, I'm just getting rolling, and I wanted to ask you what you all needed before I head your way.'

'The as-builts, if you can.'

'Of course I can. Done and done. What else?'

'We need to know how many folks are visiting your installation at the moment. How many hikers, how many birders, all that sort of stuff. A complete people count. I suppose you'll need to have some buses available to bring visitors back and forth.'

'Absolutely no chance of rail traffic today? Or tomorrow?'

'There is little to no chance of that, sir.'

'Christ. Look, I was going to run right out there to see all this mess for myself, but obviously that's not going to work. I'll talk with Monty after he's had his look-see, and we'll go from there.'

'Your operation is under the eagle eye of the NTSB, is it not? If there were to be a problem?'

'Of course. Don't tell me this is going that far. It's not as if we have a humongous plane crash on our hands or anything like that.'

'My opinion is that we're going to need all the investigative help we can get, Miles. If you can also interest the FBI, that would also be a good thing. Any interstate complication doesn't seem likely, but we're owed some favors. If nothing else, word of their presence is worth a lot. We need to monitor the service road, button it up to keep sightseers out.' She took a deep breath. 'I'd rather overreact right now than kiss this off as just a dumb prank.'

'That's easy enough.' He sighed. 'I'll say it again . . . *wow.* You know, I want to meet the little rat who did this, face to face.'

'There may be several rats, sir.'

'All of this, and nobody heard a chainsaw at work?'

'Apparently not.'

He grunted with disgust. 'You remember when they managed to cut down a couple of my power poles. Way back when I was first getting started with this project?'

'I do. Bill Gastner does too. He's the one who spotted the prairie fire that the shorted-out power line ignited.'

'What a mess. But let me get to work. We'll talk again, Estelle. And I want to touch bases with Bill Gastner, to make sure he's all right.'

'I can speak to that, Miles. He's enjoying himself at the moment.'

'Yeah, well. We'll see. I've got this vigilante job I was thinking of contracting out.'

'I didn't hear that, sir.'

'Just joking, Estelle. Just joking. Look, to expedite things, how about if I meet you at the airport? I can be there just about the time you are. I can deliver the as-builts to you, and we'll go from there.'

'Perfect, sir. Remember that there are a lot of cops out there. Watch your speed.'

'Oh, sure.' He laughed a little ruefully. 'It's the elk, deer, javalinas, and all the other suspects that I worry more about.'

Wouldn't it be a wonderful world if that were true, Estelle thought.

TWENTY-FOUR

'Ten percent left.' Gastner slid out of the chair and unlocked his Suburban. 'Exhilarating. Butt's a little sore, I have to admit.' He watched as the hydraulic lift lowered itself into position. Estelle reached out a hand to support his elbow as he struggled a little to climb back aboard the chair, but he shook his head and held up a hand. 'I need to be able to do this by myself, sweetheart.'

He settled in and turned the power key. 'A beautiful night. You're lucky that the wind isn't kicking up.'

'We're lucky in a lot of ways, sir.'

'I hear ya.' He positioned the chair and backed it on to the lift, set the brakes and power lever, and worked himself off-board. Estelle waited patiently. 'I'd hate to do all this while trying to respond to a three-alarm fire,' he muttered. 'I have to keep telling myself to take my time.' Once the chair was lifted and fully in place, he stood back with satisfaction, slid the door shut and locked it.

'What's next on your docket? Trail cam hunting?'

'The good thing is that we know where to look, *Padrino*. But we're not going to find anything in the dark. At the same time, Miles will be here shortly,' Estelle said. 'He has the as-builts, which may or may not be helpful. We'll go from there.' She looked at her watch. 'We have about two hours before dawn. Things can wait until then for Linda to work. And by then, the survey crew will have some answers.'

'How much and how many,' Gastner nodded.

'Exactly.'

'And now my curiosity is piqued.'

'How so?'

'How about a civilian ride-along? I promise to behave. I might even be useful, although how I don't know.'

'*Padrino*, I have no idea where this day is going to take me.'

'That's part of the fun.'

'I mean you might end up stranded in my unit for hours and hours if I become involved in something.'

'Just leave me the keys.'

Estelle pointed east, where the paved road skirted the airport and took travelers to the NightZone train terminal. The midnight-blue locomotive, sleek and almost futuristic, was bathed in muted lighting under its train-port, a building that housed not only the engine but its four passenger cars as well. 'Like this guy driving too fast our way.'

'That would be Miles, his own self. Estelle, I have nowhere else I have to be, nothing I have to do. And let's face it . . . this is an interesting case from any angle. It's the sort of entertainment I need.'

'Camille might think otherwise, *Padrino*.'

His brow furrowed. 'Much as I love my busybody daughter, sweetheart, I don't feel that I'm required to check in with her every time I turn around. Better forgiveness than permission. And asking forgiveness isn't on my agenda anyway.'

'I know that, sir.' She took a deep breath. It would be easy to just say, 'No', but on the other hand, she genuinely enjoyed – even treasured – his company. Having a living gazetteer at her disposal was a plus, when the old man's memory cooperated. 'Let's see what Miles can tell us.'

Gastner heard and correctly interpreted that last word, and nodded his thanks. Miles Waddell stepped out of his black NightZone plac-arded Expedition, looking as if he were headed to attend a swank dinner party – or a round-up of mustangs. His official dress code rarely varied. Crisp blue jeans just breaking over the arch of his brown cowboy boots, a dark blue denim long-sleeve shirt with pearl buttons, and his trademark purple scarf around his throat were complemented this time not by his black Stetson, but instead by a plain black ball-cap with the NightZone emblem above the brim.

A four-foot cardboard tube was tucked under his left arm, and he was in animated conversation on his phone. He kept his eyes on the ground as he walked toward Estelle, shaking his head. Whether his expression was in disgust, consternation or disagreement wasn't clear.

'That was Monty,' he announced when he broke the connection. 'Bill, how are you doing?' He thrust his hand out to grasp Gastner's.

'Not the important question of the day,' the former sheriff said. 'This is a frustrating mess you've got here, though.'

'You aren't kidding about that. Monty says there is no apparent damage to the second trestle. That's the low trestle over the wash that takes a turn to the west near mile marker seven. That's the good news. Let's find a flat spot to spread this map out, and I'll show you the bad news. What *is* going to give us headaches.' He gestured toward what looked like a tidy, western-style clapboard farmhouse, but was in fact the train station and waiting area and – in typical Waddell fashion – included a small but efficient café that operated whenever the train did, a punishing twenty-four-seven schedule. But, as Waddell had discovered during the past five years of his operation, the 'always open' policy paid dividends. A dozen cars filled the parking lot, only one with a New Mexico license plate.

He reached out a hand and took Estelle by the elbow. 'Sheriff Guzman, I'm always delighted to see you, even in these circumstances.' In deference to Gastner, Waddell kept his pace toward the station more of a casual stroll.

'The first issue to consider right now includes a head count of fifty-seven visitors – that's forty-one adults and sixteen kids – who are visiting NightZone at the moment. Of those fifty-seven, twenty-two arrived in their own vehicles, so no worries about them. The remaining thirty-two arrived by train. Of *those* thirty-two, twenty-one are staying for two days or more. That leaves eleven who were planning to ride the train back here to the airport station later today.'

Always impressed with Waddell's fluency with statistics, Estelle glanced at the cars parked in the airport lot. 'You'll bus them back here?'

'I certainly hope so. A handful of them were perfectly cheerful about changing their plans and staying with us for another day or so as our guests. But five need to head out today. Monty will make sure that someone provides transportation with one of our vehicles, whenever they need to go. That gives us a day or so to arrange a couple of nine-passenger vehicles to run back and forth, in lieu of the train. *That's* not a worry. The issue so far, and I say "so far", is the trestle at mile marker twelve point five. That's where the deputies and Monty are now.'

'Red Slade Gulch,' Gastner said. He shuffled through the café door that Waddell held for him. 'Red thought that he'd build a nice cabin on the side of the arroyo, that big one that winds down from the flank of Cat Mesa up there north of us and then feeds the Salinas yet again. Picturesque spot with maybe some gold to be had. Trouble is, he didn't pay attention to where the high-water marks were.'

Waddell reached one of the six four-tops that graced the café's dining area. Three teenagers and two adults were eagerly engaged with the largest cheeseburgers Estelle had ever seen. Even those at the Broken Spur Saloon were no competition. At four in the morning. Her stomach churned, but she noticed that Bill Gastner looked interested. The three youngsters, animated and loud as Waddell, Estelle and Gastner entered, immediately lowered their voices to hushed tones. Estelle guessed the Philippines as their home port.

'And?' Waddell prompted Gastner's tale.

'And he drowned one night in 1954 when we had a frog-strangler that took out the cabin, him in his bed, the whole ball of wax.'

Waddell tried to laugh. 'I feel so much better now.' He turned to the young lady who had appeared from the serving area. With her coiled black hair and maybe a hint of too much dark lipstick, she might have been mistaken for goth in her black NightZone garb. Her smile, however, was radiant, which in itself was an accomplishment at four in the morning. Her name tag announced Tracie.

'I know it's the middle of the night,' Waddell said, 'but how about something? Coffee? Tea? Probably the world's best green chile cheeseburger?'

'The menudo is to die for,' the girl said. 'I think it's ready.'

'Menudo,' Gastner said wistfully. 'But no. Just coffee for me. Black, please.'

To Tracie's apparent disappointment, Estelle held up a hand. 'Just some water, please, Tracie.'

'You two are cheap dates,' Waddell said, then lowered his voice. 'You know my waitress, Estelle?'

'Tracie? Sure. Miss Steiger applied to work dispatch for us a year or so ago.'

'No go?'

'I think we would have hired her, but then she had boyfriend issues. He worked days for the Highway Department, and she would have started graveyard with us.'

'Ah.' He looked toward the kitchen where Tracie was assembling the coffee and water.

'Interesting how things turn out. She's sure as hell working graveyard here! She lose the boyfriend?'

'I believe so.'

'But she didn't reapply to you folks?'

Estelle smiled at Waddell's fascination with other people's trivia. 'No. You headhunted her away.'

Waddell looked philosophical. 'See? I bet we pay more than Posadas County does.'

'I bet you do, too, sir.' She nodded at the rolled-up maps and he eagerly took the hint.

'OK. Show-and-tell time.' He unrolled the bulky blueprint as if he'd done it a thousand times – which he probably had. 'The trestle at mile marker four,' and he tapped the map. He sat back as Tracie approached with a serving tray.

'Where can I put this so you won't spill on the paperwork?' she asked, not a bit intimidated by Waddell's boss status, but obviously familiar with the potential disaster of blunt cowboy fingers trying to manage a heavy porcelain coffee cup. Without waiting for a response, she said, 'How about over here?' She set the tray on a nearby table.

'Perfect.' Waddell then ignored the coffee and started right in. 'Trestle two, I'm told, is undamaged. It's low, and pretty short. It's only about sixty feet long, enough to allow passage underneath by Forest Road Twenty-Six. It's around twelve feet high, enough for a standard livestock trailer or a Forest Service fire truck. But . . .' and he adjusted the set of plans. 'Damage at trestle three is potentially a real headache for us. The damage impacts six supports, Monty says. But now, number three – what did you call it?'

'Red Slade Gulch,' Gastner said.

'That's picturesque. We gotta get a nice sign built beside the tracks for that. Anyway, *that* trestle has a high point of sixty-seven feet. And its span is a hundred and ninety feet long. It has about a million dollars in spruce beams alone.' He separated out a smaller sheet, a schematic of the Red Slade Gulch trestle. 'Here's the problem.' He drew out a silver Cross ballpoint and used it as a pointer. 'This center span, bridging the main watercourse and arroyo cut, is sixty-eight feet wide.'

He touched his pen to six points, three on either side of the arroyo. 'Monty tells me that they cut these supports.' He ran his pen up the damaged beams above the cuts. 'Same . . . what do you cops call it? Same m.o. That's a lot of weight, a lot of potential sheer, a lot of what engineers call "arm moment" at work, with beams that long and heavy. Lots of force if you let heavy things pivot. They couldn't have chosen a more dangerous spot.'

'And this is the tallest of the trestles?' Estelle asked.

'Yes, it is. By far.'

'And the rest?'

Waddell shrugged in frustration. 'We don't know yet. They're finishing up at three – the Red Slade – and they're about to head on west. It's another four miles to number four, then a long stretch, almost fifteen miles, on west to five. That's the major span that crosses the big arroyo just east of the old Torrance ranch. It becomes the Rio Guijarro when it crosses the state highway, east of the Broken Spur.'

He rolled part of the map out of the way. 'The last one, number six? That's the much photographed trestle just east of the NightZone complex. At that point, the tracks have to round a tight curve where the engine slows to five or six miles an hour or so. Train barely has time to straighten out before entering the terminal at the parking lot.'

'If this were an isolated thing,' Gastner said. 'If it were just a single attack on a single trestle, I could imagine chalking it up to some bozo who gets his kicks out of brainless vandalism. Most vandals are lazy sons of bitches, you know. A spray can here, another one there, trash tossed. Nothing like this, where real *work* is involved.'

'Interesting point. You know, all the time I've spent behind a chain saw, I've never timed how long it takes to cut through a ten- or twelve-inch-diameter log. With a good saw and a new chain, a couple of minutes maybe? But six cuts? And those big spruce poles are creosoted and that takes the life out of a chain. On top of that, a lot of times the chain will bind, and there you are, stuck. That would have happened for sure if they'd tried to saw all the way through. But they got smart. There's enough wood left that the beam doesn't sag and vise the saw tight.'

He rose from his chair, and as he rolled up the schematics, he waved off Tracie's efforts to replenish the coffee carafe. 'I want to take the loop,' he said. 'You folks have time?'

'We do,' Estelle said. 'But we need to take my unit. I need my office with me.'

'That'll work. I need to bend your ears, so can I ride along?'

'Of course. And just so you know, I have a suspicion that whoever did this damage might have wanted to preserve the results for posterity. We'll be looking for a good place to mount a trail cam. They're simple, they're cheap. Or like the cameras that a grocery store parking lot might use. Or a surveillance camera against shoplifters.'

'Well, shit,' Waddell whispered. He let that thought deter him for a handful of seconds, then turned and put on a cheerful face for the Philippine family as he stepped to their table. 'I hope you folks had a good time at NightZone,' he said, and received energetic nods in response. 'What did you like the best?'

The rapid fire and heavily accented answers were incomprehensible, but Waddell nodded as if he understood every syllable. The youngest boy, perhaps twelve years old, pointed at the remains of his burger, and said clearly, 'This is the best. Yes.'

Waddell turned to Estelle. 'I guess, as a former rancher, I should be pleased to hear that, eh?' No ticket had appeared, but he dropped a tip-boosting twenty on the serving platter as they left.

TWENTY-FIVE

B y the time they reached the sharp turn in the service road that rounded a sea of boulders and the arroyo that had taken Red Slade's life more than three-quarters of a century before, the sun had cracked the horizon, starting the slow burn that would evaporate any cloud that tried to form.

After using yellow crime-scene tape to visually secure the scene at the first trestle, a site she now fondly referred to as 'Gastner's Trestle', Sheriff Jackie Taber had headed back to the airport train terminal to meet photographer Linda Pasquale. Linda's work would be tedious, but her organization meticulous as she documented each slash by the chainsaw.

At the same time, the team of Lieutenant Tom Mears and Deputy Dwayne Bishop accompanied Linda, their task being to provide backup for Linda, and then to collect, bag and tag generous samples of any sawdust left behind – and the chain oil that that sawdust would contain. Collected as well would be samples of wood caulk used at each scene to disguise the saw cuts.

The service road cobbled across Red Slade arroyo, and Estelle jounced the Tahoe across and parked on the west side, staying well clear of the impressive trestle. The view, if that's what the vandals were after, was spectacular. The arroyo opened a window to the southwest, and she could see the San Cristóbals down near the border. To the north, the face of Cat Mesa, the second tallest landmark in Posadas County, reared nearly vertical from the prairie. Its lower surface was littered with ragged boulders that had calved off the rimrock and tumbled down the mesa face, ripping through trees and leaving the scree scars of talus deposits all the way down the flank.

The trestle itself was banded with lengths of bright yellow crime-scene tape that Pasquale had used to mark the damaged logs. Estelle had walked around the Tahoe to assist Gastner, who slid out of the seat without problems, but as Estelle approached, quipped, 'I may need a crane to lift me back in.'

She started to answer when a loud crack like a rifle shot made her duck.

'I saw it!' Waddell shouted. 'Holy smokes!'

Without waiting, he set off at a fast trot toward the trestle base, stopping when he was a dozen feet from the structure. He turned toward Estelle and Gastner. 'You gotta see this.'

He hauled his phone out of its holster and started shooting photos. As Estelle approached, he reached out a finger to touch one of the giant spruce vertical supports.

'Right there. It gave way right there, moved enough to see. I happened to be looking at it. It broke the rest of the cut and I saw it move.' He stroked the support as if he could heal it. 'Gave way a good quarter of an inch out of line.'

Waddell's almost childlike excitement prompted a retired Marine Corps sergeant's command bark from Gastner. Waddell backed off a couple of steps and craned his neck to look upward at the towering, sixty-seven-foot-high log structure, now scarred by damage. If it collapsed and fell toward the north, the structure would bury them in tons of spruce logs snapped like kindling wood.

'Right now!' Estelle shouted, and was relieved when Waddell finally reacted and backed away, turning to trot back toward the Tahoe. By the time he'd jumped inside, Estelle had pulled the truck into gear, and accelerated hard out of the arroyo. Once safe on top, at the same elevation as the tracks, she stopped the truck.

'Wow,' Waddell said. 'Now what?'

'First, we need to close this area. People need to stay out of range of that trestle, and that means off the service road. Some "Danger, Road Closed" signs at both ends. What engineering firm designed the trestle?'

'Baker and Melrose, out of El Paso.'

'How fast can they get here?'

'The amount I paid them, they can be here in a couple of hours.'

'That's good. That noise we heard may be a single release of strain. Maybe it's stable now. And maybe it isn't. The engineers need to take the maybes out of the equation.'

'And in the meantime,' Gastner said, and paused.

'In the meantime, we need to post a deputy here.'

'The service road is fenced. You'd think that would be enough.' Estelle shot him a dark look. 'They even let wheelchairs in.'

'Well, that's true.' He didn't look the least bit guilty. 'But then again . . .' He let it drop with that, but Miles Waddell was prompt.

'My friend, you discovered this whole mess, so take credit where it's due. If you hadn't tried to dirt-bike an arroyo, we wouldn't know about the damage to my trestles. Look, I can post someone here, if that will help. I mean, I *should* post someone, twenty-four seven, until all this is resolved. We can keep the end gates locked, but there's nothing to stop some hunter from wandering where he shouldn't be wandering. Or anyone at all that drives down the Forest Road at the second trestle.'

'Right-of-way fences won't stop them,' Gastner said. 'Even the new barbed-wire fence that Boyd's got underway won't make a difference if someone's determined.'

'It's the unwary birdwatchers who hike along the railroad that worry me,' Waddell said.

Estelle opened her phone and dialed, waiting for half a dozen rings while Sergeant Pasquale dug out his phone and activated it.

'Pasquale.'

'Tom, we've got some instability here at number three, the Red Slade trestle. Until we can come up with an alternative, we're going to have to post somebody out here around the clock.'

'OK.' He didn't sound enthused. 'The gates at either end of the service road won't be enough? Well, no,' he added, answering his own question. 'Forest Road Twenty-Eight crosses right through.'

'That's exactly right. There are too many miles, too many ways to access the site. When we walked up to the trestle, it let out a bang and one of the girders showed signs of slipping.'

'Does Linda know that?'

'Not yet. But she shouldn't be far behind us, so we can advise her. How are you coming along? What are we looking at with the other sites?'

'Clear as far as we can see. We're just on site by the sixth trestle, just east of the parking lot terminal. No damage to four or five, though.'

'Good news. I need a deputy to spring free for this site, though. Do you have someone who wants some overtime?'

'Let me check and get back to you in a few minutes. We're looking at a full shift?'

'I think so. Until the engineers get here and do what they need to do to call it safe.'

'Is Mr Waddell going to find somebody as well?'

'He will. But we can't just leave him holding the bag when it's a public safety issue. The only way to make sure that no one trespasses and puts themselves in danger is to be on site.'

'Leona is going to have kittens at all the overtime.'

'Fortunately, our county manager loves kittens,' Estelle said. 'Get back to me ASAP, Thomas. And just so you know, keep this front and center. I have a suspicion that we might have someone using a trail cam, or some gadget like that. It doesn't make sense to me that someone would go to all this work, and not want to record it. So we're going to be looking for something like that. There'd even be some evidence if they've taken the thing down. I might be wrong, but we have to look.'

'What, they're planning to sell something to YouTube, or TikTok, or someplace like that? I don't know how that works.'

'Nor do I.'

'Spectacular train crash on tonight's news at eleven,' Pasquale announced in his best imitation of a newscaster, then added, 'That's just what we need.'

TWENTY-SIX

'Linda,' Estelle phoned, 'when you come to the east edge of the arroyo, stop there. Do not drive down into the arroyo. I'll meet you over there to give you a heads-up.'

'Alllllllll right,' Linda said. 'Water, or what?'

'The "or what" part. The trestle isn't safe. I'll explain.' She watched the dust cloud behind Linda Pasquale's SUV dissipate as the photographer pulled to a stop, joined after a moment by Lieutenant Mears and Deputy Bishop. She beckoned to Miles Waddell.

'Miles, there's no damage to the intermediate trestles, so there's little point in us going on. If there's damage to the terminal trestle, Sergeant Pasquale will let us know. You'll no doubt want to visit even the undamaged trestles with your engineers when they arrive on site.'

'No doubt about that,' Miles agreed. 'You know, when I first started with this whole railroad thing, the engineers told me that steel trestles were more practical than wood. I should have believed them.'

'But then,' Gastner chimed in, 'you didn't suppose that you'd have some mental freak cutting down your trestles with a chain saw.'

'Some solace in that, I suppose,' Miles said. 'Anyway, we have a logistical mess now for you folks.'

'They're waiting for us.' Estelle keyed the phone again. 'Linda, we'll be over in a few minutes.' She gestured to the Tahoe when she disconnected. 'Buckle up, gents. It won't be a smooth ride.'

After she turned around, she headed down into the arroyo, staying on the service road, but then turned immediately to the north, away from the trestle and the service road. The Tahoe walked over the rocky arroyo bottom without much difficulty, until reaching the two-foot vertical banks of the dried watercourse. They jounced down, across, and back out of the ditch with all undercarriage parts of the Tahoe scraped and dented, but still attached.

'Leona wants us driving Priuses,' she laughed. They rejoined the service road just as it ramped up and out of the arroyo.

Her phone buzzed again, and Pasquale's voice sounded pleased. 'Six is all right,' he said. 'Maybe too close to the terminal for 'em to mess with a chain saw unnoticed. I'm sending Thompson back to your location to sit the trestle. She's willing to spend all day there, no worries.'

'Excellent.'

'She wants to know if you're going to be there. Apparently she wants to talk to you.'

'I'll be here. Both Miles and Bill Gastner are with me. I'm about to rendezvous with Linda.'

'Good enough. It'll take Thompson a while, even using the shortcut of the service road. It's in pretty good shape most of the way, but it ain't pavement. Sutherland is going to ride with me. His vehicle is back at the airport terminal. We'll take Fifty-Six back to town to save some time, and meet up at the airport.'

'The green chile cheeseburgers look good, and the menudo is ready for you. Use the county credit card.'

'Leona will scream,' Pasquale laughed.

'The exercise is good for her.'

She joined Linda. The two officers were walking the tracks with Miles as far as the lip of the arroyo, and they returned promptly.

'Can't see well from up here,' Mears said. 'What's the plan?'

'The plan is that the trestle is unsafe, pure and simple,' Estelle replied. 'We heard one of the girders snap just as we got out of the vehicle. Miles actually saw some tiny movement. For the present, I don't want anyone near it. Not on it, or under it, or even beside it.'

'I was thinking of a holiday excursion in Bermuda,' Linda said. 'I have no desire to be buried under a million pounds of splintered firewood. But look. Where are the cut beams?'

'Let me show you the schematic,' Waddell said. When he returned, he spread out an eighteen-by-twenty-four engineering drawing of the trestle. 'The cuts are these six beams. Right along the upriver side, right in the middle.'

'So if it falls, it'll be because those beams collapse, and the whole thing will pitch upstream.'

'Maybe,' Estelle said. 'We will settle for what you can get from a safe distance.'

'I could approach on the downstream side.'

'No.'

Linda smiled at that. 'That had the ring of finality, Undersheriff Reyes-Guzman.'

'Yes. If you were replaceable, I'd say, "Go right ahead. Risk it." But you aren't, so I won't. Do as best as you can via telephoto. That suits me. The engineers can provide close-ups and sawdust samples later, when it's stabilized.'

'There's got to be a better way,' Deputy Bishop said. 'I mean for pictures and stuff. The train ran over it, after all. It didn't collapse then.' Estelle could see that, with the enthusiasm of youth, the young deputy would have charged right to the source of the ruined trestle supports, trusting to luck. But he hadn't heard it crack like a rifle shot.

'There is a better way,' she said. 'Stay away from it. Be patient.'

'Amen,' Miles Waddell muttered.

'Another better way,' Linda said. 'Time to break out the toys.' The toy she referred to was a 1200-millimeter lens for one of the Nikons, an enormous fat gadget that sat on a tripod with the camera hanging off the back. 'If I follow your tracks, upstream from the service road, I'll be all right? You're happy with that?'

'Yes.'

Linda looked hard at Estelle. 'You don't sound happy.'

'I'm happy enough. Right now, I'm tired and hungry.'

'We can fix that right up,' Waddell said enthusiastically. 'The terminal is the place to be. Tracie will take care of us. My treat.'

'He has the right idea,' Mears said, not meaning Miles Waddell. The lieutenant nodded at the Tahoe, where Bill Gastner had pulled himself up into the passenger seat and now sat with his head back against the rest, eyes closed, jaw slack.

An hour and a half later, Estelle's phone burped at the same time as the dust cloud from Lydia Thompson's Tahoe roiled up from the west.

'Guzman.'

'Estelle, I see you on the east side. Is that where you want me to be?'

'Yes. If you follow my tracks across the arroyo, that would be good. Stay well away from the trestle. Stay north of it, upstream of it. Don't follow the service road across. That route is too close to the trestle.'

'Roger that. I see Linda and Lieutenant Mears down in the arroyo with the camera gear, and I can see your tracks.'

'If this thing ever does collapse, it'll be well documented,' Waddell said when Estelle got off the phone. '*I'll* be able to sell the pictures to help pay for the repairs.' His eyebrows cocked at a sudden thought. 'I can scoop the jerks with the trail cam, if that's what they used.'

'You don't need to give anyone else any ideas, Miles.' She turned and scanned the surrounding country. Rugged terrain, a smattering of runty, water-stressed piñons and junipers, creosote bush, cacti and salt-brush. Just to the west, and on the north side of the railroad tracks, the ground climbed in a sharp hump, overlooking Red Slade Gulch.

'Just the place,' she said to herself. 'Deputy Bishop, I have a job for you.' She quickly explained what she wanted, and added, 'As soon as I have more personnel, I'll send up reinforcements. But keep in mind that if they were using a trail cam, this,' she nodded at the trestle, 'is the target. They'd want a clear shot.'

'I'll go up with him,' Waddell volunteered.

Estelle turned as another vehicle, this one a bright blue compact pickup, approached from the east. 'Thanks, but your challenge just arrived. That's Rik Chang from the *Register*, Miles. You might want to think very carefully what you wish to say to him. You're front-page news.'

TWENTY-SEVEN

Rik Chang confused people, and Estelle suspected that the young man knew it. He would talk without hesitation about the spectacular southwestern country, and never mentioned that he was originally from the Bronx. His four years in the Navy, including two years on board the nuclear submarine USS *Mississippi*, was known to Estelle only because the *Posadas Register* publisher, Frank Dayan, had mentioned the young man's service after reading Chang's brief résumé. He didn't talk about his years in college, or his university journalism degree. What he *did* do was become a human fountain of questions, fascinated by what everyone else did or knew.

Now pushing thirty years old, Chang dated a petite, utterly gorgeous Mexican national who worked in the county assessor's office. County Manager Leona Spears, herself a master at prying information out of recalcitrant people, had learned that Chang and his fiancée, Yolanda Garcia, were planning a wedding in November – a traditional ceremony in Old Mexico hosted by Yolanda's relatives in Huachile.

Posadas, like most small villages, thrived on the grapevine, the ever-blooming gossip circles. Rik Chang did not partake of the gossip fountain, and that endeared him to some members of the community – especially the Posadas County Sheriff's Department.

Estelle turned her attention away from Chang's approach and watched Lydia Thompson navigate the rocks and boulders littering the Red Slade arroyo before rejoining the service road and topping out to park beside Estelle's unit.

'It looks like she's done this before,' Miles Waddell said.

'Probably many times.' Estelle watched Chang's careful approach, evidence that he had yet to put a scratch on his new 4x4 Tacoma. 'As opposed to our friend from the media.'

'Should I talk with him?'

'That's up to you, Miles. If you do, please do *not* discuss any of the investigative work . . . that the deputies are taking samples of oil and sawdust, that sort of thing. No speculation. And please

. . . do *not* mention the notion of a possible game cam. Or a trail camera, or anything of the sort. The old wartime adage about loose lips sinking ships holds true today.'

'He'll want to know about the cost, I bet. Everybody wants to know that. They'll want to know how much repairs will cost, and how shutting down the railroad will affect my business.'

'For sure. All that's for you to decide.'

'He'll want photos. That I know. He interviewed me half a dozen times out at the Zone.' He grinned. 'I'd call it "inquisitive" coverage. He never runs out of questions.'

'Of course. Not here, though, unless he's got a telephoto as powerful as Linda's.' As Chang left his truck and talked toward them, Estelle saw the professional-grade digital camera hanging from its shoulder strap. 'Which he probably does.'

She extended her hand to Chang. His grip was deferential, brief but strong, and he also shook hands with Miles Waddell. 'I spoke with Sheriff Taber at the terminal, and she referred me out here,' Chang said. 'I can't believe someone would damage this facility.'

'I can't either,' Waddell said. 'But there you have it. There's no telling what goes through little minds.' He flashed a smile. 'Don't quote me on that.'

'Ron Esposito is at the first trestle with a couple of his crew,' Chang said as he opened his slender notebook. 'He says he's exploring ways to make repairs. But he said that the major damage is out here, at this site.'

'Correct.'

'The train won't be running until further notice?'

'Also correct.'

'Is that what the vandals want, do you think?'

Waddell glanced sideways at Estelle, then said, 'I wish I knew.'

'Have there been threats?'

'No. None made to me, anyway.'

'Or serious complaints?'

Waddell laughed quietly. 'As opposed to *unserious* complaints?'

'Sure.' Chang smiled engagingly.

'We have complaints all the time. Any business that serves people, any service? I'm sure we all have complaints. No matter how hard we work. The train is too slow – that's a common one. We should serve meals on the train. We should focus all the telescopes on incoming rogue asteroids that threaten all of mankind. People think that the radio telescope is eavesdropping on them . . . or on aliens. Or they think that the radio telescope causes cancer.'

'You're kidding, sir.'

'No, Mr Chang, I'm not kidding. The list is long. It's something we live with every day.'

Estelle could see that Miles Waddell was working hard to wind himself down.

Fortunately for him, Rik Chang changed tacks. 'Sheriff,' he said to Estelle, 'I see someone in your unit. Have you made an arrest already?'

Miles Waddell exploded into laughter. 'Caught with chain saw in hand, Mr Chang. I think you should go over and interview him.'

Before Chang could do that very thing, Estelle interrupted. 'That's Bill Gastner, Rik. He's riding with me. At the moment, he's taking a nap. It's been a long day, a long night.'

'Oh, OK.' He started to say something else, but Deputy Lydia Thompson approached. She offered a friendly smile to the reporter, and reached out to shake Miles Waddell's hand. 'Sheriff, can I conference with you for a bit?'

'Absolutely you can.'

Thompson nodded again at Waddell and Chang and walked off toward the arroyo bank to the north. Cattle had cut numerous trails both along the edge as well as diagonally down the embankment to the arroyo bottom. 'How about a short walk?' Lydia said.

'Sure.'

'Enough people around now, I didn't want to be interrupted. And I didn't want to be overheard by the long ears of the press.'

'You said you were OK with spending some time out here on guard duty?'

Lydia chuckled. 'It'll be a quiet day, that's for sure. Once everyone has gone home.'

'We can hope so. The squad of engineers should be here shortly.'

They reached the arroyo bottom, and could look downstream where Linda Pasquale and Lieutenant Mears worked. Lydia stopped and leaned a hip against a Volkswagen-sized boulder.

'When Johnny Rabke and I were talking the other night . . .' She stopped and looked first at Estelle, and then into the distance. 'You know . . .' She stopped again, and Estelle said nothing to prompt her. 'He was an attractive young man, Estelle.' Again, Estelle didn't respond, and Lydia turned back to gaze at her. 'You can understand that.'

'Lydia, what are you trying to tell me?'

'I'm trying to tell you that the night Mr Gastner saw us down on Fifty-Six, the day before the murders? That was not the first time I had taken time to have a private talk with Johnny Rabke.'

TWENTY-EIGHT

I f Lydia Thompson was expecting a surprised reaction – or any reaction at all – from Estelle Reyes-Guzman, she didn't get it. The undersheriff regarded her with her best poker face, and waited for Lydia to continue. In truth, Estelle was not especially surprised. Widowed now more than a couple of years, Lydia Thompson had finally found a niche with the Sheriff's Department that she apparently enjoyed and was well-suited and -trained for. She worked nights, and would have had every opportunity to cross paths with the handsome, hard-drinking bachelor cowboy.

'That night,' Lydia said. 'The night Mr Gastner and your son happened to see me during a traffic stop, Johnny Rabke was asking me to meet him later for breakfast.' She nodded at the trestle. 'He liked to eat once in a while at the terminal café at the airport.' She made a grimace, aimed at herself and her memories. 'I know. I know. I had heard all the stories about wild Johnny Rabke. And I wasn't going off the deep end for him. But he was . . . he was comfortable company. A nice guy to have a meal with.' She shrugged. 'I don't know if it would ever have gone further. Maybe. Maybe not.

'Anyway, the night Mr Gastner saw us, Johnny really was stopped for what he thought was a bad wheel bearing. And he really was parked with the ass end of his stock trailer really close to the traffic lane.' She smiled at her repetition. 'Really, he was. Really, really. So I stopped, and gave him some emergency traffic cover with my lights. When Mr Gastner came along, Johnny and I had been talking for maybe five minutes. He wasn't his usual ebullient, wacko self, either. My guess is that he was concerned about something. Maybe it was just his frustration with having truck problems. I mean, this is a guy who kisses off most problems with a grin and a shrug.' Lydia bit her lower lip. 'Just one of the happiest . . . happy-go-lucky humans I've ever met. Even his grand jury mess last year didn't faze him.'

'When you saw him Thursday morning, he was returning from town at that point?'

'Yes.'

'Did you know that he was working on the fencing crew?' Estelle asked.

'Yes. And he told he had a load of supplies and a couple of ATVs in the trailer. That's where he was headed, after a short stop and snort at the Spur, of course. That seemed to be his pattern. Two or three days before that, we'd met on the county road. I was northbound, cruising past the Zone, and he was headed south, two guesses where.'

'The Spur.'

'Sure.' She shrugged. 'Maybe it's none of my business, his drinking. Maybe it would have become an issue if we continued. I gave some thought now and then to how I could wean him away from that place, because it was no good for him. Anyway, he told me that progress on the Boyd fence was coming along, that it was what he called a bastard of a job. He invited me to join him at the Spur. I declined. He understood, I guess.'

'You said that he seemed concerned, or maybe preoccupied about something?'

'Maybe he was. I asked him how the job was going, and he frowned. Johnny Rabke hardly ever frowned, Estelle. He asked me where I was headed, and I told him I always swung into the Zone parking lot to check license plates. He said something like, "You never know, do you." When I replied something like, "No, you don't," he said something like, "Yeah, some of the guys I'm workin' with don't like that place much."'

Estelle straightened. 'Tell me more about that.'

'That's really all he said. And I didn't pursue it. At that moment, there was no reason to.' Lydia turned and looked back up the hill, where sure enough Rik Chang had managed to engage both Miles Waddell and the sleepy Bill Gastner in earnest conversation.

'I ignored his comment, because in the past several months, I've met lots of people who are of mixed minds about Waddell's dream extravagance. I usually chalk it up to them being jealous that he isn't spending his money on *them,* you know?'

'His money, his choice how he spends it,' Estelle said.

'Of course. If I didn't like what he was doing, I wouldn't have sold him our nineteen acres.' She sighed loudly. 'So what's next? With him, I mean.'

'We're still waiting on some lab work on Rabke's case. I need to talk with Arturo Ramirez's family. I was going to do that today, but,' and she shrugged, nodding at the wounded trestle. 'There's this, now. At the same time, LT and Bob Torrez are working on a ballistics schematic for our best guess about where the shots came from that killed Ramirez. There's little doubt about that in my mind, knowing what we know about Johnny Rabke's habits.'

'He almost always wore that gun, or had it handy in his truck,' Lydia said. 'That I can tell you.'

'We're well aware that he did, Lydia. We need to be sure about the sequence of events . . . that Johnny managed to fire off five rounds *after* being stabbed. And then the big puzzle. None of the pieces we have fits, primarily because the autopsy makes it clear that someone attacked Rabke a second time, *after* being stabbed, *after* firing the five shots. None of us, including my husband, and including Bob Torrez, thinks that Rabke was shooting *after* the second attack. That's just not credible. That knife initially went in straight and hard, but then was jerked sideways, nearly cutting his heart in two.'

Lydia's expression was pained, but she kept her voice steady. 'So now, what can I do?'

'First things first, with all of us working two directions at once. We're waiting on lab work, and now up here? We're waiting on engineers. We need to make sure no one wanders into *this* site and risks injury from that damaged trestle. Until the engineers figure out what to do, that's a twenty-four-seven job for us, and for Waddell's crew. The train isn't running, so all should be quiet. I'm going to pay a visit to the fencing job. We've talked to each one of the crew, but we haven't had time to pay them a visit on their home turf.'

Lydia Thompson's eyes grew hard. 'Take somebody with you, Sheriff. I'm serious. You have chain saws up there at the fencing job, you have chain saws attacking the trestles down here. You have Johnny Rabke murdered over on County Road Fourteen, and he was working on the fencing crew.' She joined the fingers of both hands together in a tight knot. 'I can't believe the two major incidents aren't conjoined. And we don't know who's still out there. So please, Sheriff. Take someone with you.'

Estelle nodded. 'Are you up for that?'

'Absolutely.'

'I'll ask Sutherland to cover the day shift here at the Trestle, freeing you up.' She smiled. 'Unless you need something like . . . sleep?'

'Lots of time for that later.'

Estelle looked at her watch. 'I need to run Miles and Bill Gastner back to the airport terminal. How about you and I meet there at two? That will give me some time to confab with Jackie.' She saw Rik Chang start down the cow trail into the arroyo, approaching them. 'And then there's this guy. He won't be satisfied until he's got photos, even if he has to sneak in close when nobody's looking.'

Lydia shook her head. 'And he's had his own brush with mortality,' she said, referring to an incident four years before when Chang had gotten in the way of a drive-by shooter's hail of gunfire.

'Some learn faster than others,' Estelle said. 'And by the way . . . that dark dot making his way up the hill to the west? That's Deputy Bishop, seeing if he can find a good place for a trail cam.' Lydia looked puzzled. 'The brainstorm hit us. Why would someone damage these trestles and not want to photograph the results? This is the most spectacular of the trestles, and is seriously damaged. So it made sense to me that if someone were to set up a camera – like a simple trail cam, or a surveillance unit like any box store would be likely to use – where would they put it? Up there is a likely choice.'

'You've got to be kidding.'

'In this crazy world,' Estelle said, 'no. I'm not kidding.' She pointed to new traffic, this time a shiny black Toyota crew cab pickup, running on rail rider bogies, wheeled mounts that fitted the width of the narrow-gage track so the pickup could effortless travel the rails from one end to the other for routine maintenance inspection. The vehicle stopped just before the trestle.

'Miles Waddell is very proud of his TacoTruck,' she said, referring to the specialty fitted Toyota Tacoma. 'If he decides to cross, let's hope the trestle doesn't notice an extra two tons of load.' Three passengers climbed out of the track truck without making any move to cross the trestle. They headed toward a conference with Miles Waddell.

TWENTY-NINE

As planned that afternoon, and without success at seeking an incriminating trail cam, the three women rode in Sheriff Jackie Taber's Expedition, heading west on State Seventeen. It was a roadway long overdue for repaving, and Taber was busy dodging the worst of the potholes. Both State Seventeen and the narrow-gage railroad crossed under the interstate – a feat of engineering that proved Miles Waddell's influential pull with a couple of legislators in Santa Fe.

After turning south on County Road Fourteen, they pounded gravel for about eight miles before Jackie slowed the Expedition to a walk and turned east on a well-worn two track. What had been a short, informal track marked by woodcutters was now beaten hard by the fence crew traffic.

Just as their tires hit the chalk-dry prairie dirt, Estelle's phone came to life. With engineers on site at the trestle with Miles Waddell and half a dozen other people, Lieutenant Tom Mears had returned to Posadas to concentrate on half a dozen unfinished tasks.

'Estelle, I finished up a pretty good profile of the murder weapon.'

'Anything new that we don't know? And just a second. Let me put you on speaker so all three of us can hear.' Jackie Taber obligingly pushed buttons and Mears's voice came loud and clear through the Expedition's audio system.

'All of the blood on the knife is Rabke's, type AB negative. No surprise there. Ditto all of the blood on him, on the truck seat, on the door, the dashboard, the steering wheel. He clearly thrashed around some, and gushed a lot.'

Estelle heard a tiny whimper from the back seat and knew that Lydia Thompson wasn't as stoic as she might want to be.

'All of the fingerprints on the knife that are readable are a match to either Arturo Ramirez or Rabke. In every case, Rabke's prints overlay Ramirez's, what we can see of them. The problem is that most of the prints are obscured. Most of them are smeared unreadable.'

'At least it's *most*, not *all*,' Jackie interjected.

'Yes. One good one of Rabke's right little finger near the hilt, just above Ramirez's, also near the hilt. All of the rest are smeared enough to be unreadable. The only explanation I can see – remember that neither Rabke nor Ramirez wore gloves – would be consistent with the attacker *using* gloves. That would account for it.'

'No surprises there,' Estelle said. 'But good to know.'

'Bobby Torrez is volunteering some time. He'll have what he thinks is a profile of the shots fired here in a little bit. Right now, everything is pointing to *all* of the rounds fired coming from Rabke's forty-five, fired from a point in front of his chest. He was left-handed, so that makes some sense to me. He's hugging himself, and he's managed to pull the gun into his left hand. The shot patterns all tell that same story. From a few inches distance for the wound in Rabke's thigh, to five feet or so for the pellets that struck the right door panel and about three feet to the pattern in Ramirez's armpit. There were no powder burns around the wound in Ramirez's skull, and that jibes with the gun a few feet away – like across the width of the truck cab. All of the fingerprints and all of the blood residue on the gun belong to Rabke. It looks like Ramirez was headed out the door when the final round hit him in the head. Any blood of his is outside the truck.'

'No one touched the gun after Rabke used it and then dropped it?'

'That appears correct,' Mears said. 'One round remained in the chamber with two in the magazine. No surprises.'

'I'm happy with no surprises,' Estelle said. 'And no word yet on finding a trail cam, either. Maybe my imagination is working overtime, expecting there to be something, LT.'

'So many ways that could have happened, Estelle. There's been enough time for someone to have removed it, if there was one.'

Estelle broke off the call just as Jackie Taber slowed to guide the Expedition around a clump of junipers and then stopped abruptly. A fence line came in from the north, the posts, wire and hardware shiny and bright, and then the fence line turned eastward. To the southwest, they could clearly see a couple of miles away the rise of Torrance Mesa. The sun winked off the NightZone buildings on the mesa top.

Just ahead, they could see a generous livestock gate that would allow traffic to cross through the new fence. A chain secured the gate, but wasn't secured with a lock.

Tracks through the gate had pounded the dirt to dust.

'If we don't go through the gate here, we're going to get caught with the mesa drop-off on ahead,' Estelle said. 'We need to be on the other side of the fence now.'

She slid out of the big SUV, and unloosened the chain from around the gate, then pushed the gate open, standing with a hand on it while the sheriff pulled through.

As she got back in, Jackie grinned at her. 'You got three guys riding in the front seat of a standard cab pickup. How do you tell who the real cowboy is?'

'I'm afraid you're going to tell us,' Estelle said.

Jackie's voice became that of a drawling Texan. ''Cause. Sittin' in the middle, you don't have to drive, and you don't have to climb out and open all the dad burn gates.'

Estelle turned to raise an eyebrow at Lydia Thompson. 'Remember that.'

'Absolutely I will.'

As they idled along the fence line, the road was almost civilized as the fence crossed a broad expanse of flat prairie between two low-browed mesas. So straight that it might have been laid out with a laser, for the first mile they crossed a half-dozen washes filled with a thick growth of sage, and then an arroyo that in places cut six feet deep. Looking for a feasible route, the two-track swung north away from the fence line, and dived across the arroyo at a spot where the tire cuts easily beat a crossing that the trucks hauling trailers could manage.

Estelle's phone alerted her and she saw the Sheriff's Department number on the screen.

'Guzman.'

'Estelle, what's your twenty?'

'Ernie, we're headed eastbound on a two-track off of County Road Fourteen. We're following the new fence line that Wallace Boyd's crew is working. About two miles in from the county road.'

'Ten four.'

She heard a soft voice in the background, and a moment later, Dispatcher Ernie Wheeler added, 'Still the three of you?'

'Affirmative.'

'Ten four.'

Wheeler cut off before Estelle could say anything else, and Estelle glanced at Jackie Taber.

'What's Ernie want?' the sheriff asked.

'He didn't say. He just wanted to know our twenty.'

'A good thing to know in any case.'

Estelle keyed the return number and Ernie Wheeler picked up on the first ring.

'Ernie, did you need anything specific from any of us? I think we got cut off before I could ask.'

After a slight pause, Wheeler said, 'Three hundred wanted to know. He's going out that way.'

'Ah. All right. To speak with one of us, or what?'

'I'm not sure.'

'Is he there, or did he just call?'

'He was here in the Sheriff's Office. He's gone now.'

'Thanks, Ernie.'

She switched off. 'Like pulling teeth. Ernie says that Bobby Torrez was asking about us. Both he and Bill use three hundred as a car contact number, and I know it wouldn't be Bill.'

'How touching that Bobby is asking about us,' Jackie said.

'He wants something, but Ernie didn't know what.'

THIRTY

Three miles of fence line brought them to the same arroyo that was crossed farther to the south under the fourth trestle. The arroyo was a low, flat scar on the prairie that issued from between two hills, and the fence line cut across the foot of both hills, diving up and down with the lay of the land, requiring the use of carefully constructed 'dead men' on the dip bottoms to keep the wire down and taut.

Each dead man was nothing more complex than the largest boulder that the fence builders could find and move, then wrapped with a nest of barbed wire. That construction was wired to the lowest point of the fence, drawing the wire down to the desired distance from the ground, in this case about eight inches.

From the dead man's low point, the fence tracked straight and true up the hillside to the band of rimrock.

'Cattle are going to come down that?' Lydia asked, and Jackie nodded.

'They will for sure. Anywhere you *don't* want them to wander, they'll wander.' She drew her binoculars from the center console and focused on the top of the rimrock. 'Driving posts into that stuff must have been a hoot,' she said.

The vehicle tracks turned to the north, away from the fence, and led along the arroyo until an easy crossing presented itself. A steep climb then took them to the hilltop and, from there, they could look east. Despite the torturous terrain, the fence maintained its straight line, climbing over whatever was in the way.

Once over the hill, they could see the obvious problem facing the fencing crew. Whether it was a choice gathering spot for clouds, or the presence of underground springs, or protection from the wind, the prairie was canopied by a thick stand of juniper – alligator bark with its characteristic reptilian bark pattern, one seed with its dense blue-green foliage, Rocky Mountain with its shaggy, messy bark – the stunted trees spread across the rolling prairie, greedily sucking groundwater. Some ranchers tried their best to control the invasive shrubs, others – like Wallace Boyd and his late father Johnny – did not bother, hoping that opening up new acreage would provide forage for the ever-hungry cattle.

In order to build the fence east from where Jackie Taber parked to survey the view, the fencing crew first would have to clear a path for both fence and vehicles. This they were doing in an organized way, cutting a straight boulevard for the fence, wide enough to allow the dirt two-track to follow close along the fence line.

'There they be,' Jackie said. 'I would guess about a mile and a half out.' She shifted to 'park', and turned to Estelle. 'Not that I'm objecting to the peace and quiet out here, some time to ponder and think, but I have to ask, Estelle. What direction is your thinking taking? Bluntly put, why are we here?'

'I thought you'd never ask,' Estelle said soberly. 'The problem with this killing is that we *know*, for sure and without any doubt, who stabbed Johnny Rabke. We *know*, beyond any reasonable doubt, who shot Arturo Ramirez.' She held up both hands. 'And here it ends. That's what we have left. *Lots* of doubts.'

'And unless we're grossly mistaken,' Jackie added, 'we have someone walking around scot-free who made sure that Rabke was finished off, beyond Ramirez's best efforts.'

'Yes. And that's confusing my thinking.'

'I can understand that, but that's a quantum leap, from killing Rabke to taking a chain saw to the railroad trestles, if the same person is responsible. What are you seeing as the connection?'

'Bill reminded me. And Miles Waddell, both.' Jackie's eyebrows shot up when Estelle mentioned Bill Gastner. 'One night, six or seven years ago, some vandals took a chain saw to the power poles along the north side of the NightZone property. Those poles were the main lines feeding the whole NightZone project. One of the sawyers who attacked the poles was killed when he was head-butted by the very power pole that he was cutting. It fell and teeter-tottered over a big old corner post in the fence line. The butt end kicked up and took him right under the chin. End of story. Broke his neck like a dry twig.

'That was Wallace Boyd's younger brother, Curtis. And after he died things went from bad to worse. One of our deputies was killed in that incident, murdered by one of Curtis Boyd's co-conspirators.

'Curtis was the late Johnny Boyd's younger son. He was an impressionable college student at NMSU at the time,' Estelle continued. 'He thought he was striking out against what he saw as the rampant development on the mesa – what became NightZone. Rick Boyd – the kid that's working with this fencing crew? He's Wallace's son. He'd be Curtis Boyd's nephew.'

Jackie made a face. 'I can't imagine pudgy little Ricky Boyd taking a chain saw to the trestle beams, Estelle. And six years ago, when the power poles were cut? He would have been, what, eleven or twelve years old? I can't see Curtis's death after a stupid prank – or even a moment of stupid environmental terrorism – brewing in Ricky's little mind for all those years, and suddenly popping into action, trying to avenge his long-dead uncle's death.'

They sat silently for a moment, gazing out across the sea of juniper. 'I've met Wallace Boyd a few times over the years,' Jackie said. 'He seemed like a pretty straight arrow to me. And at least when I talked with him, he didn't sound as if he was harboring a grudge against Miles Waddell's development. My impression is that he's come to accept living with NightZone as a neighbor.'

'It would seem so, doesn't it? And I can't see young Ricky Boyd driving the knife in and wrenching it around, to put the finish on Johnny Rabke,' Estelle mused. 'That takes a special kind of mindset. A special kind of cold-blooded mindset. But . . .'

'But?'

'Think about the fencing crew. They're the closest human beings to the trestles. A decent hike, or motoring cross-country to reach Red Slade, but easily possible. Then you're on the rail service road, and it's an easy shot east to the next trestles.'

'Johnny Rabke was on that crew.'

'And he wanted to talk to me about something that was bugging him,' Lydia said.

'But he never got around to it.' Estelle laced her fingers together. 'Somebody stopped his clock for him. Maybe he wouldn't have survived the initial wound inflicted by Arturo Ramirez. Maybe he wouldn't have. But somebody wanted to make sure.'

Jackie tapped her turquoise ring on the steering wheel. 'Or Rabke's killer could have been an unknown who dropped off the interstate.' She shook her head. 'Nah. Estelle, I see it as someone who knew where Rabke was going . . . that would be Arturo Ramirez. Johnny picks him up either at the Spur, or along the county road, and Ramirez sees his chance. Bang. Knife driven into Rabke's chest. Shots fired. Ramirez is down and out. Rabke is left sitting there,

pinned by seven inches of Ka-Bar. A third party comes along . . .
someone who *knows* Rabke, and has reason to see him dead. It's a
moment of opportunity, guys. Who's going to know? The killing
. . . the knifing . . . is going to be blamed on Ramirez, for sure. Us
dumb cops will never figure it out, right? So, why grab the knife
and worry about finishing Rabke off? Maybe to keep him from
talking, if he's still conscious when another Samaritan maybe passes
by. That's the way I see it. Who would we expect to see driving on
County Road Fourteen in the early hours? Who would have reason
to be there?'

'Any NightZone employee,' Lydia offered.

'Yep. And any one of the fencing crew,' Jackie agreed.

'That's what's drawing me,' Estelle said. 'I want to meet with
them on their own turf. See what stirs.'

THIRTY-ONE

Piles of drying juniper slash dotted the prairie along the fence line, some of the piles ten feet high and twice that distance across the base.

'Bobby Torrez calls those piles of slash "rabbit hotels",' Estelle said. 'An incredible population of critters will take up residence there.'

Jackie pointed at the stretch of barbed wire ahead. Hanging limply over the top strand was the battered carcass of a four-foot rattlesnake, its rattles amputated. 'There'll be more of those, I'm betting, when we get into some of that rocky country east of here.'

At one point where an arroyo had opened up the view to the south, they could see the glint of the narrow-gage railroad. Just as suddenly, as they rounded a gentle curve around the base of a small mesa, they came upon a crew cab pickup with horse trailer attached, parked just far enough off the two track that another vehicle could squeeze by. The trailer's tailgate was lowered.

'That truck is Jake Palmer's,' Estelle said. 'He's picked up trailer duties.' ATV tracks led away from the truck/trailer combo.

Another hundred yards on, the new fence two-track crossed a much older trail, one that was now blocked by the fence. Seeing Jackie's puzzled expression, Estelle said, 'It won't even be on the map. It's just one of the bazillion old roads in this country, used for a while to manage herds or for wood cutting, then abandoned.'

'Fresh tracks on it, though.'

'Yes. If we followed it north, it'd probably take us eventually to Forest Road Twenty-Six, or on toward the Boyd ranch on the other side of Cat Mesa. Close to it, anyway. I've driven it a couple of times, and it's a long, hard trip. Four-by-four country most of the way.'

The muted whisper of the Expedition was eclipsed by an unmuffled roar, and a battered ATV appeared around the corner, all four wheels locking in a cloud of dust when the driver saw the Sheriff's Department vehicle. Jake Palmer vaulted off the machine, tucking in the tail of his denim shirt at the same time. He stopped short, looking in at the three women.

'Oh,' he said, and ducked his head as he read the legend on the Expedition's door. 'Didn't see that. I thought maybe you was the electric company or something.'

'Not too many electric lines out this way, Jake,' Estelle said.

'Thought maybe they was going to get around to running some.' He straightened up and finished tucking his shirt. 'Anyways, I gotta get the truck and trailer and move on up the line.' He nodded in the pickup's direction. 'That's where we stashed the cans of gasoline for the ATVs.'

'Everything going all right?' Jackie asked.

'Yup. We're short-handed, but we're doin' OK. Could use some more hands to run that post driver.'

'Short-handed besides losing Johnny Rabke, you mean?'

Estelle thought that Jake looked ill at ease with that question.

'Well, sure. That and Keenan workin' on ahead, markin' the exact fence line.' His smile was sweaty in the hot weather. 'Sometimes I wish he'd find a route out of the trees, 'cause those roots give us the fits.' He glanced up at the vacant sky. 'And if it don't rain good and hard pretty soon so we can burn, we're going to have a real fire danger with all the slash piles.'

'You got that right,' Jackie said. Estelle thought that Sheriff Jackie Taber could fit in nicely with the 'boot-on-the-lower-fence-rail' gossip crowd, were she so inclined.

'You're working with who now?' Estelle asked.

'Me and EJ now, mostly. Howie works pretty good when he ain't complainin' about blisters. He's got Ricky Boyd singin' that tune, too. You'd think they were both twelve years old . . . or younger.'

'So just the four of you?'

Jake's eyebrows puckered as he computed the answer. 'Yup,' he said, 'EJ and Howie, Ricky and Keenan. Oh, and me.' He made a face. 'Forgot to count myself. That's five of us then.'

Jackie pulled the Expedition into gear. 'We'll head on up the way, if you want to move your buggy.'

'Yup. It'll just ride in the trailer. You headed on up where we're workin' now?'

'Thought we would.'

'You need to talk to us again, or what?'

'Or what,' Jackie said with an easy smile. 'We're just curious how Wallace's project is coming along.'

'It's a bitch.' Jake actually managed to blush. 'I mean, you know . . .'

'We're sure it is, Jake.'

He started to turn away. 'Oh, that big guy was out here, too. I thought maybe he was going to work with us.'

'Big guy?'

'He used to be sheriff. Mr Torrez? I know he hunts out here a lot, and him and Mr Boyd was out here talkin' earlier this morning. Mr Boyd is thinkin' of going to a permit-only hunt on his land this year, and him and Mr Torrez were talkin' about that. What it would take to post it all. Stuff like that.'

'I wish him luck with that,' Jackie said.

As Jake turned back to his ATV, Jackie glanced across at Estelle. '"Mr Torrez." I haven't heard him called that for a long time.'

'Jake Palmer is a ranch kid, you have to remember. They can be polite if need be.'

Jackie nodded. 'I think we can cross him off the list. He doesn't seem like the type who would wrench a knife through somebody's heart, up close and personal. But then again . . .'

Knowing full well what list the sheriff was talking about, Estelle nodded agreement. 'We need to keep prodding, find out what else he knows.'

THIRTY-TWO

A mile through the brush seemed more like ten, but all in all, the fencing crew had done good work. They had resisted the impulse for a quick and dirty job, where they might leave a fence that later would be more than a chore to maintain. The narrow roadway they were clearing was a lot of extra work, but it provided an avenue for cattle to saunter along without getting snarled in the fencing wire, or leaning their bovine poundage against the posts.

Juniper stumps where the road hugged the fence had been cut below ground level, with the dirt shoveled back over the stump remains. Only when the path crossed a seasonal arroyo was the Expedition's ride jolting enough to jar the eye teeth loose, and with some of the larger watercourses, the access road had to snake diagonally to make a passable route across the streambed. Through it all, the fence line itself ran straight and true, with boulder 'dead men' keeping the wire taught as it spanned the low spots.

The breeze was gentle, making virtually no sound through the juniper crowns, and when the first chain saw fired up ahead, it was a loud and raucous snarl. A second saw soon joined the first. Adding to the cacophony was a long string of shouted profanities as one young voice bellowed incomprehensible instructions over the racket.

Shortly after they had met Jake Palmer, he had been prompt to trailer his ATV and then pull the rig down the trail. Jackie had pulled as far off the pathway as she could without scraping paint, giving Jake room to pass. Now, they saw his truck and trailer parked squarely in the middle of the new two-track, blocking any further exploration.

An older Ford 350 crew cab was parked off the way, its grille nudging a runty juniper seedling. The battered license showing signs of frequent over-shoots with the trailer hitch. What was hampering progress was a grand old alligator-bark juniper, squarely in the flagged path of the proposed fence. Beside the Ford was a mud-tan Toyota Tacoma with a battered tailgate, with ATV ramps leading up to the bed.

Whether the challenge of the juniper was just Keenan Clark's idea of a practical joke on the kids working for him, or whether it actually had to be removed, was up for debate. If the tree stayed, Estelle saw that the fence would have to dodge around the massive trunk, putting a crook in the fence line. A fence too close to the tree would encourage cattle to lean or scratch, their bodies sandwiched between tree and wire. And the wire would lose.

'That old guy must be thirty-six inches DBH,' Estelle said. Seeing Jackie's blank look, she added, 'Diameter Breast High.' She grinned and deepened her lumberjack's accent. 'That's my logger talk,' she added. It appeared that the sawyers had been busy hacking off the huge tree's lower limbs, starting an enormous brush pile.

'And what saw do they have that can manage a tree like that?' Jackie mused. Ricky Boyd was struggling with one saw with what looked like an eighteen-inch bar, making a ragged and ineffectual gnawing at the tree's smoother limbwood bark. He gave up and retreated to the crew cab. 'His saw may be too small, but at least it's dull,'Jackie quipped.

Howie Stance had retreated from the battle, and was busy fueling his saw, an old-timer with a large motor that looked out of proportion to the short bar and chain. 'Let's see what else they have.' She lowered her voice and leaned toward Estelle. 'Right now, I don't see anything that I'd trust for the job of cutting creosoted trestle beams.'

'We'll see. Diligence can be an amazing thing,' Estelle said.

The moment they opened the doors of the Expedition, the noise hushed. The four young men – Howie and his older brother Elliot 'EJ' Stance, Rick Boyd and Jake Palmer – stopped what they were about, and it was Jake Palmer who turned to the others, in particular EJ Stance, and said, 'See? I told ya they was following me in here.'

'That old tree is a challenge,' Jackie said by way of greeting.

'Well, it'd be a whole lot easier if we could just build around it,' Jake allowed. 'But oh, no. We gots to have us a straight line.'

'Just gots to,' Jackie agreed, mimicking the boy's grammar. 'Is Keenan working out here today?'

EJ Stance waved a hand toward the east. 'He's working on down the line. You can see the flagging. He took the Honda.'

'You gentlemen are in the thick of it. About a million bucks' worth of firewood in this section.'

'Yup. That's next,' EJ said, and that earned a look of dismay from his younger brother, Howie. 'What,' EJ barked, seeing the boy's expression. 'You thought all this wood was just going to be left here to rot?' He shook his head in derision at his brother, and then turned his attention to the shiny Expedition. 'Nice ride you got here.'

'Your tax dollars at work,' Jackie said. 'It'll do. Not much of a wood hauler, though.'

'So how'd you find us?' The answer to that was obvious, and it sounded to Estelle as if EJ had asked the question just to have something to say, to avoid an uncomfortable silence.

'Your tracks are pretty clear, EJ,' Jackie replied. 'What with this boulevard that you've made. Hunters are going to love you for it.'

Estelle watched the young man's face for a tick of realization. If one of them had driven an ATV down to the trestles, even a single pass of those knobby tires would leave distinctive tracks across the prairie – at least until they reached the track's thoroughly graveled service road.

For the first time, Lydia Thompson spoke up. She had been watching as Ricky Boyd joined Howie Stance at the Toyota's tailgate saw shop. He poured bar oil from a battered gallon can into the saw's reservoir. His hands weren't as steady as they should have been, and a liberal slopping of the dark oil puddled on the pickup's tailgate.

'Johnny Rabke told me that you're fencing all the way over to Forest Road Twenty-Six,' Lydia said.

'Most of the way,' EJ said. 'There's some BLM land in the way.' His left hand carved a zigzag in the air. He fell silent and studied the ground, suddenly evasive at Rabke's mention. Estelle glanced from one member of the crew to the others. Rick Boyd managed a heavy oil spill as he jerked the can upright when the reservoir ran over.

Jake Palmer watched him with amusement. 'Even used engine oil ain't that cheap.'

Rick muttered a curse, more at being watched than making the spill.

'Over to Twenty-Six. That's a lot of fence,' Lydia said.

'Too much,' EJ responded. 'But it's good money for us.' He managed a smile. 'Job security. Makes it easier at round-up time, too. I mean, knowin' where the cattle *are*. They sure do wander.'

'I bet they do. Now, tell me, men,' Jackie Taber said, craning her neck back to judge the tree's crown. 'How are you going to cut that with those little saws?'

'We got bigger,' EJ said. 'That big outfit that Keenan uses? That monster'll make quick work of this. He just wants the limbs out of the way first.'

'Hard to imagine.' Jackie stepped over to the oil-puddled tailgate, and Rick Boyd shifted sideways one way, with Howie Stance scooting over the other, pulling the bar of his saw out of her way. She stood with her hands on her hips, surveying the loaded truck. She pointed at a veteran double-bit axe, tossed haphazardly among the welter of hand tools, gas and oil cans, come-alongs, and not a few empty beer cans. The axe's handle just under the head showed scars from a life of stump encounters.

'When I was a kid down in the hill country over around Fredericksburg, I got to use one of them more than I wanted. My dad had something against chain saws. I don't know what. Axes use less bar oil, I guess.'

'Yeah, they do,' Rick laughed. His glance shifted over to take in Jackie Taber's broad shoulders and heavy arms.

In the distance, another chain saw started, ran for a short time and then stopped, the engine settling into a rolling idle. After a moment, the operator goosed the throttle again.

'That's Keenan,' EJ said.

'How long's he going to work out front?' Estelle asked.

'Don't know. But not too long usually. He'll mark a good run, then come back and make sure we don't screw something up.' He shrugged. 'He don't need to. Running fence ain't rocket science, you know. But he's fussy.' He hacked his hand through the air, closing one eye as he did so. 'Got to be just right. Got to be straight. Got to have the stays put in exactly right. All that. You'd think some fence inspector was going to be comin' along with a tape measure.'

'Dad would,' Ricky Boyd said.

'And left up to you, you'd just run the wire from tree to tree,' EJ said, fishtailing his hand through the air.

Sheriff Taber turned to Estelle, holding out a hand. 'Small size sample?' she asked, and Estelle knew what she meant.

'Let me get one from my briefcase.' Estelle trudged back to the Expedition, and selected a small plastic evidence vial, its sturdy plastic already imprinted with a white label.

She handed a slender disposable wood spatula to Jackie and then, in her neat, almost architectural script, printed on the jar's label with a fine-tipped black marker the date, location, and the words *Boyd bar oil*, along with the truck's license plate number and her initials. She handed the vial to Jackie.

'Move your butt a little,' the sheriff instructed Rick.

'Wha . . .'

'I want that nice big puddle you made for me right there.' She pointed at the generous sample of bar oil caught in one of the design indents of the tailgate.

'How come you got to do that?' the young man said. He slid from his seat on the tailgate. 'I was going to clean that up.'

'It ain't illegal now to spill oil, is it?' Howie Stance blurted, and Estelle managed to keep her expression stone-cold sober, masking her amusement. After all, one never knew when the EPA official might pop out from behind a tree and catch the woodsmen at it.

'Nope, not yet, anyway.' Jackie continued her work, gathering several milliliters of spilled oil, avoiding any drips down the side of the vial.

She was about to say something else when EJ Stance's quiet voice on his cell phone surprised them.

'Keenan, you need to come back asap. The cops are here.'

THIRTY-THREE

EJ Stance stood with the cell phone in hand, the other hand
poised over its screen. Jake Palmer leaned against the side of
his truck, watching but saying nothing. Rick Boyd's eyes were
locked on the small vial as Sheriff Jackie Taber secured the top and
then handed the vial to Lydia.

'One of the padded envelopes,' she instructed.

'Don't you got to have a warrant for that?' Rick blurted.

'You've been watching too many movies, bro,' Jackie replied.
She smiled at him, unthreatening. 'Let's just relax here and see what
Mr Clark has to say. Now that he's been summoned.' As if following
some unspoken command, three of the four cell phones appeared
from their spots in the hip pockets of three sets of jeans. Only Jake
Palmer's trousers bore the double faded mark of both phone and
Copenhagen, one on each butt cheek.

EJ Stance collected his wits and stared hard at the three officers,
finally settled on Deputy Lydia Thompson as she walked back from
the Expedition. 'What'd Rabke tell you, anyways?'

One eyebrow lifted. 'And that's something I would discuss with
you, Mr Stance?'

'Well, he was always talkin' about him and you. He jawed on
about that all the time, even about a day or two ago, when you
stopped him down on the highway 'cause he was workin' on that
wheel bearing. He talked about that most of the next day.'

'You have the whole story, I guess.' Her expression was
hard.

'Well, I guess you made quite the impression on him, officer,'
EJ said. 'That's why you're here, then? 'Cause of what he told you?'
He shoved his phone in his hip pocket. 'And then he tangled with
that Mexican guy, and that was that. Not much more *he* was going
to tell you then, huh.'

'I'm surprised that you know all about how Johnny Rabke died,'
Sheriff Taber said. She now stood relaxed, both hands at her side.
'How'd you hear about it?'

'Everybody knows by now,' he said.

'I suppose they do,' Jackie said affably. 'Comes to things like that, it's a small world.'

In the distance, they heard the sound of an ATV approaching, weaving through the trees, taking its time. Estelle caught sight of the machine as it approached – a bright red Honda that was either new or treated to power-washing between jobs. But what surprised her the most was that two men were on board.

'Well, well,' Jackie said.

'That's—' Lydia began, and Estelle finished for her, 'Yes, it is.'

The side-by seating of the utility vehicle – two in front, two in back, along with a short utility bed over the engine – would have made more sense for Bill Gastner's choice, except it required an open pickup truck or trailer for carrying it to and fro. Former Sheriff Bobby Torrez might have been reasonably comfortable in the Honda, but he didn't waste time dismounting. Even before it stopped, he'd swung a boot out to skid along the ground, as if he needed the contact with earth to feel secure.

Both doors had been removed, and Keenan Clark shut down the engine before pulling himself out. He was a big man, broad through the shoulders and heavy of torso. He wore a ball cap from the local feed store, sawdust-flecked denim long-sleeved shirt, and cargo pants with pockets stuffed.

'Now, what the hell is this all about?' he demanded. He worked at keeping a quasi-smile, nodding at the three officers. 'Somebody hurt themselves?' He surveyed his four workers. 'EJ, what's going on?'

'Just visiting this big project.' Jackie stepped forward with an outthrust hand before EJ Stance could think of an answer. 'I understand you're fencing all the way to Twenty-Six?'

'Well, not quite, but almost,' Clark said. He shook perfunctorily with Taber, and offered a curt nod to Estelle and Lydia. As Clark did so, former sheriff Robert Torrez unfolded himself all the way out of the Honda, stretching all six foot four of himself and rotating both arms to ease the kinks. He wore a tan uniform shirt, the fabric unfaded where the patches had been removed. His blue jeans were faded but comfortable, his scuffed boots rugged. He wore the same brown Western-style Stetson that he'd worn for years as sheriff when he wasn't going casual with a baseball cap.

Estelle noticed that Torrez was not wearing the .45 automatic that had been his duty gun. Instead, his high-riding belt holster carried a revolver that Estelle had had occasion to shoot a few times at the department qualifications. Compared to her own Beretta .40, Torrez's .44 magnum Smith & Wesson Model 29 was a howitzer.

Clark nodded at Torrez. 'Found this guy out in the woods. We was talking, and then when one of the boys gave me a call, he offered to ride along.' Estelle was regarding Torrez when Clark said that, and she was sure that she saw the hint of a twinkle in Torrez's dark eyes. Just walking around in the rugged juniper forest, especially when there was no hunting season currently?

Before she could explore that unlikelihood with the former sheriff, Ricky Boyd found his voice. He pointed to the remains of the puddle on the tailgate. 'They took a sample of this,' he said.

'A sample of what?' Clark asked.

'This oil that I spilled. Didn't mean to.'

'What do you mean, a sample, dumbbutt?'

'Just what he said,' Sheriff Taber said, her tone easy and polite. 'A sample that we can send to the lab for quantitative testing.'

'Oh,' Clark said, as if the whole story had just dawned on him. 'So now the county says it's illegal to spill a little chain-saw oil out in the middle of the goddamn woods?'

'Nope, things haven't gotten that bad yet,' Jackie laughed. 'But it was a chain saw that cut the supports over at the train trestles. So any chain saw we find in the area, we'll test. We'll find a match-up.'

Clark was speechless – dumbfounded. 'You got to be shitting me. Is that what all this is about? The trains stopped, all kinds of people on site? I heard something about all that, about the trestle supports damaged somehow. And now, you're thinkin' . . .' His head swung as if it had come loose, swinging to glare at each officer in turn.

'Well, I don't know what you're thinkin',' he continued. 'Like maybe these kids went down there and sawed on the trestles in the middle of the night? Like they don't get their fill of woodcutting on this job?' He shot out an index finger toward where the two boys still huddled near the Toyota pickup. 'And the spilled oil there on the truck? What's that going to tell you? What a waste of goddamned time.'

'Not so. Every oil has its own molecular profile, its own distinctive signature.'

That Jackie Taber could reel off such nonsense with a straight face was remarkable, Estelle thought, equal to the notion that the county Sheriff's Department had the lab resources to accomplish such a test, or even knew of a laboratory that would respond to a request for a complete molecular profile analysis.

'That's all bullshit, and you know it,' Clark scoffed.

'Trust me, we'll find the saw that cut those trestles, one way or another. Someone messing with a railway becomes a federal matter. The NTSB will be taking a long, hard look. They have the resources, if we don't.'

'Good luck with that,' Clark guffawed. He turned to Torrez. 'All the years you was sheriff, you ever hear of such shit?' Torrez settled for a tactful shrug. 'But look, you want to start by testing our saws, you go right ahead. Start with the two in the back of the Honda, if you want.'

'I appreciate your cooperation, Mr Clark.' Jackie nodded at the deputy, and Lydia set off for the Expedition and the supply of collection vials.

'You're thinking you can scour enough bar oil for a comparison? What are you going to do, find a way to pull the oil off any sawdust that got left down by the tracks?'

'That's exactly what we do, what's being done while you and I stand here jawing.' Jackie sounded as if she had either done, or observed, the testing process dozens of times. She turned to Lydia. 'Take a sample from the saw's oil reservoir while you're at it. Both of the big saws in the back of the Honda.'

'You know, that's a crazy, screwball thing that some son-of-a-bitch did, cutting through those trestle supports, if what I hear is right.' Clark wiped the back of his hand across his mouth, trailing a little smear of tobacco juice across his cheek. 'No sense in it. Train goes off those tracks and into that arroyo, somebody's going to get killed, and that's a fact.' He swallowed hard. 'You know what I think? I think you're going to need a warrant before you go much further. This is private property you're on.'

'It's not your property, Mr Clark. So a warrant is something you don't have to worry about.'

'We'll see about that.' He glanced up at the sky and then at his four workers. 'And what are you jokers standing around for? We got cutting to do.' It didn't look as if that was something any of the four sawyers wanted to hear.

Bob Torrez caught Estelle's eye and beckoned as he ambled off toward the Expedition. When they were out of earshot, he paused and swung a boot up to rest on the back bumper.

'So tell me, Bobby. What prompts your day hike today?' Estelle asked.

'Just routine backup,' he replied. 'You know? Just kinda curious.'

'I didn't hear the SO call for backup, routine or otherwise.'

'Well, it was otherwise. Gastner called me. Kind of like one retiree to another.' He turned in a circle, stretching as he did so. 'Wild Bill was thinking of taking another jaunt with that fancy chair of his. I suggested that he do some thinkin' about that. We're a long ways from anywhere, and everybody's busy.'

'That's true. But . . .' She left the thought unfinished.

'But what? You know the different ways this could go.'

'Yes, I do.'

'All right then. Bill remembers that Forest Road Twenty-Six crosses under the railroad at that low second trestle. He got to thinkin' about how someone could access those trestles easy enough. Twenty-Six breaks off from the state highway not far west of the airport. Easy shot down to the rail access road.'

'*Padrino* gets to thinking about things,' Estelle said.

'Yeah, he does.' Torrez nodded. 'Waddell was tellin' us that he's been planning to fence the whole route. The whole rail route from the mesa to town, right along the tracks. This project here got him to thinking about it, I guess. He's going to have to do more than talk about it. But no matter. Fences can be cut easy enough.' He smiled, something Estelle had always thought that Bobby Torrez should do more often.

'Anyway,' she said, 'thanks for checking up on us.'

'Nice day for a walk.'

'Where are you parked?'

'Twenty-Six, where it goes under the tracks.'

'We can run you back down there, no problem. You must be a couple hours out, even hiking at a good clip.'

He shook his head. 'Walkin' through the woods on a nice day is one thing. Tryin' to drive your unit through all the brush is somethin' else. That's what I got to thinkin'. If one of those knuckleheads decided to drive from here down to the trestles with the ATV? No way they wouldn't leave some tracks.'

'And?'

'Not possible to tell much. Clark's been drivin' the fence line all the way to Twenty-Six. So his tracks are there. I just got curious about that, is all.' He shrugged. 'Didn't pan out.' He almost smiled. 'Thanks for the offer, anyways. With you guys having to drive back all the way around, I'll probably be back before you all. I can hike cross country.'

Keenan Clark watched with undisguised impatience while the officers gathered what samples they wanted. He didn't interfere, but he simmered. At one point he glared at Deputy Lydia Thompson and asked, 'Is this what Rabke put you up to?'

Estelle looked hard at Clark. 'That's a curious thing for you to say, Mr Clark.'

'Well, I hear these kids talkin' about it.' He swept a hand toward the others. 'What Rabke said he would do, and all the rest.'

'"And all the rest." I'd like to hear about that.'

Clark's tone was sharp. 'Well, I don't know what he meant. He was all the time shootin' off his mouth about something. About the girls he knew,' and he waved a hand at Lydia. 'All his great plans. Talk so much that I didn't even listen to him any more.'

As if realizing that he'd already said too much, Clark turned away in disgust. He jabbed a hand at Jake Palmer. 'If they're done with it, get my big saw. Let's get this tree out of the right-of-way.'

'I'll catch you later,' Torrez said, just before the saw barked into life. Keenan Clark didn't take the time to wish the officers a good day as they boarded the Expedition and maneuvered to turn it around.

The juniper/piñon woodland was fragrant as they made their way back, windows open despite the heat of the day. Content to let Lydia Thompson ride shotgun, Estelle slumped in the back seat, knees drawn up and supported against the back of the front seat. Eyelids heavy with fatigue, and in no mood for small talk, she let the long hours catch up with her, half thinking, half dreaming about the possibility of an ATV sneaking through the juniper cover down to the trestles. At one point, she almost awoke as her window buzzed up, feeling only the change of air, but unwilling to surface. She didn't feel the air conditioning switch on, or hear the rumble of the tires when they turned on to County Road Fourteen, or feel the acceleration as they reached State Seventy-Six and turned southeast toward Posadas.

THIRTY-FOUR

'My office made arrangements to ship Arturo Ramirez's body home to Janos.' Dr Francis Guzman sat on the edge of the bed, both hands working the tight muscles in Estelle's back. 'Colonel Naranjo said he'll make sure that a priest visits the family.'

'That's good of him,' Estelle muttered into her pillow.

'He wants to meet with you sometime, to talk over the case with you. He has concerns, he said.'

Estelle twisted a little to bring her face into the light. 'I bet he does. Did he say what about?' Colonel Tomás Naranjo had served with the Mexican Provinciales for as long as Estelle had been with the county, and the Mexican lawman had been of invaluable service on several occasions. Estelle had always been delighted by the way Tomás ignored the bureaucracy of borders, and the various fences that went with them.

'He wonders if we should do something about what he called "Father Anselmo's pipeline".'

She twisted some more until she could see her husband's face. 'That's what Tomás called it?'

'His words. But you know, he just mentioned it, in passing. I'm not sure how serious he was.'

'I'll make a point to contact him. He's always fun to talk to.'

'He's also a shameless flirt.'

'That too, but harmless.' She looked at the clock. 'Is that the right time?'

'I assume it is.'

'*Por díos*,' Estelle murmured. 'You let me sleep too long.'

'Doctor's orders, *mi corazón*. Jackie said you fell asleep in the car, and weren't making much sense when you woke up back at the office.'

'*Ay*.' His hands chasing the stiff muscles of her back didn't release their grip as she stretched for the phone on the night stand. The screen index of received messages brought a groan from her.

'How about a cup of tea,' Francis said. 'Or something stronger?'

She read the list again. 'Probably something stronger, *Oso*. But I'll wait for dinner.'

'You slept through dinner, *querida*.'

'*Argg*. Do I still have a family, or have they all given up on me as well?'

'Carlos and Tasha went out to dinner with Francisco and Angie, I'm not just sure where. They're invited over here for dessert, provided you'll be awake by then.'

'I'm awake. I'm awake.'

'And Bill took Camille and Mark to NightZone for dinner.'

'A peace settlement, no doubt.'

'No doubt.'

She looked at the clock again. 'Seven sixteen,' she said absently. 'I don't believe I did that.'

'Get up and move around a little. You'll feel better.'

'Let me check in with a few people. Have you eaten anything?'

'Not so's I'd notice. But we have tons of leftovers, including a bunch of that nuclear stuff that Tasha made.'

'It's just lamb, *Oso*. Lamb and curry and a hundred other things. That sounds good, though. That and ice tea, and I'll be happy. I'll get my carcass moving.'

She picked up her phone again and saw that Miles Waddell had called her four times since noon, that first call now more than seven hours old. She listened while the phone connected. 'I can't come to the phone right now, but . . .' and he interrupted his answering machine.

'Estelle! I thought you'd gone to Mexico or wherever. I think I called four or five times.'

'I was on vacation.'

He paused at that, then said, 'Good for you. Hey, guess what?'

'You're getting married.'

'I wish. No, come on. I spoke with my engineers this afternoon. They visited the trestles and said that there's enough redundancy in the design that there's no way the trestles will collapse, not even the big one that groaned at us in Red Slade. They're not saying that no damage was done, for sure. Some expensive damage, actually. But no danger of collapse.'

'That's good news. Can you run the train?'

'Ah, no. That's the bad news. They said that would be pushing my luck. I can run the Tacotracker, not the train.'

'What's the timetable for repairs?'

She could hear him suck in a long breath and hold it, then groan. 'Would you believe six weeks.'

'Ouch.'

'That's what I'm saying. And a permanent repair is going to be expensive, of course. Let's hope the perpetrator is filthy rich so I can sue the bastard. Once you catch him, that is.'

'We can always hope.'

'No ideas yet, eh?'

'I have lots of *ideas*, Miles. They don't hold up in court, though.'

'You know who's here for dinner, don't you,' he said, leaping to another subject.

'Bill and his daughter and son-in-law, I'm told.'

'Correcto. I think they're about to leave, though, so I have to go tear up the check.'

'Well done, Miles. You're a good guy. How you avoid bankruptcy I don't know, but you're a good guy.'

'Hey, I owe Bill big time. If he hadn't done that dumb stunt with his back-country wheelchair, no telling what would have happened with my trestles.'

'A helpful hint, Miles. Don't make Bill Gastner think that you're in his debt. He doesn't like that much. Better to tell him that you're thinking of arresting him for trespassing.'

Waddell laughed. 'Maybe I should try that . . . not. Anyway, you and your husband come up sometime soon, will you?'

'Guaranteed, Miles.'

'And please keep me posted on how the investigation is going.'

'Certainly.'

'Oh . . . and before I let you go . . . you don't have any ideas about who might have done this, right?'

'That would be correct. But who knows. Sometimes unexpected breaks happen.'

'I'll take 'em, unexpected or not. I worry, you know. I worry that they're sitting out there in the boonies somewhere, laughing at me and waiting for a second assault. You can believe we're going to be patrolling with the Tacotracker twenty-four seven. Monty has his twelve-gauge in the cab, loaded with double-ought buck. I hope we catch the sons a bitches.'

'Be careful with that vigilante stuff, Miles.'

'Yeah, I know. But tell Monte that. He's mighty possessive of what he calls "my train". And I'll add, tell *Bobby* that. Our former sheriff has been out there all day, you know. The deputies haven't found any trace of a game camera, but Bobby says they don't know where to look.'

'He says he does?'

'I don't doubt him,' Waddell said.

'Nor do I.' She saw that Bobby Torrez had called her, once, at 4:15 p.m. 'I'll talk with him. In the meantime, you be careful. And tell Monty to be careful with that shotgun.'

'You bet. Enjoy your "vacation", Estelle.'

That vacation lasted less than a minute, ending when Sheriff Jackie Taber picked up the phone.

THIRTY-FIVE

'Good to hear your voice,' Jackie chided gently. 'You were soooo out of it on the way home.'

'No more hours than anybody else on this investigation,' Estelle laughed. 'But it's gotten so that if I miss my nap time, I'm worthless.'

'None of us is as young as we once were, you know. My regimen is to eat enough for about four people,' the sheriff said. 'That keeps me going. It also keeps me fat, but oh well.'

'I'll try that.'

'I bet you will, my dear. So . . . do you want the very good news first, the "sort of" good news, or the not so good?'

'I'll brace myself. I obviously slept too long, Jackie. Go ahead.'

'All right. The very good. You know, I had a long chat with Lydia this afternoon. She is absolutely sure that Johnny Rabke had something he wanted to tell her, but for whatever reason, didn't. I can imagine an age-old reason. If you think that somebody's going to rat you out, rat you out for something bad that you did? You know for a fact – or at least you *think* you do – that he's on the ins with a good-lookin' deputy sheriff? You know he's going to blab to her. So. What do you do?'

She stopped there, and Estelle could run the scenario though her mind. 'Arturo sets the game in motion by attacking Johnny. He's not expecting to stop a bullet with his skull. He gets the knife in, then tries to flee this barrage of gunfire that Johnny manages. And there Johnny sits, a knife plunged into his chest.'

'But not enough to kill him right away,' Jackie said. 'Your hubby confirms that the first blow with the knife didn't lacerate the heart. Maybe cut the pericardium, maybe even nicked one of the big arteries or veins. Sliced some lung. For sure Johnny is going to bleed to death if he isn't slapped on the operating table in seconds. But he's way out *there*. Miles from your husband's skilled hands. And that's the condition he's in when along comes Mr Helpful.'

'How does the killer know that Johnny hasn't already talked to our deputy?'

'You know the answer to that,' Jackie said.

'You're right, I do. Because Lydia didn't tell *us* what Johnny might have said had he not been murdered. She didn't know. She *wouldn't* have known, because if she knew, there's no reason she would keep it to herself. If she told us, we'd be out there right away. We wouldn't be waiting for an eighty-seven-year-old man in a wheelchair to stumble on the damage.'

'But I'm willing to bet my pension, such as it is, that the killer is one of the five. It's just a matter of numbers.'

'Keenan Clark, maybe. Jake Palmer, well, maybe. He was shaken by what he saw, or he was nervous about the cops gathering around. Maybe. The Stance brothers? EJ and Howard. "Howie". Stranger things have happened. And Ricky Boyd. Although I can't see him bellying up to the side of the truck, taking a good look at the tortured face of Johnny Rabke, and reaching in to put it all together. I can't see him doing that.'

There was silence for a moment, and then Estelle could hear the tapping of the sheriff's pencil on her polished desktop.

'One more thing.'

'What's that? You're thinking of Curtis Boyd?'

'You're a mind reader, Jackie.'

'Yeah, but Ricky was only twelve years old or so when his uncle was killed. He's seventeen, going on eighteen now. That would be a hell of a long time for a kid to wait for payback.'

'Just saying. It's another connection. A *possible* connection.'

'Tell you what. It's a quiet evening. Let me paw through the records on that case and see if there's something we missed. Some little connection.'

'Other than *Padrino*.'

'Yeah. Other than him. On the one hand, I'm glad that Bill knew nothing about what might have been going on, what with Johnny's murder and all. Maybe he sees something that we're missing.'

'I don't think so,' Estelle mused. 'For one thing, if he did, he'd have told me right away. If he'd had suspicions, he'd have said something. I don't like coincidences, but in this case, I think that's all we have.'

'Here's my plan, then,' Jackie said. 'I've been thinking about it all afternoon, since the test results came back . . .'

'Wait. When we first started this conversation, you said good news, and bad. Or at least not so good.'

'Ah, the bad. I have an acquaintance at Quantico. I asked him what the chances were of a test on the chain-saw oil pulled either from wood chips, or from the oil reservoir of the saw. He laughed.'

'*That's* encouraging.'

'Well, actually it is. He said that the FBI lab could probably do an oil profile that established the brand of the oil . . . even the used oil, or the oil residue centrifuged from the oily chips. But he doubted that, barring a long and expensive analysis, that he could do much better than that. And certainly zero results on short notice. Weeks, maybe.'

'What about *with* a long and expensive analysis? What could they tell us then?'

'Probably they could tell us anything we wanted to know. I think. He thinks. You know why he's not particularly excited about going that route?'

'Because the trestles didn't collapse, a train didn't plunge into an arroyo with a resulting loss of many lives, and there was no good evidence that the sabotage was caused by some terrorist dirtbag with foreign connections.'

The sheriff crooned a drawn-out *ooooh*. 'You're getting cynical in your dotage, Estelle.'

'*Dotage.* That's not a word I've used in a long time.'

'But you're absolutely right, nail on the head, win the bet. That's almost *exactly* what my FBI friend said. That's why he doesn't want to tie into a long and expensive analysis of any oil.'

'Even if a murder is somehow involved.'

'Even if. And that's *even if* we knew that to be true.'

'So your plan? I have one, but . . .'

'Let's hear yours first,' Jackie said.

'Simple. We're dealing, for the most part, with someone who did something stupid, then tried to cover it up, right? My inclination is to revisit the fence crew, during the early morning hours when they're not thinking straight, and see what we can accomplish with some careful bluffing. Some careful arm twisting. Some threats. Maybe even stretch the truth a little here and there.'

'As you're fond of saying, my dear, '*¡Ay, caramba!* You've read my mind. I would suggest using three cars, not one. Lots of flashing lights and spotlights are both impressive and unhinging, especially if the perp is guilty. Three cars gives us that edge.'

'All the lights you want, Jackie. But I don't want anyone hurt.'

'Especially not one of us.'

'Especially.'

'If we leave the Sheriff's Office at oh four hundred and hustle a little, that should get us to the fence camp around five thirty.'

'As far as I know, only the Stance brothers, Jake Palmer, and sometimes Rick Boyd spend the night there, depending on the weather. But that's a start.

'Sergeant Pasquale and Lydia to bring in Clark, while you, me and LT take the others.'

'Think on it overnight, Jackie. There's a fly in our ointment, though.'

'I'm listening.'

'Tomorrow is Sunday. They're working on Sunday? They'll be in camp?'

'The answer to that is "yes". I gave Wallace Boyd a call, told him I had concerns. It's likely he'll show up out there as well.'

'That should be interesting. And something else that I think about during wakeful moments . . .'

'And that is?'

'*Someone* cut the trestle supports. That's a given.'

'Yes.'

'Either that person, or persons, is a member of Wallace Boyd's fencing crew – one of the kids, for want of a better word – or . . .'

'Or there's someone else out there with a chain saw. You know why I don't believe that?'

'Probably the same reason I don't believe it,' Estelle said. 'If someone *else* was running a saw, the kids would have heard it. They'd be curious. It's possible for me to imagine a scenario like that – sawing at night, a couple miles away from their camp? Or sawing in the daytime, when the fence crew is also working. I can imagine all that. But it doesn't fit. And I'm trying not to be driven by assumptions.'

Jackie hummed a little tune to accompany her thoughts. 'In the meantime, let's try something that sometimes works, especially with the young, the eager, the restless. Let's add a little bluff to the mix.'

'Meaning?'

'We've talked to Wallace, we've talked to Keenan. We've talked to each one of the kids. Let's you and I take a little drive up to Newton. I want to talk with Orrin Stance – the guy who wanted to give his mules the opportunity to shit all over Miles Waddell's pet NightZone.'

Estelle looked hard at the sheriff for a moment, then smiled. 'OK.'

THIRTY-SIX

Bobby Torrez's phone rang half a dozen times, long enough that Estelle thought that the former sheriff and now confirmed family man might be in his spacious backyard, playing charbroiler chef along with son Gabe. But the circuit clicked, and Estelle was greeted by the familiar greeting.

'Yup?' That was followed by a brief pause, and he added, 'I thought you was going to sleep all night.'

'That would have been nice,' Estelle said. 'Miles said you spent the day out hiking.'

'Yup. Did you talk to Bishop yet?'

'Not since I sent him up the hill near Red Slade Gulch to look for the game cam.'

'Yeah, well.'

'Did you find it?'

'Yup.'

Estelle's pulse jumped. 'You *did?*'

'Yup.' Then, as if he had decided rightly that monosyllabic responses were going to eat into his free time, he added, 'It's set up south of the trestle, not on that hill to the north. That's where they were lookin'.'

'Did you confiscate it? Or at least tell Deputy Bishop that you found it?'

'Nope. I'll sit on it until you get here. You might want some pictures of it in place. And I don't have an evidence bag with me.'

Estelle glanced at her watch. 'It's five after eight, Bobby. How long have you been out there?'

'Don't know. Probably since about four this afternoon or so.'

'*Ay.* You should have called sooner.'

'I did. Nice evening, and I got some entertainment just now.'

'Who?'

'More like *what.* There's a herd of javelina thinks it might be a good thing to bed down under the trestle. So, no hurry. I'll wait until you get here.'

'I . . .' and then she stopped. Bobby Torrez had his own agenda, not always understandable by others.

'Bishop is over there in the parking area. No need to bother him,' Torrez said. 'He'll just call you. Or worse yet, he might want to take the thing down. Easier I just wait. You coming directly?'

'I'm on my way.'

'Almost directly, then,' Torrez chuckled, and hung up.

Sheriff Jackie Taber sounded surprised when she answered her phone. 'Our four o'clock rendezvous is going to be here before we know it,' she said. 'But this is a game changer. Let's not keep the man waiting.'

She and Estelle took Jackie's Expedition, calling ahead so that the train terminal gate was open when they arrived. Monty Schaffer, the head railroad engineer, was there to greet them, but they settled for a quick wave and shot through to the service road.

Twelve and a half miles of gravel road took them twenty-five minutes, and Jackie made constant use of the spotlight, shooting it ahead to catch critters who might be in the way. They pulled to a stop near the lip of Red Slade Gulch.

Estelle's phone vibrated.

'Scoot through the trestle,' Bobby instructed. 'Ain't going to fall on you. Come about fifty yards south, and there's a pretty good grove of piñon in the east side of the arroyo. I'll meet you there. Watch your step. It's gettin' dark.'

'It ain't gonna fall on us,' Jackie muttered. 'I love that. I have a packet of evidence stuff, if you'll schlep the camera bag.' She opened the door and greeted Deputy Bishop, who had strolled from his unit over to their Expedition. 'Quiet night, Dwayne?'

'Very,' the young man said. 'Monty Schaffer was here for a bit, then he went back to the terminal. No other traffic, nobody coming to visit until you folks arrived.'

'That's good. You didn't talk with Bobby Torrez?'

'Haven't seen him, Sheriff.'

'Ah.' Taber smiled at Estelle. 'What a trip he is, no?'

'So what's going on, Sheriff?' Bishop asked, puzzled.

'Do you feel like climbing a tree?'

'Well, I guess so.'

'Good. Bring your gloves. Piñon can be a real pitch.'

Deputy Bishop didn't respond to the lame joke, and remained silent as they made their way down into the arroyo, and passed underneath the wounded trestles. Torrez was right, Estelle thought gratefully. The trestle didn't collapse. By the time they reached

Torrez, who was seated comfortably atop a shed-sized boulder, the last of the day's twilight had cast the arroyo into darkness.

Torrez stood up on the rock, and pivoted in place. He turned on his pencil-beam flashlight, and ran it up the bole of a burly piñon twenty yards up the hill. The beam held steady at a spot in the upper branches. He drew small circles with the beam, framing the target. The camera was about the size of a shoebox, and appeared to be held in place with a couple of Velcro straps encircling a stout limb.

'So there it be,' Sheriff Taber said.

'I should have awakened Linda,' Estelle said. 'She would have loved to add a credit for this in her diary. But my efforts are going to have to do. Let's see what we have.'

The piñon was squat and overly studded with racks of limbs, with abundant trailing limbs that might provide secure footing for a creature designed for climbing. Estelle looked at Deputy Dwayne Bishop. 'We need photos of that thing in place, Dwayne. Using full flash, a portrait of the whole tree that clearly shows the trail camera in place. And then, nice detailed close-ups, with the flash setting turned low so we don't just get a fireball.'

'OooOK.'

'If I might make a suggestion,' Jackie said. 'Shed that utility belt, gun, and all the extraneous gear. You won't need that up a tree. There's nothing to shoot up there.'

As he shucked the gear, Bishop eyed the tree. 'Actually, it looks pretty easy. I can see the scuff marks where somebody's gone up before me.'

After photo-documenting the scuff marks, Estelle adjusted the camera settings, then handed it to the deputy, who folded one of the camera straps around one of his belt loops. 'Take your time. We have all night, Dwayne.' He tucked the larger plastic evidence bag through the back of his belt, and pulled on his gloves.

They held their three flashlights for him, keeping the beams focused where they would do the most good without blinding the climber.

'Bobby, a question,' Estelle said at one point. 'Where did you park?'

'On west a ways.'

'The birders' drop-off?'

'Yup.'

'How did you happen to see this spot?'

'Where I woulda put the camera, probably.'

She looked over her shoulder at the trestle. 'That would be dramatic.'

'That's what they were hopin',' Torrez said.

Deputy Bishop looked down at them and grinned. He was twenty feet off the ground, with no more large limbs to take him higher. 'I can get it from here,' he announced, then shook one gloved hand. 'And you're right about the pitch.' Even with the electronic flash set on its lowest setting, the halo of light was bright enough to make them flinch. After five exposures, adjusting his position a bit for each one, Bishop paused. Estelle could see the light of the review monitor on the camera's back, flicking on and off as Bishop scrolled through the images.

'It worked,' he announced.

For a generation used to taking selfies at every opportunity, Estelle thought, how hard could this be? 'Before you remove the trail cam, take another set of photos. Double-check the settings to make sure you're on close-up. This is a one-time deal, Dwayne. If we don't get it this time, once you remove the trail cam, we don't get another chance. So take your time.'

When he was finished, he looked down at Estelle. 'You want me to bring it down for you to check?'

'No. You've got a good eye, Dwayne. If you say the pictures are good, then they're good. Pack the camera up, make sure it's secure on your belt, and then remove the trail cam and secure it in the evidence bag. Remember when you do that, we'll be looking for fingerprints. Handle it as little as possible, maybe just holding it by the straps. *Then* bring everything down.'

'I suppose you don't want piñon pitch all over it,' Bishop said.

'We love you, Dwayne,' Jackie Taber said.

With both of the deputy's feet on the ground, Estelle suddenly realized that she had been holding her breath – the feeling a puzzle master might have as a final, critical piece dropped into place.

'This,' Estelle said as she held the evidence bag, 'goes to LT for processing.'

'Tonight?' Jackie asked.

'Tonight. I'll print up a set of Dwayne's photos as well.' She smiled at the silent Bobby Torrez. 'Thank you.' She already knew what he'd say.

'Yup.'

'With a little luck, we have enough for a warrant,' the sheriff said. 'I'll take care of that.'

THIRTY-SEVEN

The shortest route to the tiny village of Newton was by no means the fastest. Sheriff Jackie Taber eschewed the paved roads like NM76, calling them 'boring'. Forest Road Twenty-Six, on the other hand, wound northward from its intersection with Miles Waddell's railroad service road, then visited every nook and cranny in the prairie before curving around the western hump of Cat Mesa. Winding through a peninsula of Oria National Forest, FR26 finally joined a county road that visited Wallace Boyd's ranch.

'Now you're talkin',' the sheriff said when they encountered their first herd of antelope, which burst across the road, two of the fleet critters turning to pace the truck for a quarter of a mile just for the fun of it before veering away.

It would have been easy to miss the Boyd Ranch, except for the invitation of the single porch light. Posadas County's maintenance of the road wasn't a good advertisement for the county road maintenance budget, or the skill of its road crews. The washboards were dense, sharply crowned, and spanned the full width of the road. Crossing out of the county didn't help.

A dozen miles north, right at the outskirts of Newton, gravel turned to pavement. The macadam was broken and potholed, with prairie grass invading across the shoulders, the roots crumbling the edges of the pavement.

'This town reminds me of a movie set for one of those apocalypse movies. Do you know where Orrin Stance lives?' Jackie asked. The first two buildings at Newton's outskirts were empty, the third was a weather-beaten clapboard church that didn't announce its denomination, or its hours. Across the street from the church was a collapsed, fire-blackened building that might have been a gas station.

'On the right,' Estelle announced. 'The place with the circle of wagons.' Despite the rest of the village's appearance, Orrin Stance's residence showed signs of life, even productivity. A large metal-paneled shop was snuggled close to the double-wide mobile home. Despite the hour, and Estelle saw that it was already going on eleven p.m., lights flooded out through the open garage door, sparks flaring and pulsing from a welding torch.

'PCS,' Jackie radioed, 'three zero eight and ten are ten six at Stance residence in Newton.'

Ernie Wheeler took a little longer than usual to digest that before giving his cryptic, 'Ten four, three zero right.'

'This place needs one of those bumper stickers that says, "Where the Hell is Newton",' Jackie said. 'Not even a dollar store.'

Estelle smiled at that. 'How do they possibly manage?'

Orrin Stance appeared, framed by the light. He'd already removed his welder's helmet, and now settled his paisley cap more firmly on his head. Long-cuffed leather gloves came off and were flopped over the gauges on top of the oxyacetylene tanks.

The last time Estelle had seen him, the year before during the 4 July parade, Orrin had been driving a six-pack of mules pulling an enormous freight wagon decorated with flag buntings. On board were a dozen fancy ladies, tossing candy to eager children.

Orrin didn't look as if he'd changed much since then, or even in the past few decades. His beard was neatly trimmed with just a frosting of gray. A big man anyway, just enough belly kept his bib overalls tight at the waist.

'Shit, don't tell me,' he said by way of greeting. 'The boys are camping down to the fence job at Boyd's. They start a forest fire or something?'

Sheriff Jackie Taber extended a hand, and he stepped forward to take it, not giving her a chance to answer his question.

'Sheriff, I've never had the pleasure. Good evening to you.' He turned to Estelle. 'And you. Don't see enough of you, Mrs Guzman.' He held up his left hand, missing half of the index finger. 'If you get a chance, tell your husband that the hand is healing up just fine.' He wiggled the index stump. 'Still hurts now and then, but I guess I'm lucky.' He turned and nodded toward the shop. 'Too hot during the day. Nighttime is just right when a man's got a whole shitload of welding to do, pardon my French. So. I don't guess you came all this way just to gab. Want to buy a mule or two? Got a pretty good choice right now. Even a couple well-trained and docile teams that are just a joy to drive.'

'Orrin,' Estelle said, keeping her tone conversational, 'does EJ or Howie either one own a game camera?' The man looked puzzled, and Estelle added, 'One of those gadgets you can set up to film wildlife? Set it on a tripod, or tie it to a tree maybe?'

'This ain't good, then.'

'Sir?'

'You coming all the way out here to ask about something like that? What's he done? Am I lookin' at a visit from the critter cops on this?'

'I don't think the Game and Fish is involved, sir.'

'Glad to hear that.' He frowned. 'Now, yes, EJ bought himself a trail camera, that's what he called it. I ain't seen the results from it yet, but I know that he took it with him down to Boyd's when he and Howie went to work fence. He was going to try it out there. Maybe get a champion elk to pose.' He laughed shortly. 'More likely to catch a bunch of peccary. But see, EJ said he was going to play a little stunt on Miles Waddell if he got the chance.' He stabbed his good index finger into the distance. 'And I told that boy that what that fancy britches does ain't *none* of our business. Not me, not EJ.'

'Did EJ happen to mention what kind of "little stunt" he was planning?' Jackie asked.

'Is this what this is all about?'

'We're just interested in what the kids are up to these days.'

For a moment, Orrin thought about that before shaking his head. 'Don't know.' He squinted at Jackie, turning his head so he was looking askance at her. 'I was in town this morning . . . old Patrick down at the feed store was telling me that a couple kids got into it down on the county road. One of 'em was Mexican. Him and that wild hair who beaned another Mexican last year at the Spur. He's dead too, somehow, he says.'

'That be true,' the sheriff said. She opened her notepad and withdrew a carefully folded document. 'Mr Stance, this is a warrant from District Judge Scott for this residence. We need to take a moment to look through EJ's things.'

Orrin bridled at that. 'That ain't right. You ain't even from this county. You got no jurisdiction here, do you?'

'Actually, we do, Mr Stance. In pursuit of a felony, boundaries don't matter much. But if you want to argue about jurisdiction, we can have one of the State Police here to help out.'

'Felony? You're shittin' me now. You after that trail camera? EJ's got that down at Boyd's. That ain't no felony, owning one of them things.'

'We'll see,' Jackie said.

'Well then, if this ain't the craziest damn thing. Look, there's the house,' Orrin said. 'No big deal. EJ's room, when he chooses to be here, it's down the hall, all the way in the back. Come along, then.' He jammed his hands into his coverall pockets and stopped short. He turned to the sheriff. 'Play straight with me now. What's this felony business that you're talkin'? You think EJ or Howie did something that warrants that?'

'We don't know, Mr Stance.'

'Ain't that the truth.' He set off toward the house. Once inside the front door, he stopped again. 'My room's to the left, then Howie's, then EJ's in back.' He made an ushering motion with both hands. 'Just snoop to your heart's content. Don't mind the dirty underwear.' He tried to smile at Estelle. 'You got two of your own, so I don't guess it'd be anything new for you.'

The two Stance boys couldn't have been more different in their personal habits. Howie's room was neat to the point of looking like something out of a military boot camp barracks. EJ's was the polar opposite, with a rumple of soiled clothing long overdue for laundry.

'When's wash day?' Jackie asked. Orrin had been standing in the doorway of the bedroom, shoulder braced against the door jamb.

'That's up to them two kids,' he said. 'When Mamie left, she took free laundry service with her. I ain't about to do that.'

Estelle's phone vibrated, and she fished it out, seeing dispatch. 'Guzman.'

'Estelle, Bob Patchett tells me he's about ten minutes out from your location.'

'Ask him to cruise this way,' she said, but then, knowing the state trooper's propensity for Code Three arrivals, added, 'But ask him to keep it quiet, Ernie. We don't need to wake up the town. Thanks.'

'He's on the way, then.'

She disconnected in time to see Jackie pulling a small rucksack from the closet. The sheriff wrinkled her nose as she opened it. 'Veteran laundry,' she said, and dumped the contents of the rucksack on the bed. Blue jeans that might stand by themselves, underwear and socks that attested to long days laboring in the hot sun, and two khaki workshirts, both ripe.

'Yeah, well,' Orrin said, 'he might be twenty-two goin' on twenty-three, but he ain't much for hygiene.'

Jackie held up one of the shirts and spread the sleeve. 'Pretty serious cut to bleed that much.' She looked at Orrin.

'My gosh, look at that. Well, they're workin' with chain saws all day, so I ain't surprised, but nevertheless . . .'

'I suppose so,' the sheriff said. 'Lots of blood, but I don't see a tear in the sleeve fabric to account for it. Mr Stance, you want to come with me for a minute?' She nodded at Estelle. 'I'll bring bags and tags. You and Orrin wait for me at the door.'

'Orrin, did EJ ever have his blood typed? Like maybe when he signed on to the Highway Department down in Deming?'

'You mean like A and O and stuff like that? Yeah, he did, and he was proud as a peacock about that. He come up with Type O, so his blood type is in short supply. He drops a pint every time there's one of those blood banks.'

'O positive, or negative?'

'Negative. I remember 'cause he was told that only some small percent of the population is O negative.'

'About seven percent,' Estelle said, eager to keep Orrin talking.

'That's right. Of course, you'd know, your husband bein' a doc and all.' He frowned hard, making the obvious conclusion. 'You're thinkin' that blood on his shirt might be somebody else's?'

'I don't know.'

He scoffed. 'Course you know, damn it. Otherwise, you wouldn't be here. Who'd he tangle with?'

'I can't tell you that.'

His voice rose. 'You damn sure can.'

'EJ is well over twenty-one, Orrin. If it were Howie, that'd be a different story.'

'Oh, Jesus. Now we got this . . .' He looked over Estelle's shoulder at the approaching black-and-white State Police cruiser. Estelle saw Jackie Taber finish packing the shirt in an evidence bag. The sheriff met Officer Patchett at the door of his unit. Their conversation was brief.

Estelle met Orrin's gaze. 'Orrin, does EBJ have a firearm? Like a handgun that he might carry with him?'

'Course he does.'

'With him down at the fencing job?'

He hesitated. 'I don't know. I'd have to check.'

'Where does he keep it?'

'Up on the shelf in the pantry. We get coyote problem more'n we need. Once in a while a rattlesnake.'

Officer Patchett settled back in his unit, apparently satisfied that things were peaceful and under control. As Jackie approached, Estelle held out a hand. 'Orrin wants to talk to you, Sheriff. If you'd do that while I go back inside?'

'Course. Patchett is going to run the sample down to the hospital for us. They'll contact us as soon as they run the tests.'

'Outstanding. Give me just a minute.'

In the living room, three long guns were racked over a bookcase, and Estelle continued on to the back where the pantry took up a small room behind the kitchen. Sure enough, a large plastic box was pushed back on the upper shelf. The label on the end announced Ruger Super Blackhawk in .44 Magnum. The box was empty.

Estelle returned to the front porch. 'You find it, ma'am?'

'It's gone. So you think either EJ or Howie has it with them?'

'Wouldn't be Howie,' Orrin said. He started to say something else, but stopped, at a loss for words.

'We'll be in touch, Mr Stance,' Estelle said. She saw the anguish on his face and felt a twinge of sadness for him. 'Stay near the phone, sir.'

'Sheriff,' he started to say, then stopped again. After a moment, he said, 'Am I about to lose a son over this? Over what's goin' on?'

'I hope not, Mr Stance. A lot of that is up to him now.'

'So he's in deep trouble, somehow.'

'Yes, sir. Most likely he is.'

THIRTY-EIGHT

What had been the ancient, spreading alligator bark juniper cut by the fence line crew was now a mountain of branches, spookily pale in the glare of the spotlights. The massive bole was cut into one eight-foot length, and then a second log of six feet, taking the trunk to the point where it branched into a medusa-like head of twisted limbs. The carcass had been pulled away from the fence line. The stump had been cut as low as possible without sawing dirt and rocks.

The fence line itself had been extended for a hundred feet beyond, tracks from the vehicles pounding the duff to powder. The service road the cutters had fashioned disappeared to the left just beyond the new fence. Where the fence ended was stashed a pile of fragrant peeled juniper logs, ready to be positioned as a fence corner brace.

'Looks as if they worked off some anxiety.' Estelle had pulled the Tahoe door to door with Jackie's Expedition, and with all windows lowered, they could converse in near whispers. Both of them worked their spotlights, the beam crisscrossing the site.

'We have enough moon and stars. Let's go dark from here.' Jackie spoke quietly on the car-to-car channel. Both spots clicked off, along with all lights from the three vehicles. The dark and quiet were comfortable, Estelle thought. 'Let's ease up to the end of the fence and see what's what.'

'We have company.' Lieutenant Tom Mears's voice was metallic coming through the vehicles' speakers, just barely loud enough to hear.

The muffled growl of a diesel engine worked its way at walking speed through the trees. A slight rise in the roadway blocked it from the officers' view, then it first appeared as a row of cabtop running lights, and then the sweep of headlights. Even before it appeared, Sheriff Taber accelerated hard, nosing her Expedition first forward a little, and then backing off the fenceline path, parking beside the slash and limbwood. Estelle did the same, but parking on the opposite side of the pile. Mears followed, pulling well away from the road, on the far side of Estelle's truck.

Any possibility of stealth was abandoned now. The four vehicles – three with the officers, another unknown approaching, made enough noise to cancel the peace and quiet of the night. They doused the lights and shut off the engines, waiting. The approaching diesel paused, and its own spotlight flared out, bathing an H-brace. The driver moved the light here and there, as if inspecting the job, then snapped off.

'Right now,' Jackie said, this time using the car-to-car radio channel. Her lights burst on bright, followed a heartbeat later by Estelle's and Mears's. The older model GMC dually was caught in the blaze of light, and its driver stopped so abruptly that the truck's tires plowed ruts in the soft dirt. If the driver had had initial doubts, they vanished when Jackie Taber lit the roof rack on the Expedition, the rainbow of blue and red bouncing off the trees.

He opened the driver's door and the interior light came on. Wallace Boyd eased himself out of the truck, both hands in sight. Once clear of the truck, he left the door open.

'You boys lost?' he said, voice loud enough to be easily heard, but courteous.

He perhaps recognized Jackie Taber's wrestler's build as she dismounted and approached with flashlight in hand. 'Pardon me, Sheriff. You're on the prowl early.'

Estelle kept her light down, and saw Lieutenant Mears angling off to the left. 'I know that this land isn't posted yet, but you folks are all on the wrong side of the fence.'

He pointed off to the east, the sun still many minutes away from dawn. 'They got the camp on down about a quarter of a mile, if that's what you're lookin' for.'

'Mr Boyd, we have a problem here,' the sheriff said. 'Like I told you yesterday on the phone, we've got some serious concerns. It's not something we wanted to wait on.'

'That so? Concerns about what?'

'We were out here yesterday.' Jackie swung her light past Boyd, carefully advancing past him, moving around him on his left, toward the back of his truck. She stopped and flashed the light to illuminate the truck's bed. It was empty.

'Undersheriff Guzman, this must be serious if you're out here.'

'Yes, sir. I wouldn't be surprised to hear that Orrin Stance called you.'

'He did that.' He smiled, not altogether pleasantly. 'I always half expect to see Bobby when I see you.' She didn't reply. After the camera recovery, Torrez had been happy to hike back to his pickup – not interested in playing another round of law-dog. 'So, what's going on?'

'Mr Boyd, we have direct evidence that the person involved with the death of Johnny Rabke is also working on your fencing crew.'

He looked sideways at the sheriff. 'That'd be a surprise.'

'Why is that?'

'I ain't got any Mexican nationals working up here. That's who Rabke tangled with the other night. That's what I heard.'

'What was it you planned on doing out here this early in the morning?' Jackie asked.

'Now listen here,' Boyd said, and Estelle could hear the sharpness in his tone that reminded her of the man's father, the surly Johnny Boyd, a rancher who couldn't talk without a fresh cigarette hanging between his lips. 'There isn't some law that says I have to report what I do on my own land, any time, come day or night. And I could ask you the same goddamn question. Here it is, what, about five o'clock on a Sunday morning? Five o'clock and we got half of the goddamn Sheriff's Department out here. Orrin tells me there's trouble of some sort. That late last night you've been up to Newton to see him.'

'Mr Boyd,' Estelle said, 'as you well know, someone assaulted Rabke, just down the county road from here. We're following a trail, and that trail leads us right to here. That's definite, and reason enough for our early morning visit.' Boyd started to say something, but she interrupted him.

'We're also looking at evidence that points to one of your people having a hand in damaging some of the NightZone railroad infrastructure.'

Boyd looked incredulous. 'I think you guys have been smokin' that funny weed that's gettin' so damn popular, is what I think. Look, you wanted to know, I'll tell you. I'm headed out to pick up my son, Ricky. He's got a doctor's appointment 'cause of a bad elbow he's got, and I ain't about to let him drive into Albuquerque all by himself.'

'Finding a doc on a Sunday is quite the trick,' Jackie said. 'And yet here Ricky is, working on the fence crew? With a bad elbow? And he's still camping out with his friends?'

'He don't have to have permission to do that, 'cept maybe from me or his mother. He's favoring that bad elbow anyways, and we figured some exercise wasn't going to hurt. I told him I'd pick him up, to be ready going on five thirty, and here I am. He'll be ready to go. Unless I need permission from you to do that. And he don't see the doc *today*. His appointment is tomorrow. He's staying the night in Albuquerque with an aunt.'

'We'll need to talk with him.'

'Better make it quick. We got just time for him to make a quick stop at home, get himself cleaned up, and we'll be on our way.'

'Mr Boyd,' Lieutenant Mears said, and they were his first words since the conversation between the officers and landowner had begun, 'I know this is your property, but when we go on down this lane, it'd be best if you stow some of the guns in a safe place . . . for your safety and ours.'

The AR-15 clone was obvious in the rack beside the transmission tunnel, and when Boyd turned toward his truck, as if he needed to check on the rifle, the handgun in his belt holster was apparent.

'They *are* in a safe place, Mr Mears. This is my property, and the guns will stay right where they are. Unless you want to make an issue of it. Now I got to roll. If you're comin' with me, don't tarry.'

And so four trucks rumbled up dust on the new two-track, Sheriff Taber slipping quickly in front to provide an effective road block, then Boyd, tailed by Estelle and Tom Mears.

THIRTY-NINE

T he trucks and trailers were parked in a rough semi-circle, protecting the campsite from the likely breeze. One small pup tent, big enough for two if they were friendly campers, was situated with its door facing a small, tidy fire ring. A red tarp thrown on the ground and then folded loosely over sleeping bags provided some shelter for two of the other campers.

One of them, Jake Palmer, was crouched by the fire, blowing on smoldering kindling. He turned to see the cavalcade of trucks, uttered a yelp, and dived back toward the tarp, where he hastily dug out his trousers, shirt and shoes. He stood up, partially buttoned together, when the campsite turned into a parking lot.

'Morning all,' Sheriff Taber announced in her best reveille voice. She had left the Expedition's roof rack flashing, and the red and blue lights bounced off the tent walls. The first one out of the tent was Ricky Boyd, not particularly cleaned up, but dressed for work.

'Ricky,' Jackie called, walking toward the remains of the campfire. 'Your dad's here to take you to town.'

'Wha . . .'

'Your elbow. Remember? Your lame elbow?'

Estelle watched the boy's face, and saw nothing that suggested he'd heard anything about a trip to town, or maybe for that matter, a lame elbow. He turned toward his father, and in the growing light, Estelle could see an ugly scar running along the outside of Ricky's left elbow, just below the sleeve of his graying T-shirt.

'Well, shit,' Wallace Boyd muttered. Estelle caught Lieutenant Mears's eye, and took a second to point two fingers at her own eyes, then swung the pointed fingers to indicate Boyd. As she exited her unit, she saw that he hadn't stashed his handgun. Before closing the door of her vehicle, she removed a clear plastic evidence bag.

She walked to the little smudge pot that was Jake Palmer's attempt at a campfire and held up the bagged shirt . . . the second work shirt from EJ's laundry. The shirt with the blood-soaked sleeve was secure in the evidence locker at the sheriff's office.

Estelle caught movement out of the corner of her eye, and glanced to see Mears moving within easy arm's reach of Wallace Boyd. She watched the man's face and lowered her voice to barely a whisper. 'Wallace, do you want to rethink the story you're telling me?'

The rancher turned his glare fully on Estelle. 'What are you sayin'?'

'I'm saying that someone killed Johnny Rabke. And I don't mean Arturo Ramirez. I'm talking about the person who wrenched that big knife so hard that it finished the job that Ramirez started. The dying man sprayed blood all over the cab of his truck. All over the sleeve of this shirt.' She paused for a moment to give Boyd a chance to say something. He didn't.

'I'm saying that before all of that, someone also worked pretty hard trying to sabotage the trestles of the NightZone train. Handy chain-saw work. Johnny Rabke learned about that either sitting around the campfire or over drinks at the Broken Spur, and knowing Johnny as I do . . . as I did . . . I can imagine him using that information as leverage to impress one of my deputies.' Estelle saw a slight slumping of Boyd's shoulders.

'Now, I may be wrong in some of that, but the DNA testing is going to give us a lot of the answer, Wallace. By later this afternoon, the tests will tell us who wore this shirt. Whose sweat permeated the fabric inside.' Estelle knew perfectly well that DNA tests completed in a day was a pipe-dream, but Wallace Boyd probably didn't. 'Mr Boyd, we already know whose blood type is staining the fabric. Those kinds of tests are simple and quick.'

The tent door parted, and Howie Stance appeared, bleary-eyed and tousle-headed. Whoever was still under the tarp had yet to make a move, and Jackie Taber stepped forward and jabbed at the lump with the toe of her boot. 'Rise and shine, sleepy-head,' she said, and then backed away at the first signs of motion. Her hand had dropped so that the fingers of her hand touched the black stocks of her duty automatic.

'Blood on the shirt is one thing, and maybe we'll find some piñon pitch as well, huh? Not surprising after all,' the sheriff said. 'But something else to interest you.' She hefted the evidence bag she'd carried from her truck. 'I'll willing to bet there's quite the story told by the fingerprints on this game camera that some brilliant soul strapped to a piñon down below the Red Slade arroyo trestle . . . that big trestle that's going to make a hell of a film when it collapses?'

She hefted the camera. 'Who was going to sell that to some internet clown, do you suppose?' She scanned the group.

'I also figure a nice unit like this one,' and she eyed the camera, 'probably has a review feature. Whatever you all shot movies of, probably is still on preview.'

The first one to find his voice, and apparently finding something he was good at, Ricky Boyd pointed at the emerging figure of Elliot EJ Stance, as the young man unwound himself from his sleeping bag. His hands were empty. 'He said we'd be able to sell video of the train thing on the internet, easy,' Ricky said. 'Like there are all kinds of sites that buy stuff like that.'

'Well, shit,' Wallace Boyd said matter-of-factly. He stepped forward before Mears could grab him, and delivered a world-class soccer kick to the unsuspecting EJ's midsection. 'You know what I'd like to do, Stance? I'd sure as hell like to lock you in a room with Miles Waddell and let him just beat the holy shit out of you.'

'Was Johnny Rabke going to rat you out, Elliot? Letting us know about your plan to cut the trestles?' Sheriff Taber's voice was low and dangerous. 'Is that why you killed him?'

For the first time EJ found his voice. With one hand clutching his gut and propped up by the other, he coughed, then looked up at Estelle. 'He was already dead when I found him. You can ask Jake.'

'Hey, no,' Jake Palmer said, and jumped to his feet. 'I didn't have nothing to do with that. I *found* Rabke in his truck by the side of the road, dead for sure, and the other guy shot all to hell.' He pointed at Estelle. 'You interviewed me right there, so you know.' He held out both hands. 'You can test me all you want. I didn't touch Johnny Rabke. Or that knife. Or . . .' He gave up, his head shaking from side to side as if the screws holding it had come loose.

'So tell me, EJ,' Estelle said, watching the young man's hands. 'What do you think Keenan Clark is going to say when we talk to him in a little bit?'

'He didn't have nothing to do with the railroad thing, honest, ma'am,' Ricky chirped. 'He didn't. We used his ATV cause it held the three of us and the saws and stuff.'

'A little night-time recreation, huh.' She handed the bagged trail cam to Mears, who stowed it in his unit, returning with a good inventory of slip ties. 'The prints on that camera will tell us for sure. But gentlemen, finish up getting dressed. Then we're going to take a ride and have us a nice, long talk.'

EJ Stance staggered to his feet and pulled on his trousers and slipped on his T-shirt. He bent over and fussed with his boots, maybe having a hard time seeing the laces as the fire's smoke blew in his face. When EJ was still off balance, Jackie stepped forward, reached down, and yanked first one of EJ's arms and then the other, drawing them tight behind his back. Her voice was no longer soft and pleasant. 'It gives me great pleasure to say this, EJ. You're under arrest, son.' She turned him so she could look him in the eye.

'Where's the gun, son?'

'I don't have—'

'Don't be stupid, son. Ruger forty-four. It's not at the house on the pantry shelf. You have it here somewhere?'

They all waited while EJ gave that some thought. Finally, he murmured, 'It's under my pillow.'

'Smart lad.' Jackie stepped past him and toed his pillow out of the way. The revolver was huge and black.

'Well, shit,' Wallace Boyd said. 'All of this heartache so they could put something on the internet? That's enough to make me goddamn sick. Worse'n that, it'll probably put my ranch right out of business. Forty years of life blood right down the goddamn sewer.' He started toward EJ Stance, but Tom Mears grabbed him hard from behind by both forearms, keeping Boyd's right hand away from the handgun he wore.

At the same time, EJ Stance sat down with a hard thump beside the fire, his hands locked behind his back. His eyes lost themselves in the small dance of flame that Jake Palmer's efforts had started. When he spoke, his voice shook, barely a whisper. 'It ain't just about the video,' he said. 'Rabke knew about the game camera and stuff, and he was sure enough going to tell.'

'The game camera and stuff,' Estelle echoed. 'You consider destroying the railroad bridges just a bunch of stuff?'

'He woulda gone to that big shot and told,' EJ cried. 'He woulda.' He jerked his head down, chin hard against his chest, and then said no more.

FORTY

B ill Gastner entered the front door of the Posadas County District Court, an annex to the county building. He wore his best – his only – dark gray suit and his favorite of the three ties he owned. Just for fun, he covered his close-cropped, now white hair with a baseball cap with the legend advertising the Air Force's almost-ready-to-retire A-10 Warthog.

He took his time negotiating the three shallow steps, maneuvering the duck-footed one-handed walker. One of the court bailiff's, Owen Tynes, saw him coming and punched the automatic door actuator.

'Morning, Sheriff. I guess you know where you're supposed to go.'

'Owen, lots of things I might forget, but not that. How's Gladys doing?'

'Any finer and I might start worrying that she's going to leave me in her dust.'

He offered a hand as Gastner headed toward the second-floor stairway. 'Elevator works if you'd prefer that.'

'No challenge,' Gastner said gruffly. He regarded the fourteen steps with resignation. 'You know, I have a wheelchair that could negotiate this.'

'I heard about that, sir. I'm headed up that way. How about I keep you company?'

'I won't say no.'

'I know that the newspaper kid is waiting for you, by the way.'

'Let's hope he's patient.'

Rik Chang was patient. He waited near the drinking fountain, giving him an unrestricted view of both the stairway up from the Sheriff's Office and from the main county building lobby. His face brightened when he saw Gastner conquering the final steps.

'Sir,' the *Posadas Register* reporter said, 'Would you take a few minutes to talk with me?'

Gastner looked to Tynes, who nodded. 'I'll come fetch you when it's time, sir.'

'Then let's grab one of those benches.' Gastner indicated one of the antique polished-wood benches that had listened to whispered conversations since the courthouse was built in 1933 as a WPA project. He settled on the bench with a sigh and grinned at Chang. 'There's not much that I can tell you, you know. You know how grand juries work. All hush-hush and stuff.'

Chang nodded eagerly and held up his phone. 'I'd like to record us, if that's all right with you.'

'Forgot your pencil?'

Chang's smile was fleeting. 'I don't have a permit to carry one of those, sir.'

Gastner held up both hands in surrender.

'I'm hearing that the grand jury is looking at seeking indictments against three of the men involved in this incident. Will you comment on that?'

'No. I'm not privy to what the grand jury is doing. Or what the DA wants to accomplish. You'd have to ask him.'

Chang looked down at his phone as if he didn't quite trust it. 'You were the first person to discover the damage to the railroad trestles.'

A slow smile spread across Gastner's face, and after a moment he asked, 'Is there a question there? Or just a statement of fact.'

'*Is* it a statement of fact? Were you first on the scene?'

'That sounds more dramatic than it was, Mr Chang. I stopped my wheelchair so that I could take a piss, old prostates being what they are. I walked over into the shade of the nearest trestle to do my business, and saw the chain-saw cuts.'

'What did you think when you saw them?'

'First things first. I had to relieve myself. And then I had to figure out how to get my carcass out of the arroyo.'

'How'd you do that?'

'The way porcupines kiss. Very carefully. I left the chair at the bottom. It was rescued later.'

'How did that happen? I mean, you were rescued somehow.'

'I was reported by a concerned citizen who happened to be passing by on board a train.'

Chang looked pole-axed. 'They were driving over a trestle that had had some of its supports cut?'

'Yes. Sometimes us humans get lucky.'

'I don't understand who would do a thing like that.'

'Join the club, Mr Chang. Now it's up to the grand jury to make sense of everything.' Just as he said that, the elevator chimed and the door slid open. Undersheriff Estelle Reyes-Guzman stepped out, followed by Sheriff Jackie Taber.

'Rik, how are you?' Jackie said. 'Busy day for you.'

He stood up abruptly, gathering in his phone as he did so. 'Yes, ma'am.'

He nodded a greeting to Estelle, and she extended her hand.

'Rik, I need a few minutes with Mr Gastner. Would you excuse us for a little bit?'

'Let's go use the bailiff's chambers,' Taber said. She nodded at Chang. 'Are you going to need a statement from me?' When he nodded eagerly, she took him by the arm. 'Let's go talk.'

'Last-minute plans, *Padrino*,' Estelle said. 'Francisco just got the word that he's needed in New York.' She sighed. 'He made me promise not to tell anyone why. They're headed out tomorrow morning. I was hoping that you could join us for a farewell dinner.'

'Food? Me? Surely you jest. Food and intrigue. Nothing better.'

She smiled. 'A Carlos special.'

'Double me.'

'Good. Come anytime. We're going to eat around six. Has Shearson spoken with you?'

'Only in the most vague way.'

'I think that's the new district attorney's trademark.'

'I prefer the job that Schroeder did. I always knew where I stood with him.'

'Changes, changes,' Estelle said. 'District Attorney Shearson is leaning toward seeking an indictment for second degree murder, rather than voluntary manslaughter.'

'Murder is a tough call, sweetheart.'

'With the victim just sitting there, pinned through the chest, it would be hard to imagine involuntary manslaughter when the knife was wrenched this way and that, inflicting grievous injury.'

'And *voluntary* manslaughter implies that there was no malice aforethought, just a fit of rage, or some sort of heat of passion. It would be hard to argue that, under the circumstances. But hey, we're not lawyers.'

'If the grand jury indicts Elliot Stance for second degree murder, then it'll be the job for the petit jury to establish proof. Rabke's blood type on EJ's shirtsleeve puts him there, finding his prints on the trail cam puts a lock on it. EJ's statement fills in the holes. Did you know that Stance's father wanted to work for Waddell?'

'I suppose that wouldn't surprise me. Everybody in the county wants to work for Miles, it seems.'

'Stance wanted to use his mule train – his mules and his fancy wagons – up on the NightZone mesa. He pictured it as a real tourist draw.'

'I can imagine what Miles said to that, and I vaguely remember. Not only no, but hell no. Miles didn't want piles of mule crap all over his mesa, with all the flies that come with it. Stance didn't take that kindly. I can imagine he held a grudge ever since. Especially when he saw how successful the train was . . . what a tourist draw. You really think that's why the boy wanted to sabotage the train? To help out his old man?'

'He says it is,' Estelle said. 'Personally, I don't think so. Just a handy excuse, when it comes down to it. I think it was just the fun of playing with the game cam. Make a great film if it succeeds. Johnny Rabke found out about all that, and was trying to figure out a way to tell the cops without sounding like a rat. He was going to talk with Lydia, we think. Or maybe directly to Miles when he got the chance.'

'And there's lots of shadows of doubt,' Gastner said. 'Your husband's testimony is going to be a key, proving for the grand jury whether or not Johnny Rabke was still alive when Elliot went to work with that Ka-Bar.'

'The geyser of blood on EJ's shirt says that Johnny's heart was still hammering away.'

'True enough. Be interesting to see on down the line how all the lawyers spin it. But first things first. I don't see much chance that the grand jury will *not* indict.'

'How about a bit of news that you might not like, *Padrino.*'

He looked at her askance. 'Now what?'

'Miles Waddell doesn't want to press charges against Ricky Boyd and Howie Stance for the trestle damage. Not criminal charges, anyway. He's willing to let EJ Stance go it alone as the mastermind, and then on the murder rap.'

'You've got to be kidding me.'

'No. He *might* . . . and he says *might* . . . consider civil damages, but he's waffling on that. His logic is that coming down hard on those kids would create more ill will against his project than letting them off. He was thinking of hiring them to be part of the trestle repair crew.'

'He thinks that's going to appease old man Stance?'

'Probably not. Fancy britches, Orrin called him. But I really don't think Miles is much worried about what Orrin Stance thinks. I think he's harmless.'

'Ye gods,' Gastner said, shaking his head. 'So by Waddell's way of thinking, Ricky Boyd and Howie Stance could take a walk on what they've done, and end up with a job to boot.'

'But that's vintage Miles, *Padrino*. If the law allows it, Miles will put 'em to work and try to develop a sense of decency in them. Try to work some sense into their little heads. He's done that before, if you'll recall. Years ago, when the young man sprayed the graffiti on the radio telescope dish, for instance.'

'Well, good luck with that. He can't go that route with Elliot Stance, though. He's nailed for sure. You know what Monty Schaffer said when he heard about the arrests. Good thing he didn't get there first with his shotgun.'

'Yes. But of course, then the grand jury would be deliberating about *him*.'

'I suppose so. You did a first-rate job, sweetheart. You and your crew. And most important, everybody is safe and goes home afterward. On top of that, I have complete faith in our medical examiner, sweetheart. And I stand corrected. With any luck at all, Elliot Stance *won't* be going home.'

He grinned at something behind Estelle, and at the same moment she felt a finger probing between her ribs. She turned to see Linda Pasquale, black eyebrows knit with an uncharacteristic glower on her face.

'I am *sooooo* mad at you, Undersheriff Guzman.' Even as Estelle was opening her mouth to ask 'what for', Linda continued. 'You let young Bishop climb that piñon tree, in the dark, to take photos of the dumb game camera? I'm not sour about missing the chance to get covered with pine pitch and covered with ants, but I really miss taking pictures of Dwayne being miserable. What a calendar photo that might have made!' Linda's gift calendars, each year focusing on a dozen staff photos taken most often during some embarrassing moment throughout the years, were legendary.

The glower left Linda's face, and she wrapped an arm around Estelle's shoulder for a strong hug. 'I forgive you.'

'That's nice to know,' Estelle said. 'I feel better now.' She nodded toward the courtroom door, opened now by Bailiff Owen Tynes, who announced loudly to Bill Gastner, 'Sheriff, we're ready for you.'